IN WOLVES' CLOTHING

GREG LEVIN

CHAPTER ONE

The handcuffs cut into me more than usual. These things would be tight even on a man half my size. Why the cop with his knee on my neck didn't leave more room for my wrists, I have no idea. It's not like we haven't been over this.

To my right, Barrett's lying flat on his belly just like me. Only he doesn't appear to be in much discomfort. Of course, Barrett could have his leg crushed by a steamroller and he wouldn't appear to be in much discomfort. Still, it looks like the officer who nabbed him was kind enough to let Barrett's carpal bones breathe. Barrett's lucky like that. Whether we're in Puerto Plata, Bangkok or Mumbai, the local cops always seem to take a shine to him whenever we get busted.

Barrett turns his head to face me, his right cheek pressed to the marble floor. He gives me a wink and a smile. Of course he does.

The girls. They're screaming their heads off. Many of the younger ones—eight or nine or ten years old—are crying. The ones who aren't screaming or crying are giggling or yawning or just staring at the walls. I'm guessing they're newer. They've yet to build up much of a tolerance to the morphine the pimps have been feeding them. One of these girls, she's laughing at how far the bubblegum she's pulled out of her mouth can stretch. This would be adorable if it weren't horrific.

Three of the police officers are now trying to wrangle all the girls and get them out the door of our rented mansion, where no doubt a van or small bus awaits. Not as easy a job as you'd think. These girls have learned to trust no one, especially the cops. A few of them make a break toward the pool out back, with one of the cops chasing after them the way you'd chase kittens who've escaped from a box. Another girl kicks one of the other officers in the shin and shouts, "*Pendejo!*" The bubblegum girl clutches the armrest of the black leather sofa while an officer tugs tentatively at her legs. She's still laughing, but not as much as before.

Of the remaining cops, one pretends to keep an eye on Barrett and me, one pretends to keep an eye on our cohorts Drew and Malik, and the other three tend to the two local men who helped us make this party happen. Nice hombres, if you take away the kidnapping and the pedophilia. And the resisting arrest. The shorter, fatter one takes a shot to the ribs from a cop's baton and drops. The taller, skinnier one—the one putting up more of a fight—two of his teeth just skittered across the floor and under the billiard table. It will be a while before he smiles like he smiled two days ago when we told him how many girls we wanted. Or maybe he'll luck out with a prison that has a good dentist.

Señor Gaptooth looks over at me as he gets cuffed, and I shake my head like I can't believe this is happening to us. But really I'm just concerned his blood won't wash out of the hand-woven Zapotec rug he's pinned to. Our boss, Fynn, she'll be pissed if we lose our damage deposit. Not pissed enough to change our modus operandi, though. Convincing pimps to bring their girls to us is the best way to make them believe we are what we say we are—rich American businessmen who need to keep our perverted activities out of the public eye. After hearing what we creeps are willing to pay for a private party at a location of our choosing, even the most wary pimp will agree to our terms.

The only thing louder than Señor Gaptooth cursing at the cops right now is Drew begging them not to issue a report. Shouting and crying about how his wife is going to kill him. How he'll be forced to resign as CIO of his company if this leaks. How he'll lose his pension.

Drew's by far the best actor among us.

Malik takes a quieter approach. He has to. He's black in Acapulco. Even though the police know he didn't lay a finger on any of the girls, they're ready to treat him like a legitimate criminal if he so much as looks at them funny. If this were Haiti or Uganda, Malik would be able to relax and almost be himself. But Haiti and Uganda were last month.

After the two bruised, bloodied pimps get dragged out and all eleven girls are safely removed from the party hall, Drew stops crying. Barrett starts laughing. Malik continues to lie on the ground and keep his mouth shut. Me, I'm just hoping the three oxy pills in my pocket are intact.

The four of us stand up, still cuffed, and brush the dust and debris from our knock-off Armani and Versace and Gucci and Canali suits.

"Nice work, guys," I say to my crew. "*Gracias, agentes*," I say to the cops who took us down.

"*Gracias a Ustedes*," one of the cops replies. As he's removing my handcuffs, I go, "*Demasiado apretadas*," then show him the red indents ringing my wrists.

"*Lo siento*," he says. But I know he's not sorry. And I don't blame him. Seeing what he sees every day, he needs to inflict a little pain to feel alive—and to keep from doing much worse. Besides, I can handle the hurt. Makes the oxy go down easier.

Barrett shakes the hand of the cop who cuffed him, then turns to me and the guys. "Let's blow this shithole and grab a poolside drink somewhere."

"No way," says Drew before blowing his nose into a silk handkerchief. "Ain't worth getting whacked for a margarita. Besides, our flight's in three hours."

Malik nods. "I'm getting out of dodge and heading straight for the airport."

"Jesus, you guys are never any fun," says Barrett as he adjusts his Rolex that isn't a Rolex. He looks at me. "How about you, Zero?"

"They have margaritas in the club lounge," I say.

Barrett shakes his head. "It's not the same, man."

"You're right," I say. "It's just, I find it hard to enjoy a cocktail when I'm in the crosshairs of a rifle scope."

One of the cops walks over to the door, opens it and looks outside.

"Okay, you can go," he says in a thick Spanish accent. "I recommend you gather your bags and get to the airport."

"See?" Malik says to Barrett while pointing at the cop. "Dude knows what's up."

Barrett gives a dismissive wave. "Right," he says under his breath, "because you should always do what a Mexican cop says."

The four of us grab our carry-ons from the closet behind the bar in the game room and roll them out of the house to our taxi parked on the circular driveway. The men we were five minutes ago would never be caught dead in a yellow minivan like this, all dinged up and covered in scratches. Those guys would have demanded a stretch limo. Or a private helicopter. But the party's over now, and we're all just a bunch of Cinderellas.

"*El aeropuerto, por favor*," I say to the driver, Mateo, as he gets out to load our bags.

"*Por supuesto*," says Mateo. He came highly recommended, and has not disappointed. He didn't ask any questions on the way here, was right where he was supposed to be for the ride back, and just offered us each a bottle of water.

"To Mateo," says Drew, holding up his plastic bottle.

The rest of us raise our bottles and bounce them together in the back of the minivan.

Mateo blushes and grins. "*Gracias, caballeros*," he says as he pulls away from the curb.

I down my water and tap the shoulder of Drew, who's sitting next to Malik in the row of seats in front of me and Barrett. "Another Oscar-worthy performance," I say. "I thought you were going to go full Brando and piss your pants in there."

"Who says I didn't?" Drew says. "You know, you guys could stand to up your game a bit. It wouldn't kill you to feel your character's shame."

"My character's on Zoloft," says Barrett. "He doesn't feel much of anything."

And we all laugh.

And then we don't.

Drew stares out the window, or perhaps at the swollen face reflecting back. Malik bows his head and runs his fingers along his side fade. Barrett closes his eyes and cracks his giant knuckles.

Me, I yawn. Then pop two oxy into my mouth and grind them into dust.

CHAPTER TWO

Guadalajara.

The guys and I ogle the dozen or so pre-teen prostitutes being led into our villa by three slim, scowling men. Each of the men is wearing a different soccer jersey that looks the same. Each of the girls is wearing whatever discount-rack party dress the pimps forced them into. The room smells like Drakkar Noir and sweat mixed with Cotton Candy and fear. Some of the girls look at us and try to smile. The rest of them probably aren't aware we exist.

We offer the girls some sodas as they plop onto couches and chairs in the huge open living room. Barrett says something silly in broken Spanish and several of the girls giggle. Even one of the pimps is smiling. I pour myself a glass of tequila and wink at a ten-year-old.

The trick to looking excited when children are presented to you for sex is to remember you are saving their lives. If you don't look excited, the pimps will get suspicious. Show your anger and disgust, and you ruin everything.

I take a sip of tequila and grin at a child and would kill for an oxy. The one I ate an hour ago is losing its luster. But two on the job, that's a no-no.

For help getting into character, think about the biggest douchebag frat guy you've ever met, imagine him with several million dollars, multiply his money and demeanor by ten, and then act like *that* guy. Right up until the cops remove your handcuffs and thank you.

This mission is a little bigger than the one in Acapulco yesterday, so there are six of us. Barrett, Malik, Drew and I have been joined by Anders and Scott from Seattle, who arrived in Guadalajara two days ago to get everything set up. Anders and Scott look more refreshed than the rest of us right now because they're not finishing up a doubleheader. None of us at Operation Emancipation like doubleheaders—shooting off to a city to complete a jump immediately after finishing one in the same or similar time zone. Doubleheaders may be practical from a cost and logistics standpoint, but they're never fun. For one, fitting a second pseudo-designer suit inside a valise is next to impossible. Secondly, if you play a pedophile too often, your face might stay that way. But Fynn makes the schedule, and you don't fuck with Fynn or her schedule.

The guys and I are chatting and laughing with the girls, warming up to them slowly with a *"Qué guapa!"* here and a *"Muy bonita!"* there, making sure not to lock eyes or look at their mouths or do anything else that might invite a kiss. If one of the pimps sees any of us rejecting an advance, they'll know something's up. Fortunately, these girls, just like all the other girls in all the other cities and countries we work in, almost never make the first move. They may be smiling and giggling, but they're not. Sadly, their terror works in our favor. They think they're about to be raped for the tenth or hundredth or thousandth time, so they aren't in any rush to get things started. They're waiting on us.

I'm not wearing a watch, what with my wrists still sore from yesterday, but the cops are a little late. We can stall only so long before the pimps will start getting nervous. And you don't want a nervous pimp. Anders and Scott may have asked them nicely the other day not to bring any weapons to the party, but the thing about pimps is you can't always trust them to respect house rules. The good news is these three clowns aren't even paying attention to us. They're too busy marveling over the size of the place, trying to fathom its value in their heads, wondering what knickknacks they might be able to nab when nobody's looking. It's not often they get to see the inside of a house on this side of town. We are in Puerta de Hierro, one of the most affluent neighborhoods in the greater Guadalajara Metropolitan Area. A twenty-minute drive and a million miles away from the pimps' brothel on Avenida Chapultepec, where Anders and Scott went to arrange this party two days ago.

Another sip of tequila. Less winking and grinning. And we're running out of stupid, flirtatious phrases to say to the girls. The watch I'm not wearing tells me we should definitely be getting arrested by now. It tells me it's time for what we at OE call the tourniquet.

"Okay boys, let's get busy!" I shout with glee at the guys.

You never get used to nearly throwing up in your mouth.

I grab the hand of one of the youngest girls—she's not a day over nine—and place my other hand on the back of another girl who isn't much older. Their forced smiles fall to the floor as we head toward the wide granite staircase. The other guys follow my lead, each picking the two girls closest to them and guiding them to the stairs. We look like teachers on a field trip, collectively accounting for all the children in our charge as we tour an historic home. If only it were that simple.

In about a minute, the girls will wonder why we aren't

removing any of our clothing or theirs. Our lack of sexual interest and aggression might even make some of them more uncomfortable than usual. We'll just tell them we like it slow. What we *won't* tell them is we're here to rescue them. All it takes is one doped-up eleven-year old with a confused allegiance to her pimp to ruin a perfectly planned emancipation.

In this job, you learn to ignore the urge to comfort those you're protecting.

From the middle of the staircase, I peer back at the three pimps. They're still paying us no mind, just nudging one another and giggling as they drool over the palatial environs, pointing at art and gold statuettes and other items of seemingly excessive value. What they don't know is all that stuff is just like the six of us men heading upstairs:

Fake.

As my foot lands on the second step from the top, one of the pimps yells, "*CORRE!*"

RUN.

He's not talking to us. I know this because he and his two colleagues are dashing for the exit.

Funny, 'cause I didn't hear any vehicles coming up the driveway, and I have a very good ear for such sounds.

Not funny, 'cause I've seen this all before. And know just what to do.

Nothing.

Our two friends nearly collide in the doorway, then disappear. My reflexes scream for me to slide down the banister. Sprint after them. Bash their faces against the concrete driveway. You learn to ignore all that, suppress your natural instincts.

"*Cálmase,*" I say to the two girls screaming on the top step as I hold them so they don't try to catch up with their captors.

Barrett and the rest of the crew retain and try to calm their girls, too, but most of the girls continue shouting and crying and trying to break loose. Our Spanish, while decent, isn't quite at the level needed to cut through the collective panic and confusion of being abandoned. We're all a few Rosetta Stone lessons away from transitioning gracefully from pedophile to savior.

Outside, whatever truck or van these girls arrived in peels out and speeds off. Honking follows the screech of a distant skid.

We continue trying to tell the girls what we're usually not allowed to. That everything is going to be okay. That they're going to be taken someplace safe.

And still they cry and squirm. Some swear at us. Some pinch us, kick us, spit at us. Anyone in their shoes would do the same. They always do.

It's awful, and it's fine by us. We're not here for hugs and applause.

"Watch these two," I say to Barrett a few steps below me. "I'm gonna keep an eye out for the cops."

Barrett nods and I maneuver down the stairs through the cursing and the kicking and the tears. Through this cluster of broken children struggling to get free. None of them yet able to comprehend they already are.

One of the girls Malik is guarding on the lower steps scratches my hand as I pass. I get it. She's probably wondering why men as large as us—if we truly are here to help them—just let three guys half our size escape without a chase or even a word. And if she's not wondering that now, one day she will.

Not risking everything for these girls is the toughest part of the job. We are trained never to confront or get physical with any of the traffickers or pimps we rub shoulders with, no matter how tempting it may be. Not unless our life or that of one of the girls is in perilous danger. Like gun-to-the-head, hammer-cocked, counting-down-from-five, blood-building-up-in-the-trigger-finger type of danger. Breaking faces and ribs and teeth is solely the job of the local police forces OE partners with.

The cops who just now rolled up the driveway in four unmarked sedans, they missed their chance.

I step out the door the pimps left wide open, and show two thumbs-down to several overweight, mustached officers in shorts as they get out of their cars and head up the walkway.

"*Qué pasó?*" one of them asks, glancing all around the property, his hands out to the side.

"*Demasiado tarde,*" I say, and tell him the pimps split. I ask if he knows what might have prompted that.

Like I don't know the answer.

No matter how good OE's relationship is with the authorities in the various regions where we work, there's always the risk of at least one crooked cop tipping off the traffickers before a bust can be completed. A quick text from an officer whose wallet gets fatter every second these pimps' ramshackle slave pits stay open. That's all it takes to undo weeks or months of reconnaissance, collaboration and strategic planning. At least today the tip didn't come until after the pimps arrived, so they were forced to leave the girls behind. That's certainly better than a no-show. Still, those scumbags will no doubt reemerge within a week. Split up to start several new brothels in the city. Replace every girl they just handed over with an exact replica. Times three.

After mumbling some excuses and apologizing for the mix-up, the cop out on the walkway with me joins his men inside to peel the girls from the banister. One of the officers comes back out with a bloody nose and a bite wound on his hand. To keep from pitying him, I convince myself he's the one—the reason nobody's getting arrested today. I point at his hand and say, "That looks like it hurts," then smile and suggest he call for back-up.

***

Everyone at Gate A-11 of Guadalajara International Airport is pissed off.

Everyone except us. Malik, Drew, Barrett and I couldn't care less about an hour-and-a-half delay due to heavy wind and rain back home in Los Angeles, our destination. First off, thunderstorms in LA are cause for celebration. Parades even. Our fellow passengers, many of whom are American, should all be applauding the gate agent, not shouting at her and grunting. She just helped end a deadly drought with nothing more than a microphone.

Secondly, fuck it. The gate agent could have announced that we'd be flying in a plane infested with wasps and fire ants, and still I wouldn't have been too bothered. Fuck it comes easily after you've gotten chummy with human trafficking. Roll around in the bowels of the child sex trade for a while, and everything else is Christmas morning. It's all about perspective. Whenever people say, "It could always be worse," they're right … unless they're talking about what the Lost Girls have been through. That's where worse ends.

Fuck it is one of the biggest perks of my job. Before I joined Operation Emancipation, I was just like the dozens of people fuming at Gate A-11 right now. Flight delays would ruin my day. So would morning alarms and traffic and taxes and head colds and commercial interruptions and the mold you can't see growing on the strawberries in the middle of the plastic container they come packed in. Now? Now I can smile and whistle while walking through a pediatric cancer ward.

12

Drew suggests heading to one of the airport bars to wait out the delay. Malik and Barrett are down. I decline. I'd rather sit here amidst the sulking and the whining and the grumbling. It cheers me up. I love that these people have no idea what an honor it is to have a ticket to fly somewhere. Anywhere. It's infuriating. And hilarious.

"Ma'am, if I don't get to Los Angeles by midnight, I'm going to miss my friend's bachelor party," a guy in a Dodgers jacket tells the gate agent.

Poor guy. I want to help him. I want to show him a picture of an eight-year-old Vietnamese girl whose pimp locked her in a cage and shocked her with a loose electrical wire for trying to escape his brothel.

And that lady two seats over from me on her phone complaining about how this always happens to her and how she's going to demand the airline give her some free travel vouchers, she just needs me to tell her about the ten-year-old Indian girl whose pimp shoved a hot metal rod inside her when she refused to perform oral sex on her very first client.

To make things easier, maybe I'll just ask the gate agent if I can borrow her microphone. I can put an end to everyone's misery at once. Efficiently spread the joy of fuck it. I've got tons of material to help everyone through this agonizing inconvenience, these ninety painful minutes of air conditioning and Wi-Fi and freedom. Maybe I'll open with all the seven- and eight- and nine-year-old Cambodian girls who have their virginity sold to sex tourists before getting stitched up to be sold as virgins again. And again. And again.

On second thought, it's probably better to close with that.

"Passengers waiting for flight one eighty-two," the gate agent announces over the loudspeaker, "we have an update on the estimated departure time. The storm in Los Angeles is moving more slowly than anticipated. We don't expect to start boarding until approximately eleven thirty tonight."

Three hours from now.

Shouts of profanity and protest fill the gate area, followed by an aftershock of sighs and snorts, followed by soft taps and clicks as everyone takes to social media to advertise their outrage.

It's digital pandemonium. The online exasperation and indignation is palpable. But it's not long before the people begin receiving likes and supportive comments and emojis from their friends and followers. And just like that, peace and order and sanity are restored.

Too bad. I was really starting to enjoy myself.

CHAPTER THREE

I can't remember if I took an oxy during the flight, so I eat two. They pair nicely with the scotch.

It's good to be home.

I should be upstairs sleeping, especially since I didn't catch a single wink on the flight from Guadalajara. But there's something I have to finish first.

An eight-letter word for gradually losing one's edge.

Slipping.

I fill in each box of 27 Down with my black pen and take another sip of scotch. It's times like these I turn into God. The crossword squares fill up by themselves in a secret blurry code. A few of the answers might even be correct.

The black pleather couch makes love to me as I solve 32 Across.

A four-letter word for spouse.

Neda.

She's leaning on the banister, wearing a white T-shirt and gray sweatpants that might have fit me when I was ten. Her eyes, almond-shaped during waking hours, are half open.

"You're home?" she says, pre-dawn gravel in her voice.

"Hi, baby," I say while trying to conceal the nearly empty

lowball glass in my hand. "Sorry to wake you. I'll be up in a sec."

Neda yawns and combs her hand through a shining cascade of black hair. "What time d'you get in?"

I scratch my shaved dome, feeling the perspiration forming, and say, "Uh, a little after one maybe."

Neda opens her eyes the rest of the way. "You've been here for nearly *two hours*? Why didn't—"

"Baby, I just needed to unwind a bit before bed."

Neda's eyes open wider than the manual recommends. "Why must unwinding always involve single malt and a crossword?" she asks. "You know, some men unwind by spooning their beautiful wife. Especially when they haven't seen her in four days."

I ponder the answer to 36 Across.

"Zero!" Neda shouts.

The sound knocks the pen from my fingers, and I go, "I didn't want to wake you."

"And look how that worked out for you," says Neda. "At least if you'd come up when you got home you wouldn't be getting yelled at."

I tell her not to be mad, then get up from the couch as gracefully as a man two drinks and twenty milligrams in can. "I knew if I woke you right when I got home, you'd want to talk about the mission."

I realize this is not what God would say. I can tell by Neda's face.

"And would that have been so horrible?" she asks. "Us actually *talking*? About something other than your dry cleaning and where you're flying off to next?"

What I want to say is, "Yes." What I actually say is, "Baby, come on. I don't want to get into it."

"I know, I know," says Neda, pulling on the banister railing like she wants to replace it. "You never want to 'get into it.' I stopped asking you to 'get into it' a while ago, Zero, in case you hadn't noticed."

I tell her let's talk about it in the morning, and she says we already are. Then she says, "You know what, forget it. Come up whenever. Or pass out on the couch. I don't really care."

Neda stomps up the hardwood stairs like gravity has doubled. I inhale in preparation to call out to her, but swallow the words. Neda has stormed off in similar fashion countless times before, but right now I can't remember the protocol. Leave her alone for a while until she cools off? Go after her immediately and talk her down? Go after her immediately and just hold her? Wait a few minutes and then tear her clothes off?

There's a good reason why I can't remember the rules: They keep changing. I've tried each of the aforementioned approaches an equal number of times in the past, and was successful with each roughly half the time.

I feel like a bomb defuser who's received minimal training. Do I snip the red wire first or the green one? Or the yellow one or the blue one? If I choose right, I'll be a hero, saving the day and winning the heart of the princess. If I choose wrong, I'll blow the whole goddamn kingdom to bits.

Or at least ruin breakfast.

I go with the red wire and pour another two fingers of scotch. The couch is softer than before, the crossword clues easier. If only the little boxes would stop blurring and bending, I'd be able write my answers inside them instead of somewhere over in the sports section.

The girls. They're still screaming, only now no sound is coming out of their mouths.

I wonder how many of the girls from the two Mexico missions will stick around their safe houses long enough to be reunited with their family, or at least to learn a trade that doesn't entail being raped thirty or more times a day. Hopefully more than half of them. Unfortunately, that would be considered a success. If only nine or ten of the girls we liberated in Acapulco and Guadalajara end up running off to find another brothel where they can get their daily fix of the drugs their previous pimp got them hooked on, victory would be ours.

You can imagine what *losing* looks like in my line of work.

Good thing I don't lose when I'm two-and-a-half drinks and twenty milligrams in. I'm cozy and invincible. I'm satin wrapped in Kevlar. I'm—

"Zero, what the fuck are you doing?" Neda shouts from the top of the stairs. "Get your ass up here now and hold me!"

Damn it. I knew it was the yellow wire.

***

From pedophilia, pimps and corruption to brunches, beach days and dinner parties. It's always such a painful transition.

I'm not built for civilian life. Especially in Los Angeles. But LA makes sense for me from a logistical standpoint. It provides me with relatively easy access to a major airport offering nonstop or one-stop flights to every epicenter of child sex slavery. Not exactly a selling point used by local realtors, but it's what got me to plant roots here. If you can call them roots. I'm gone three to four months a year, three to five days at a time. As for all the sunshine and hip restaurants and gorgeous people, I've learned to cope.

Besides, Neda loves it here. And I love Neda. So much so, I haven't complained once about all the time we've spent with our friends since my return from Guadalajara three days ago. But then I've had a lot of practice pretending to be someone else.

Whenever out with others, I can do pleasant. I can do content. I'm even able to muster empathy and interest on occasion. It's not as easy as doing conniving, creepy, sleazy and sinister, but sometimes you just have to leave work at the office.

I'm having a hard time with that at the birthday party I'm attending right now. Mine. I've never liked celebrating my birthday. Neda knows this, but she couldn't resist organizing something when she found out April twenty-ninth fell on a Saturday this year, and that I was actually going to be home for it. Personally, I was starting to like our seemingly annual tradition of her baking cupcakes and eating one for me naked during a video chat while I'm on the other end of the earth wearing what looks like a Brioni suit.

It beats the hell out of talking to Neda's boss, Bert, in my living room.

"How go things on the child rescue front?" Bert asks.

Bert is the principal at the public high school where Neda teaches, so at least he knows a *little* something about the unspeakable horrors kids face. Still, he always smells like Aqua Velva and bouillon cubes.

"It's going, and going," I say, working a clenched-teeth grin.

Bert asks me when I'm heading out again, and I say tomorrow. Then I change the subject. "How 'bout you? How are things over in the hormone factory?"

"Eh, you know," says Bert. "Pretty much business as usual. We haven't had any stabbings or drug arrests in over a month—not on school grounds anyway. So there's that."

That's the first time Bert has ever made me laugh even a little, and he wasn't joking.

"Keep up the good work," I say as I raise my glass to clink his.

"Speaking of good work," says Bert, "Neda's having a fine, fine year. Did she tell you two of her students have essays in the final round of the statewide competition?"

"Yes, she did," I say, lying through my teeth. "I couldn't be prouder."

My next seven conversations more or less go the same way. Birthday greetings and a question or two about my work with OE. Where I just returned from. Where I'm heading next. How I deal with the jet lag.

Then me deflecting the attention back to them. Asking them about their job, their kids, their spouse or significant other. I act intrigued. Or at least try. It's not as easy as acting like a millionaire sex tourist eager for an eight-year-old.

We need new friends. Or fewer.

Whenever someone I'm conversing with at parties like this tries to bring the conversation back to human trafficking, I just smile and say, "Aw, you don't want to hear about that." If they insist, I tell them something to help them realize I'm right.

"Well, on my last mission, we liberated a really sweet eleven-year-old girl. And her unborn child."

Or

"I'm not sure what's worse—when a girl finds out her mother sold her for a couple hundred dollars to a pimp, or when the girl is freed and finds out her mother doesn't want her back."

Or

"Some of the girls are lucky enough to get AIDS and don't have much longer to relive everything."

That last one I use only on the most persistent and annoying inquisitors. Most of them, after hearing it, not only stop talking to me; they finish their drink and go home.

That's exactly what I want to do now. Except I *am* home. And I want another drink.

Barrett and Malik just arrived. A former Navy Seal and recovering coke addict, and a former Secret Service agent who got fired for punching a senator in the throat.

Finally, some people I can relate to.

As drunk as everyone is, they all part for the two giants making their way to me by the mini-bar. "Happy birthday," says Barrett as we clasp hands and bro hug. "Ready to get arrested halfway around the world?"

"As I'll ever be," I say, then bro hug Malik. "Glad you two could make it."

I pour Malik a scotch rocks. Barrett a scotch neat. I hand them each their glass and the three of us clink and sip. Barrett looks around and goes, "Drew here?" I shake my head and say Drew texted earlier saying he couldn't make it. In unison they say, "That's bullshit." I remind them Drew's got three kids and is flying out again with us tomorrow night. "I'm sure he's busy packing, picking up Legos and making sure Stephanie doesn't pull all her hair out," I say.

"I don't know how he does it," says Malik. "Our work's hard enough with just a wife or girlfriend. A whole damn family? Fuck that noise." Barrett raises his glass and says, "Or husband or boyfriend."

Through the crowd, Neda points to her empty champagne flute and smiles. I open the micro-fridge beneath the mini-bar, pull out a half-empty bottle of sparkling rosé, and fill a fresh flute nearly to the rim. Usually after three glasses, Neda goes from school teacher to freshman sorority pledge. This will be her fifth.

"Gotta bring this over to Neda," I say to Barrett and Malik as I hold up the fizzy glass.

"Looks like she's going to save you the trip," says Barrett.

I turn and Neda's wobbling toward us, like a child trying to walk in her mother's high heels. Reminds me too much of work.

"Well, at least *one* of you is enjoying your birthday," says Malik.

"Hi guys!" Neda shouts when she reaches us. She places her empty glass on the kitchen counter and gives Barrett and Malik each a hug. "I didn't see you two come in!"

Barrett tells Neda she's looking as beautiful as usual. Malik says amen.

"Oh, stop it," says Neda, slurring. She reaches out to take the drink I poured her, and I go, "You sure?" as I draw the glass back, instantly regretting my actions. Would have been better off just breaking the champagne flute on the granite countertop and shoving one of the shards into my abdomen.

"Yup," says Neda, landing hard on the *p*. "I'm sure. I'm fucking positive."

I hand her the glass like I'm surrendering a pocket knife to a cop pointing a loaded Glock at my head.

Neda's smile reappears as she turns to Barrett. "I need to steal you for a second," she says to him. "A friend of mine's dying to meet you. He's gorgeous. You're still single, right?"

Barrett smiles and with a wink says, "Always."

Neda grabs his hand and drags him through the throng of our closest friends whose names escape me. Barrett, grinning like a jackal, glances back at us and shrugs.

Malik laughs and shakes his head. "Dude's such a player." Then he turns to me and says, "You seem more somber than usual. Cheer the hell up, man, it's your birthday."

I say I'm fine. I tell him I'll be back to my old self once we're getting handcuffed in Phnom Penh.

CHAPTER FOUR

You skip an entire day whenever traveling from LA to Southeast Asia.

If only you got to choose *which* day.

We've got about three hours left on our five-hour flight from Shanghai to Phnom Penh following a fourteen-hour flight from LA to Shanghai. It's Tuesday, even though we took off on Sunday only fifteen hours ago. I'll understand quantum mechanics and the rules of cricket before I understand the International Date Line.

I've hardly slept since leaving LA, thanks to constant turbulence and Barrett talking my ear off on both flights. He's snoring now, the bastard. I bend over to reach my backpack shoved under the seat in front of me, and from the small front pocket I pull out a vial of diazepam. I twist off the cap, tap two pills into my palm, put my palm to my mouth and gnash the tiny tablets before taking a sip from one of my FAA-approved single-serving vodka bottles. Swallowing prescription drugs whole with water is for amateurs. The same people who order salmon at a steakhouse, or buy a Ferrari with an automatic transmission.

Playing on my mini entertainment monitor is an action film that grossed two-hundred million in three days two months ago.

It's about a team of superheroes on a mission to save the President of the United States. It's about Lycra overcoming evil. It's about the stupidest thing I've ever seen. But who can blame the studio execs or the producers or the director or the actors? These flicks are why they each have four homes across three continents.

Maybe if we at OE started wearing tights and capes, they'd make a summer blockbuster about *us*. God knows we each have an intriguing origin story.

Malik. Faster than a speeding bullet. Became a superhero after losing his Secret Service job guarding the life of prominent politicians he secretly wished would die.

Barrett. More powerful than a locomotive. Became a superhero following a dishonorable discharge from the Navy for using coke to help him deal with his heroism.

Me. Able to leap tall bottles in a single bender. Became a superhero after not using enough of my central intelligence during a two-year stint with the CIA.

Drew, Scott, Anders and the fourteen other Jump Team superheroes headquartered across the U.S., their origin stories are equally impressive. The point is, you'd be hard-pressed to find a finer, fiercer group of failures than the crew we've managed to assemble. Not to brag.

The captain announces we'll be landing twenty minutes late due to headwinds.

The flight attendant comes through with her cart and asks if I want another mini-vodka.

I say, "Sure."

I say, "Why not."

I say, "I'm on vacation."

Nothing wrong with getting into character a little early.

***

The bad news is there's Smirnoff all over the crotch of my pants. The good news is I missed the rest of the movie. And we're here.

No matter how tired or out of sorts you are upon landing in Phnom Penh, all the genuine smiles on the locals' faces will soon snap you out of it and make you glad to be alive. Most Cambodians have nothing, but that doesn't stop them from offering you everything. It's goddamn beautiful, and shaming.

I wish I had more time to spend with the 99.9 percent of Cambodians who aren't perpetrators of child sex slavery. Then again, all their warmth and kindness and humility might rub off on me and render me useless in the field. So it's probably a good thing I'll be staying at a fancy hotel tonight, moving to a secluded luxury villa tomorrow, then going wheels up after the party there in two days.

Malik, Drew, Barrett and I spot our driver holding up a sign that reads "Tomlinson Party" just outside the customs area. Naturally, Tomlinson is the surname of none of us. We walk over to the driver and each try but fail to match the width and authenticity of the grin he's flashing.

"That's us," I say to the driver as I point at the sign. The driver shakes my hand and says, "Hello! Welcome! I am Heng! Your journey was good?"

I say, "Yes, very good, thank you." The others nod their heads.

"I take your bags," says Heng, who lays the sign on the floor and starts to place our luggage on the cart beside him. Malik bends over to help out with his own bag, but Heng says, "No, no," and motions for him to drop it. "I do all work, you rest," he adds as he hoists the bag onto the cart.

It's Malik's first time in Cambodia. We should have warned him. Never try to lessen the burden of a Khmer man joyfully doing his duty. Offering assistance is one of the few ways to make a Cambodian *stop* smiling.

"Okay," says Heng. "Everybody ready?"

We all nod, and Heng starts pushing the cart toward the exit with us in tow.

If all the happy faces don't tip you off that you've arrived in Cambodia, the heat and humidity will. If you've ever opened a commercial oven turned on high while someone splashes you with bathwater, that's the forecast for the entire trip. And it's not even supposed to rain. A good thing, since our Rolexes that aren't Rolexes aren't waterproof.

Two words to live by in Phnom Penh: talcum powder. Especially if you are going to be wearing a fake designer suit while negotiating with possibly armed pimps.

Heng is unloading our bags from the trunk of his minivan under the overhang out front of the Sofitel, which means I got about a half-hour of sleep in. We all thank Heng, and I hand him a crisp twenty. That's US dollars—the unofficial currency of Cambodia. The riel has played second fiddle to the dollar ever since the United Nations Peacekeeping Operation of 1993 pumped a ton of greenbacks into the economy. It was the least we could do after all the Agent Orange we dumped on the country's rubber tree plantations during the Vietnam War.

The twenty I gave Heng will cover his breakfast, lunch and dinner for the next three days. Or his drinks this afternoon. I'm not one to judge.

"Thank you very much, sir!" says Heng, bowing then smiling almost wider than his thin face will allow.

"Thank YOU," I say. "And, uh, *mien tingay la-aw.*"

Heng's eyes light up. "Oh! Thank you! You have a nice day, also!"

This is my fifth or sixth time in Cambodia. Forgive me if I want to show off a little.

Two bellhops load our bags onto a brass cart and escort us inside to the lobby. There we hear a familiar deep voice behind us.

"Fuck, I guess they'll let *anyone* stay here."

We all turn around to see Anders with his perfect blonde hair and pleated shorts, standing with his arms folded, shaking his head in mocking disapproval. Standing beside him is Scott, laughing.

"What's up, boys?" I ask. "Looks like you beat us to paradise." The five of us exchange bro-hugs while the bellhops wait patiently near the check-in area. Barrett asks Anders and Scott when they got in. They say seven yesterday morning. "Didn't want to miss the breakfast buffet," says Anders. I pat his stomach and say it looks like he succeeded. Anders smirks, then holds up a middle finger.

"The others here yet?" I ask.

Scott says Nick and Lance are, and that Trent, Gil and Zack will get in a little later this afternoon.

Add us all up and you get ten. That may sound like a lot, but it's not. Not here. We're in the world capital of child trafficking. A Mecca for sexual tourists. Disneyland for well-heeled pedophiles.

On this mission, we'll be aiming to free two dozen girls from a life worse than death.

We could use a few more despicable men.

***

The cops burst into the villa with Berettas aimed at our heads. They shout for all of us to get the fuck down in both Khmer and broken English, and promise to put a bullet in our brains if we don't comply. Meanwhile, children dressed like porn shriek and scatter throughout the atrium.

All in all, a normal day at the office. Except for one thing.

One of the girls won't let go of me.

According to the pimp Anders arranged this party with, the girl is five. That's a new record.

"Give her!" yells a cop with a military mohawk, taking closer aim than I'm comfortable with.

I release my hands from the waist of the child's black cocktail dress to show Officer Mohawk she's the one clinging to me. Black kitten heels that would fit a Barbie doll slip off her feet and plop onto the mahogany floor. Red fake fingernails cut into both sides of my neck, and I'm not sure how much longer my floating ribs can withstand the tiny toes working their way into them through my Neil Barrett button-down.

The pain is almost enough to drown out the panic of the other girls being rounded up. Almost enough for me not to notice one of the four pimps just had his shoulder jerked out of its socket by two cops.

"Give her NOW!" Officer Mohawk screams at me, and then there's the click of a cocked hammer. It seems someone wasn't paying attention during rehearsal.

I hold my hands up, shake my head and say, "She won't let go" as the little girl digs in deeper and sobs harder, her face buried in my chest. One of the spaghetti straps of her dress has slipped off her shoulder and rests in the crook of her arm. She smells like bubblegum mixed with crayons mixed with Chanel.

Officer Mohawk shouts again, so I lower my hands and try to peel the girl off me without bruising any of her bird bones, hoping my half-assed effort will at least get this asshole to lower his weapon. The girl cries out as I pry her fingers from my jugular. I stop and tell her shhh and whisper in Khmer, "It be okay. Nobody to hurt you." She lifts her head just long enough to see a herd of cops slapping cuffs on her owners and my crew, and then buries her face again. Normally I go to great lengths to keep lipstick and eye shadow and mucous off my best shirt, but right now it doesn't really bother me. I press a finger to my shirt pocket to make sure both my pills are intact.

Ignoring Officer Mohawk's continued barking and his tight grip on the gun, I again whisper to the girl it's going to be okay. When she lifts her head, I look her in the pupils.

Such a rookie mistake.

Strands of straight black hair are plastered to her forehead with sweat. There's as much blue and red and black smearing her face as there is my shirt collar. Under the makeup her complexion's a touch lighter than that of most of the other girls, eyes a bit rounder. Tough to tell if she's Cambodian or Laotian or Thai or Vietnamese. Or some combination. Could also have some tourist or Marine mixed in.

Officer Mohawk shouts something and the child shrinks into me again, squeezing and clawing. Forget the Beretta. Right now these fingernails pose the bigger threat.

"Jesus Christ, hand her over!" shouts Barrett from the floor over by the bar, lying on his stomach in handcuffs aside the rest of our team and the pimps.

In Khmer, I say to Officer Mohawk, "Please, you're frightening her." The look on his face says I'm not speaking Khmer. He lunges at the girl's leg with his gun-free hand, but I step back before he's able to get a grip on her. Then I extend my arm and in English say, "Stop." Barrett shouts something to remind me I'm fucking up left and right today. Like I needed a reminder.

Officer Mohawk reaches for his holster. I know what's coming and almost deserve it. The baton cracks against my forearm just hard enough to take my mind off my neck and ribs.

"Fuuuck!" I shout through gritted teeth into the girl's ear. She screams and brings the attention back to my neck and ribs. I prop her up with my good arm and raise the hand of my throbbing one, signaling for Officer Mohawk to give me a moment. Barrett shouts something again, but I can't make it out over the crying.

"You go with the nice policeman," I say to the girl in English while pointing at our assailant. Her soaked eyes expand and try to swallow me. I point at Officer Mohawk again and give the girl a thumbs-up. "He won't hurt you," I say, doubtful she's getting any of this. "He will take you to a safe place. No more bad men."

The girl stops crying, but resists as I try to release her nails from my neck and her legs from my ribcage. I force the biggest smile I can muster and she begins to loosen her grip. After setting her bare feet on the floor, I squat down in front of her, hold her hand, and with a finger lift her fallen dress strap back into place.

"*Akrak nih ku mean cheang*," I say to her, praying I got it right. Needing her to know. Willing her to believe the worst is over.

She squeezes my hand and almost smiles, then lets go and allows Officer Mohawk to scoop her up. He carries her across the atrium toward the huge cypress double doors leading to something close to freedom. I wave to her just as one of the other cops tells me to get on my knees and put my hands behind my back.

I can't expect special treatment just so what's left of a little girl doesn't evaporate.

CHAPTER FIVE

At the bus station in Siem Reap, a slim boy-almost-man in white Capri pants and a white short-sleeved shirt holds up a sign with my surname on it. He spelled "Slade" as "Slayed," but I'm not about to nitpick. The sign could say "Shithead" and I wouldn't mind. The two oxy I ate as the bus pulled in have me in a decent mood.

"Mr. Slayed?" the boy-man asks when we lock eyes. His brown complexion is like a *Vogue* cover.

"Close enough," I say, pointing at the sign.

The boy-man smiles and bows before taking my valise, pretending not to notice the scabbed scratch marks on my neck and the purple-black welt on my forearm. "I'm Pich!" he says with a level of exuberance that would make me wary if we were in any other country. "Please, follow me."

Pich leads me out of the station to his tuk-tuk parked on a patch of dirt just off the road. He motions for me to have a seat in the back, then loads my bag next to me.

"We go to LifeLong Center, yes?" he asks as he takes his seat up front.

"Yes," I say, picking at the itch of one of my neck scabs. "That's right."

Pich starts the engine and gives it a little gas. "Hold on," he shouts over the rev, his voice vibrating with the motor. "Road there a little bumpy."

According to OE's Recovery Team member Sarah, who set this little impromptu side-trip up for me, it's a twenty-minute ride to the safe house. It would be more like a five-minute one were it not for all the potholes Pich is weaving around, leaving me somewhat carsick. The sun that just decided to come out of hiding doesn't help.

After what the girls I'm going to visit have been through, I'd hate to start off by vomiting on or near any of them. Not that they haven't experienced much worse.

The tuk-tuk's rearview mirror shows me looking paler than all the other Caucasian tourists we've passed on the street.

"You okay?" Pich asks me through the mirror.

I nod to keep things simple, then inhale deeply. Exhale slowly. Throwing up isn't the end of the world, unless you've ingested forty milligrams of quality opioids that are just beginning to kiss your system.

Pich reaches into a small Styrofoam cooler on the seat next to him and pulls out a can of Coca-Cola. He holds the can up behind his head and says, "Here, take."

I say thanks as I grab the can and rub its cool condensation all over my forehead, then pop the tab and take a sip. Pich probably spent a quarter of his daily wages on this soda. That's like a perfect stranger back home buying me lunch at Spago.

One more sip and I try to hand the can back to Pich. "No, no, all for you," he says, smiling wide in the rearview, then swerving sharply to dodge a crater.

"Sorry, sorry!" he says to the mirror.

"It's okay," I say, using my hand to wipe the bit of cola that spilled on the seat, thankful the can and I didn't end up on the road.

This is the problem with Cambodians. They'll kill you with kindness.

I place the can in the console's cup holder, then sit back and close my eyes to recapture my high. The massaging hum of the motor and Pich's improved driving are helping my cause. Then Pich starts speaking in Khmer, too fast for me to follow. I open my eyes and he's got a cell phone circa 2002 to his ear. He sounds much more subdued than when speaking to me in English, and the mirror confirms he's lost his happy. Based on the short stops and starts in his speech, he's being interrupted. A lot. I don't like the way the person I can't hear is talking to him. Pich catches me in the mirror, and I look away, up at the tuk-tuk's canvas covering, like that's convincing. I close my eyes again to find my light while Pich continues not getting a word in edgewise on the phone.

"We are here!" is the next thing in my ears. It's Pich and he's talking to me and damn it. Falling asleep is almost as bad as throwing up. My little nap cost me ten or fifteen minutes of near perfection I'll never get back.

The here Pich is referring to is just inside the gates of The LifeLong Center. It's a different here than I expected. Instead of a muddy field, there's grass and flowers and palm trees. Instead of drab tenements, there's a cluster of cottages painted bright blue and yellow, each with curtained windows.

And there's a playground. A playground with slides and seesaws and a swing set and a merry-go-round. But no children.

A door of one of the cottages swings open, and out comes a woman old enough to be the great grandmother of most of the girls who live here. Except she's white and, according to Sarah, from Ohio. Sarah told me the woman's name, but it's lost in my oxy fog.

Pich waves at her as she walks toward us along a stone path. He shouts, "Good afternoon, Miss Alice!"

This kid's good to have around.

Alice waves back to him, then waves to me and calls out, "Welcome, Mr. Slade" in a voice much bigger and stronger than her frame.

I get out of the tuk-tuk and close the gap between us before extending my hand.

"Hello, Alice," I say as we shake. "Thank you for agreeing to my visit on such short notice."

"Not a problem," says Alice, brushing from her weathered cheeks a few strands of white hair that escaped from her ponytail. "Come, I'll show you around."

With my good arm, I go to grab my valise from the rear luggage rack of the tuk-tuk. Alice says, "Just leave it. Pich here can look after your bag until our visit's over. Don't worry, he won't run off with it."

I'm not worried. For two reasons. First, my remaining oxy's on me, not in the valise. And second, Pich is the only male with regular access to these grounds. I'd trust him with more than just my luggage.

Alice points at my neck and asks, "What happened there?"

"Nothing," I say. "Just the hazards of the job."

She then points to the welt on my forearm, and before she asks I say, "Same."

Alice leads me down a stone path through a garden. Impossible reds and yellows and greens. The smell of gardenias and ginger. So tranquil, I almost don't need what I ate at the bus station.

"That house there on the left," says Alice as she points to one of the blue and yellow cottages, "that's our art and healing center. That's where the girls spend a large majority of their day, and where they all are right now."

"And over here," she says, "is the play space. It's very popular with the younger girls. Actually, with the older ones, too. They like to push their little sisters on the swings, organize games, things like that."

And I go, "Brings back some schoolyard memories." Like an idiot. I just compared my little yellow bus, kickball, capture-the-flag days to the Lost Girls' lives. That's one of the drawbacks of good narcotics—they often cause you to say cheerful things.

"It's not often we get visit requests from any of you Jump Team guys," says Alice as we walk past a jungle gym. "I think it's good for you to see what happens to these girls after your work is done."

Maybe, but I don't plan on making this a habit. The less I know about these girls, the easier it is for me to imagine they're doing just fine. If I don't stay in touch, there's no way I can hear about them getting back into prostitution or dying of an accidental drug overdose or dying of an intentional one. And if I don't hear about such things, they never happen. In a way, I'm saving them a second time by dropping out of sight.

Denial is how I show my love.

I keep my distance to keep them safe.

So why I just rode five hours from Phnom Penh to a safe house in Siem Reap is unclear. As is why I lied to Barrett and the guys yesterday, telling them I left my passport at the hotel and would have to catch another flight home.

"I just hope the girls aren't frightened by me," I say to Alice.

What I'm thinking is vice versa.

"Don't worry," Alice says. "I already told them you were

coming, and they know anyone I bring to see them is no one to fear."

We walk toward the art and healing center, the largest of the six cottages on the grounds. The front and the sides are decorated with hand-painted murals and words. Stars. Suns. Rainbows. Girls holding hands in a circle, dancing. "Hope" and "Love" and "Strength" and "Forgiveness."

It's a place no child would ever want to leave. A fairy tale I'm afraid to ruin.

Ten feet from the front door, there's laughter. Five feet from the door, the laughter's louder. Alice opens the door. And the laughter ceases.

Call me the evil stepmother. Call me the wicked witch.

Call me The Big. Bad. Wolf.

A couple dozen girls ranging in age from impossibly too young to far too young stand in front of easels, paint brushes hanging by their sides, paint from the brushes dripping on the floor. Most of them are wearing masks made of colorful feathers that extend far from their faces. Through the sequin-lined eyeholes, they—along with the mask-less girls—look at me, then at Alice, then at me again. The look in their eyes, it's the look they were beaten to conceal whenever men entered the place where they used to live.

"Girls," says Alice, her voice piercing the silence, "I would like you all to meet a friend of mine. His name is ... Bob. Bob helps girls just like you get to places just like this."

Some of the girls just continue staring, motionless. Others cup their mouths and whisper to their neighbors. A girl whose face is pale-white grabs a mask from a chair and slips it on. The handful of Khmer women who help care for the girls, they smile at me as if to say don't come any closer.

"Can everyone please say hello to our friend?" says Alice.

After receiving a chorus of half-hearted greetings, I wave to everyone, then lean toward Alice and murmur, "So, they all speak English?"

"Oh yes," she says to me. "Well, most of them. A few of the younger ones, not really. But they're learning."

The girls go back to painting. Most look over every few seconds like they're doing my portrait, and I keep trying to smile for the canvas. Not easy when your lips are stuck to your teeth due to lack of saliva.

I ask Alice what's with the masks.

"Oh, yes, those," says Alice, beaming. "Those were a gift from a lovely bunch of ladies—a church group—who visited us from New Orleans a few months ago." She says the masks help the girls feel new, feel safe. She says the masks allow them to hide without disappearing.

I say the masks are scary as hell, but not out loud.

Alice looks at my shirt and goes, "Oops, I forgot to get you a name badge." She asks me to run over to the office with her to retrieve it, and says we'll come right back to chat with some of the girls. She starts for the door and I say, "Wait. Give me just a minute, please, if you don't mind."

Alice says, "Well, we really do need to get—"

"I assure you, it's okay," I say as I start to walk along the wall toward the back of the room, my eyes fixed on the only girl painting with her fingers rather than a brush. I didn't notice her during the introduction even though she's one of the few not wearing a mask. She and her toy easel were eclipsed by the taller girls and easels. Now that I have noticed her, I barely recognize her.

She's got on a baby-blue cotton T-shirt, pink leggings that

end just below the knee, and white canvas sneakers with pink laces. Her fine black hair is in pigtails. For the first time in who knows how long, she looks like a little girl.

I stop a shadow's length away from her profile and watch as she smears a red yellow green masterpiece over every inch of the easel sheet. Alice, who must have trailed my every step, taps me on the shoulder. "Uh, I'm sorry," she says, "but it's our policy to—"

"What's her name?" I ask, keeping my eyes on the girl.

"That's Sung," says Alice. "She's one of the girls you—"

"Hello, Sung."

She turns her head and looks up at me, her hand still smearing colors, then sucks her lower lip in and tucks her chin.

Alice leans over and again taps me on the shoulder. "Perhaps it's better if we—"

"It's okay, it's me," I say to Sung. I squat down and point at my face, then at the scratches on my neck. "Remember?"

Sung wrinkles her face and grimaces as she touches her own neck and shouts, "Ow, ew!"

"No, no," I say, caressing one of my fresh scabs with a fingertip and forcing a smile. "See, doesn't hurt."

And Sung hisses at me.

"You're scaring her," snaps Alice. She tugs on me to stand up, then tells Sung something in a language I don't know, and Sung's face softens. To me, Alice says, "Maybe this was a mistake."

I say sorry. I say I've never been good with kids I'm not rescuing.

"It's okay," says Alice. "Let's just go to my office." As I turn to follow her, I wave to Sung, who shouts something at me, her voice high-pitched like helium. She doesn't seem angry. I smile and wave again, slowly walking backward behind Alice. And Sung shouts what sounds like a question.

"What's she saying?" I ask.

Alice stops and turns around. "She wants to know if the police are still mad at you."

I take a step toward Sung, then squat down and shake my head while smiling. To Alice, I say, "Tell her the thing with the police was just playing, a game to help her get away. I say, "Tell her I'm one of the good guys."

Upon hearing the translation, Sung makes a wow face, then a confused face, and then scratches her cheek, leaving a red yellow green smudge behind.

"What is that, Thai?" I ask Alice as she wipes Sung's face with a tissue. She nods and tells me they're pretty sure Sung was trafficked from a small town outside of Chiang Mai just a few months ago. She says Sung's smart. "She's already picked up some basic Khmer and a bit of English."

Still squatting, I inch a few steps closer and have Alice ask Sung, "Do you like it here?"

Sung averts her eyes and nods, and I give a thumbs-up. Then she reaches out and rubs the two days of stubble atop my head.

I usually go to great lengths to keep finger-paint off my scalp, but right now I really don't mind.

Alice apologizes and hands me a tissue. I say thanks but then I just tuck the tissue in my pants pocket.

Sung asks my name through Alice, and I say Bob. Sung asks something else and Alice says to me, "She wants to know if you live here."

"No," I say to Sung, shaking my head. "America. USA." Sung frowns and then, according to Alice, asks when I'm going home. I say tomorrow, and Alice tells Sung, and Sung frowns again.

"Fuck I didn't think this through" is the look on my face, but Alice doesn't translate it.

I say, "Don't worry, Alice here will take good care of you," and Alice passes it on. It would be great if Alice would add a little something of her own here. Maybe tell Sung something like she'll soon be reunited with her family. But Alice would never lie like that. Not to Sung or any of these girls.

The next question I get from Sung through Alice is, "Will you come visit again?" The look I give Alice says if Sung keeps this up, I'll have to kill the messenger.

"Absolutely," I say, but Alice doesn't say anything. She assumes I'm lying. She knows it's what I do for a living. So I bypass the middleman and just give Sung a big nod.

And Alice says Sung says, "Promise?"

This would be the perfect time to point to something shiny or offer some candy or even ask Sung to pull my finger.

"I promise I'll try to come soon," I say. And Alice gives me the benefit of the doubt.

Sung smiles, steps in and wraps her arms around my shoulders, pressing her cheek to my chest. She smells like finger-paint and baby shampoo. And not a hint of Chanel.

My eyes water and my nose burns, and not because Sung just destroyed another one of my favorite shirts. To fend off the tears, I think about things that piss me off. Like the man who trafficked Sung. Like the madams who dressed her and applied her makeup. Like the tourists who've created a market for her.

To dial back the anger, I pull back from our hug and look into her dark brown eyes—what got me into this mess in the first place.

It's a vicious cycle.

Sung lets go and runs over to a little play nook in the back corner of the room. She grabs a naked Barbie doll off one of the shelves and then plops down on a tall white wooden chair with it. I try to think of a worse toy for this place, but nothing comes to mind.

After another wave to Sung, I dab my eyes and pretend to forget Alice is right behind me. She rests her hand on my shoulder and says, "There is no shame in crying." She tells me she can't remember the last day she didn't, and points out she's been at this for over fifteen years. I say she must be dehydrated. Alice laughs, then asks if I'd like to meet some of the other girls.

"Sure," I say, "but what about my name badge?"

Alice gives a dismissive wave and goes, "I think we can make an exception this time."

She leads me over to a girl who is twice Sung's height and still a child. Through a peacock plume mask, the girl keeps her eyes fixed on her easel sheet, where she's putting the finishing touches on what looks like a clown. A clown with Xs for eyes and a snake for a tongue.

"Very creative, Kannitha," Alice says to the girl. Kannitha smiles, but I can see her brush strokes have stiffened in the few seconds I've been standing near her. I say, "Very nice work," and Kanittha's brush strokes tighten even more.

Alice takes me around and introduces me to several of the others, encouraging them to practice their English. I recognize a couple of the girls from the Phnom Penh rescue two days ago. I smile at them, but not too widely. Afraid of looking eager or aggressive or psychotic. Everything they're accustomed to.

Each girl Alice introduces me to, I say "Nice to meet you" and praise them on their terrifying art. But what I really want to do is apologize. On behalf of my entire gender. For my Adam's apple. My five o'clock shadow. For having anything in common with the people who've tricked and abducted and bought and sold and rented them.

I'm going for cheerful and solemn, but fear my expression says distracted and tense. I want to be present for these girls, but every five … ten … fifteen seconds I can't help but glance over at the nook to catch Sung talking to Brothel Barbie.

I say hi to a masked girl named Chenda who's painting a sun setting behind a house on fire, and all I can think is what is my face doing and why didn't I bring more diazepam on this trip.

Any look of discomfort I may be showing, I hope to hell Chenda and the others realize it's not aimed at them. Aside from the artwork and the dolls, this is a hopeful environment, and interacting with these girls here shouldn't be so awkward. I hate that playing a pedophile comes more naturally to me than being myself.

Alice asks if I'm ready to tour the rest of the grounds, and I say yes please. Then I turn around to take one more look at Sung playing. And all the tension in my face and neck and shoulders ceases.

CHAPTER SIX

The gun in my hand, the muzzle of it nearly chips my tooth. As usual.

And then I wake up.

My suicide dream has been recurring with increased frequency of late. At least this time I awoke before the crowd shouted, "Do it!"

I take it as a sign it's going to be a good day.

Despite the insomnia.

I remove my black satin sleep mask, the same one I wear at thirty-thousand feet, and look over at Neda out cold halfway under the covers, her back to me. Every few seconds, she whistles from her nostrils.

Neda never fails to get a solid eight or nine hours, even after waking up due to my late arrivals. Even after not hearing from me for days when I'm away on a mission. Even after going to bed angry.

Her ability to sleep off everything, that's a survival instinct. Her hypothalamus making sure she gets forty winks before sending her in to manage a host of walking hormones in a publicly funded institution. Anything less than seven hours of delta-wave dormancy, and she's as good as dead.

I don't bother to look at the time on my phone. It's between 4:27 a.m. and 4:48 a.m. It always is.

I nudge closer to Neda and spoon her, burying my nose in her hair, inhaling more of her cinnamon-vanilla than I deserve. My lips feel the warm smooth impossible of her neck, her shoulder, her back. She tastes like salted honey. I kiss the edge of a shoulder blade, then a little lower and am hit with flashes of Santo Domingo, where we last vacationed too long ago. At the small of her back she lets out a soft, semiconscious groan. At where things can get interesting she snorts and shifts toward her edge of the bed. Then goes back to whistling.

It was worth a shot.

Hell, I'm just lucky to be in the same bed with this woman.

I'd give sleep another go, but what's the point with all this whistling and silence and faraway girls screaming and crying. I roll off my side of the bed, straighten the sheets and comforter the way Neda likes to wake up to, then tiptoe toward the medicine cabinet in the master bathroom. If I have to be conscious, I might as well enjoy it.

All there is behind the mirror over the sink is nothing. Just four plastic shelves crammed with vials you can get over-the-counter or from a doctor when you have a cough. My oxy ran out on the way home from Cambodia. Pretty sure there's some Percocet somewhere. Ten tabs prescribed for Neda following her gum surgery last summer. She took only one and complained it made her feel lightheaded and out of sorts. Some people don't know a good thing even when it bites them on the pleasure receptor.

I go through the drawers on Neda's side of the bathroom vanity. Nothing. Check the drawers on my side. Nope. Search the shelves in the nook next to the shower. Fuck.

I slink out of the bathroom and into our walk-in closet.

Experts might say looking for drugs in your wife's panty drawer at five in the morning is a warning sign. Experts need to learn to keep their mouths shut. There's nothing wrong with making sure prescription medication you paid good money for doesn't go to waste. Call me thrifty. Call me resourceful.

Call me if you have any Percocet. Or Percodan. Or Vicodin or Demerol or Lortab.

There's nothing enticing mixed in with Neda's thongs and boy shorts. I check the next drawer of the dresser and find just a bunch of petite T-shirts and tiny balled up socks. No luck in the bottom drawer, either. Only an assortment of yoga pants.

This would be a lot more enjoyable if I had some sort of clothing fetish.

I search the rest of the walk-in closet, scouring shelves of shoes and casual tops and shit. Peek behind a wall of designer jeans and blouses and dresses and goddamn it. Sift through a small chest filled with costume jewelry and retired perfume and motherfucker. Motherfucker and a neatly rolled-up necktie. It's burgundy—my least favorite color—with cream polka dots. Fine silk. I unroll it and wrap it around my face to think.

The tie must have belonged to Neda's father. But it smells very Dior or Versace or Clive Christian. Neda's father was an Old Spice guy until the day he died.

Well this is very upsetting.

Seems Neda has finally wised up. Stopped taking me for an answer. Realized she can do better.

Also, I was sure we had some Percocet.

***

I don't make the best decisions when I miss my morning narcotics.

For instance, I had two shots of bourbon for breakfast.

And forgot to add oil to the hot iron skillet I just cracked two eggs into.

The whites hiss and pop and spit at me. I lift the skillet off the flame and dig the spatula under the already-crispy edges of the eggs, causing the white bubbling mass to tear and one of the yolks to rupture. Under the spatula, the bottom of the skillet looks like we're getting a new skillet. A Teflon-coated one. I don't care what Neda says about cancer and thyroid disease and infertility.

"Fuck!" I shout as loud as the clanging of the skillet denting the bottom of the stainless steel kitchen sink.

"What's going on down there?" Neda asks from above. And I go, "Nothing, I just burned myself a little," then give the crusted skillet two middle fingers like it just cut me off on the 405.

Down the stairs comes Neda weighing much less than she did stomping up them last night. She enters the kitchen in nothing but her white tank top and black Brazilian-cut panties. Oh, and her imitation Uggs, but who's looking at her feet. This sexy on a Sunday morning after an argument. It's how she punishes me.

"Good morning, beautiful," I say, standing with my back to the sink to conceal the murder.

She yawns and stretches, then sniffs the air and goes, "You burned the eggs again, didn't you?"

I blame it on the goddamn skillet. She blames it on the goddamn bourbon. I tell her I didn't have any bourbon and she says, "Then what's that smell?"

"Oh, I dumped the little bit left in my glass from last night while washing it this morning," I say, then walk over to the table where she's sitting and kiss her forehead.

Neda nods, snatches the Arts section from the morning paper and goes, "Then why's the smell coming from your face?"

I shrug and head back to the sink to chisel the first attempt at breakfast off the surface of the skillet. But even with the chipping and scraping and the hot water spraying full blast from the faucet, Neda's still audible behind me.

"I know the trip was stressful, Zero, but c'mon. Liquor at eight thirty?"

I grab some steel wool and go to town.

"Zero!"

I stop scrubbing, then turn to face Neda and remind her I'm still on Cambodia time.

Neda snaps the Arts section open with both hands and holds it up to shut me out. "You've got a problem," she says from behind a Klimt exhibit at the LACMA. "There's no excuse for drinking this early."

She needs to learn to be more accountable. None of this would have happened if she'd held on to her Percocet.

"Let me make you a nice breakfast," I say as I glide over to the fridge to retrieve two new eggs.

Neda flips the newspaper around and snaps the pages again. Then from behind the opening of a new gallery on East 4th she says she's not hungry.

"Some tea then?"

The Arts don't move but I can tell Neda's shaking her head.

I open the fridge and return the eggs to the carton on the top shelf, then grab a container of strawberries from the middle shelf and a bottle of orange juice from the side ledge. "How about a nice smoothie?"

The new gallery smacks against the table, and Neda, her face twisted like a Picasso, looks at me and says, "I. Am. Not. Hungry."

She then snatches up the paper and goes back into hiding.

With the strawberries and juice in hand, I kick the fridge door closed, walk over to the table, and sit down across from her. "Why are you so upset?"

Neda just laughs, hard enough to punch something, and flips the paper again.

To a three-star review of the latest Tarantino film, I say, "Talk to me."

Neda taps one of her fake Uggs on the kitchen tile and turns a page.

I crinkle the flimsy plastic container of strawberries and say, "Please don't be like this."

Neda turns another page, tearing it.

I give the container a hard squeeze and a bit of red juice and pulp oozes from one of the small holes on the side. I wipe my hand on my sweatpants and, raising my voice to the Los Angeles Ballet, I go, "I finally get a full week off from jumps, and this is how you want to start things off?"

Neda crumples up the entire city's cultural scene into a large ball and throws it at me, but the Tropicana bottle deflects it to the floor. She shouts either fuck you or fuck off or fuck a camel in Farsi, then slaps the top of the table hard enough to make the strawberries bounce.

"Hey, hey, ease up," I say, as I slide my chair away from the table, both hands raised.

The look on her face is why Thorazine was invented.

I say sorry three times and not enough. Neda jumps up from the table, every inch of her brown skin brick red, and looking down at me she launches into a "First off."

First off, our full week together dropped to five days the second I skipped my first flight home from Phnom Penh.

"Yeah, but—"

Second off, I could have at least had the decency to respond to her texts and emails telling me how much she missed me loved me wanted me with text and emails telling her how much I missed her loved her wanted her.

"You already know how I—"

Third off, no she *doesn't* "already know how I" because I haven't said it or shown it in she doesn't know how long.

"I promise I'll—"

Fourth off, my drinking.

"What? I don't drink nearly—"

Fourth off, my drinking.

"It's just to help take the edge—"

Fifth off, do I have any idea what it's like to have a spouse who is even farther away the few days a month he's home?

"Aw, baby. That's not—"

Sixth off, I'll have plenty of time to think about all this. While she's living at her sister's.

I'm guessing the look on my face is why defibrillators were invented.

Neda just stands there and watches as sawdust fills my mouth. As a sponge lodges in my throat. All that, and the dizziness.

My chance to get a word in edgewise and I can't.

"Zero!" shouts Neda, bending down to my level. "Did you hear what I said?"

I go to stand up from my chair but the knees aren't having it. My hands sweat like they're still in Cambodia and brace the edge of the table to keep the rest of me from slipping under it.

All I can do is blink with my eyes wet like my mouth should be.

It opens and just more sawdust.

Neda shakes her head and mutters asshole or shithead or divorce in Farsi. With my finger I say give me a sec, then reach for the orange juice on the table and unscrew the green plastic cap. I need both hands to lift the plastic bottle to my mouth. The citrus burns off the sawdust enough to speak as Neda turns to leave the kitchen. I wasn't going to bring this up.

"Are you having an affair?"

Neda jerks to a halt, and with the back of her black panties to me, goes, "*Excuse* me?"

More sawdust. So more orange juice, and in a voice like a quarry I ask her about the tie in her jewelry chest. Without turning around, Neda drops her chin to her chest. And laughs.

"Something funny?" I ask, still seated despite my efforts.

Neda laughs again and goes, "No, not funny at all." She turns to face me and tugs at the hem of her tank top like it might cover up what she's never had to hide. "Very sad," she says. "Pathetic, in fact."

"So," I say, "*Are* you? *Did* you?"

Neda scoffs and looks away.

I spring from my chair and shout, "Answer me!" as the back of the chair slams against the fridge door behind me.

Tears now accompany Neda's smile. She covers her eyes with her thumb and forefinger, then shakes her head and goes, "What were you doing going through my jewelry chest?"

I tell her not to worry about that. I tell her to just answer the goddamn question.

Watching her grin and cry like this, seeing her caught so off guard she can't even look at or take a step closer to me, I almost feel sorry for her.

Through a clenched jaw I tell her I deserve to know the truth.

"Okay," says Neda all teeth and tears as she traipses back

toward the table. "But I don't think you're going to like it."

She leans on the table with both hands, her head down, and takes a long breath while every man she's ever met flashes through my mind. I brace for impact.

"Before I tell you," she says, looking me in the eyes at last, "I need to know what you're going to do to the guy."

I can't be honest, so I just fold my arms across my chest, dig my fingertips into my side ribs, and say, "I won't lay a hand on him."

And Neda goes, "That's a shame. I was hoping you'd kill him."

She laughs and says, "The tie? It's the tie you were wearing the night you proposed to me."

She cries and says, "I wouldn't expect you to remember that."

Then she screams and brings her fist like a sledgehammer down on the container of strawberries, spattering red all over the table and her and me. And us.

"I was having an affair with my husband," she says as she removes her tank top covered in crime scene and drops it on the floor. "But don't worry," she adds, backing out of the kitchen in just her Uggs and black panties, a crimson drop trickling down her breast, "that's all over now."

CHAPTER SEVEN

Fynn is two thousand miles away and all up in my face.

As usual, her silver hair is pulled back as far and as tight as it can go. This is so you catch every word her eyes shout.

"I don't run a travel agency, Zero," Fynn says, occupying almost my entire screen. The glare on the screen, it's her. "You don't get to extend a mission just because you're enjoying yourself."

"I wasn't enjoying myself," I say, checking the little box in the corner of my screen to make sure my strawberry-stained sweatpants aren't visible. "I simply forgot my passport back at the hotel and couldn't get an affordable flight home for a couple of days."

The little box in the corner shows me lying to my face.

"Bullshit," Fynn says softly but only because of my volume controls. "You're too good at what you do to space on your passport like that. And besides, you've got platinum status with the airline, so you could have gotten on the next flight out of there at minimum or no extra cost."

I shrug and throw my hands out to the side, then point out that if I wanted to work a vacation out of the Cambodia trip, I would have gone to Koh Ker, not to a safe house in Siem Reap.

And she goes, "That was just to cover your ass. I'm sure you squeezed in plenty of R and R, maybe a tour of Angkor Wat."

"I assure you I didn't," I say. The trouble is, the camera always takes five pounds off the truth.

I use the brightness controls to dim Fynn's contempt, then tell her sorry and it won't happen again.

"That's *right* it won't," she says as she lifts a white mug and takes a sip of tea or coffee or motor oil. "You know I don't like unapproved variations of the schedule. Unless you get captured or killed, I expect you to stick to the itinerary on every mission."

There's a reason Fynn doesn't write our help-wanted ads.

To get a little reprieve from Fynn's audiovisual reaming, and from the sight of Neda's absence everywhere, I click on my news tab and catch video coverage of a school shooting by an eighth-grader in Tulsa. Putting the video on mute and keeping my eyes on the center of the screen makes Fynn think I'm listening to and watching her every word.

"Zero, are you paying attention?" my invisible boss asks through a yearbook photo of the gunman.

I minimize the news and tell Fynn's head and shoulders, "Yes, yes. Like I said, it won't happen again."

"What? I'm talking about the new recruit I just mentioned."

I apologize to her for being distracted and say it's been a rough day. I don't go into detail. I can't tell Fynn my wife left three hours ago and I'm fresh out of painkillers. She'll assume I don't have my shit together.

"Well," says Fynn, "get your shit together. I don't like repeating myself." And she goes on to tell me about the new recruit named Caleb Klein she wants me to train. How he is, or *was*, some young hotshot with the LA FBI. How his career there was just starting to take off when *bam*, out of nowhere he decides to call it quits and come work for us.

Already I don't trust Caleb. Nobody decides to work for OE "out of nowhere." They are pushed to us by something stronger than them, something dark they can no longer control or conceal. Something like rage or addiction or PTSD. Something like bipolarity or panic disorder or masochism. But maybe I'm wrong in this case. Maybe Caleb really is the bright and shining star Fynn has described. Maybe he's self-actualized and stable and moral. Maybe he's undamaged goods.

If so, he'll never fit in.

"Have you fully vetted him?" I ask.

Fynn says of course. Says she's read every report on him ever submitted by his superiors, and has personally Skyped with him three times. "The kid's a golden boy," says Fynn. "He's goddamn Joe DiMaggio."

I turn away from the screen and throw up a little in my mouth. But then I remember Joe DiMaggio had friends in the mob. Joe DiMaggio had his heart ripped out by Marilyn Monroe. Joe DiMaggio batted just .111 in the 1949 World Series.

Maybe there's hope for Caleb yet.

"So when would you like me to start with him?" I ask.

"Tomorrow," says Fynn.

I turn away from the screen and throw up a little in my mouth again. This time it's less Caleb and more the half bottle of bourbon I drank after Neda slammed the front door behind her.

"*Tomorrow?*" I say. "I haven't even—"

"Yes, tomorrow. I want you to work with Caleb all week at the satellite office there in LA, and then have him shadow you in Mumbai this weekend."

I switch back to the school shooting while Fynn drones on

about what time I need to be at the office and what I should highlight in training and how I should remind Caleb to pack Imodium for the trip. She says she just emailed me his contact info and résumé.

"Roger that," I say as I wince at a live shot of the school cafeteria.

"You okay?" Fynn's voice asks through all the scattered lunch trays and the abandoned backpacks and the blood.

I switch back to her face and say everything's just fine. Then click off the call.

I check my phone and it says my dealer hasn't texted me back yet. My laptop and I get off the couch and trudge upstairs to the bedroom. I lie down on my back, propping my head up with the pillow next to the pillow with Neda's indent, and un-mute the laptop.

The newswoman tells me twelve students so far have been confirmed dead, including the shooter. She says nobody in the quiet little community saw it coming. She says the shooter had reportedly been bullied for years.

Such a waste of young, mostly innocent lives. If only someone could have convinced the kid to get some help. Or at least to spare his peers and shoot me instead.

Anything to get me out of sitting on the 101 during rush hour tomorrow.

***

After child sex slavery, the thing I hate most is what I'm doing today. Imparting knowledge. Sharing experience and wisdom. When your life bears a resemblance to a trailer park following a Category Five hurricane, you don't want to be depended upon to bring out the best in others.

Right behind training on my hate list is OE's downtown office. My Jetta and I are less than two miles away right now, so we'll be arriving in a little over half an hour. I reach for my travel mug and take a sip of coffee Neda didn't make, then switch on the radio and press the scan button. Every other station is saying the number of fatalities from the school shooting has risen to fourteen, and every *other* station is playing the number-one song in the nation. I switch the radio off again.

To keep from getting frustrated in the bumper-to-bumper traffic, I think about young girls suffering. About how abominable it is that a job like mine must exist. About the reason why Fynn has hired this Caleb guy to join our team, and the reason why she'll likely hire another new member within the next month or so.

The reason is this: market growth. Our industry is forever expanding. It's becoming increasingly more lucrative. Human trafficking has a tremendous future. Even brighter than drug trafficking. It's why many big-time drug dealers are diversifying—dipping their toes into the sex trade. They're starting to realize how seventy- and eighty-pound girls are worth more than thousands of kilos of coke.

The Audi to my right cuts me off, and instead of flipping him the bird I picture the lashing scars on a Venezuelan girl's back.

The Infiniti behind me lays on his horn, and rather than curse his stupidity I reminisce about the acid burns on a Laotian girl's forearm.

The Porsche to my left has been revving his engine for the three minutes it's taken us to move fifty feet, and as I start to roll down my window to scream, into my mind pops a Bangladeshi girl brain-dead from an opium overdose.

And I relax.

You don't need a therapist when you have countless raped and abused children to put everything in perspective. If it weren't for these girls I refuse to forget, I'd probably be in prison for vehicular manslaughter. All the drivers of these fancy coupes and sedans and SUVs surrounding me, advertising their asininity at five miles per hour, they don't realize how the international sex trade is saving their lives.

And giving meaning to mine. Fortunately, and unfortunately, there's a lot of job security in my line of work.

That's not to say there isn't also a lot of turnover. Caleb, like any new recruit, will either be with us for years or be gone before his second or third mission. It all depends on how fucked up he is. If he's as solid as Fynn says, he won't make it out of training. If he's as defective as I suspect, he'll be getting a gold watch from us when he finally retires.

I crawl off the freeway onto the exit for North Hill Street, then pull into the parking garage beneath the seven-story building housing our satellite office. It's 8:41. Later than when Fynn asked me to arrive but earlier than when Caleb is set to. Of course, him being former FBI, he probably got here an hour ago. Then again, him being former FBI who's opted to work for OE, he may very well have overslept after binge-drinking and waking up at the LA Zoo.

The office is on the fifth floor, between a social worker's private practice and another social worker's private practice. Nearly all of the businesses on our floor and every other floor are dedicated to making the world a better place. None of them, however, have applied that dedication to their own office space. They don't seem to understand there's only so much positive social transformation that can be accomplished beneath industrial drop-ceilings and fluorescent lighting. There's a real limit to the amount of human suffering you can relieve while sitting in a cramped gray cubicle surrounded by beige carpet.

Changing the world is a lot easier with the help of some interior decoration.

Fynn likes having a satellite office in LA because, after Denver, LA is where OE has the most employees. In addition to Barrett, Malik, Drew and me, three administrative staff members make their home here in the City of Angels. All three of the staffers have to commute to and sit in the satellite office every day, sometimes even on Saturdays. It makes me appreciate just how lucky I am to be able to do my job from the comfort of third-world sex-tour destinations.

One of the aforementioned staff members, Patrick, is sitting behind the front desk when I enter the office.

"Good morning, Mr. Slade!" he shouts as he jumps up from his seat. "Long time no see!"

I say hi and tell him I have a nine o'clock with a new Jump Team guy.

Patrick shouts, "I know!" He shouts, "Fynn emailed me about it!" He shouts, "Aren't you excited?"

I say sure.

How Patrick is able to maintain such pep and enthusiasm in these surroundings is beyond me. Most young gay men in LA would commit suicide or murder if forced to endure such a daily aesthetic assault. That Patrick shows no signs he might harm himself or others leads me to believe he's clinically insane.

I tell him I'm going to get set up in the conference room, and ask him to please escort Mr. Klein back there when he arrives.

"No problem!" shouts Patrick. "It would be my pleasure!"

The conference room. We call it that, but it's really just a large closet toward the back of the office. I'm pretty sure it's where the previous business kept its cleaning supplies. Or where it hid its clients from immigration officers.

I remove my laptop from its case and place it on the conference room table, which is just big enough to play couples bridge on. While waiting for the laptop to boot, I pull out my cell phone and text, "I'm still in need of supplies—lost mine at the airport" to my best friend.

Why I bother to lie to a drug dealer, I don't know. Can't imagine he likes me insulting his intelligence.

Thirty seconds later, he texts, "Come by around 8 tonight."

If only all my relationships were this easy.

I text Neda. For the fifth time this morning. "I'm sorry. Please just come home."

She has ignored each of my previous four messages. She also ignored the eight I sent yesterday after she left for her sister's in Culver City. And I'm guessing she'll ignore the ones I send tonight.

My laptop signals it's open for business and my new wallpaper image fills the screen. A photo of Sung, one Alice took of her playing with her stuffed tiger and emailed to me. Lucky for me, we always keep a box of tissues in the conference room.

"Hello! You must be Caleb!" Even with the door closed, Patrick sounds like a normal human standing in the same room as me. I can't hear if Caleb has responded, but assume so. Or maybe he's too confused to speak, wondering if he's mistakenly entered the office of a cheerleading association whose employees possess psychic abilities.

"Mr. Slade is expecting you!" Patrick shouts. "Please, right this way!"

I pull up a training file on my laptop and practice various pleasant facial expressions. My phone buzzes. A text from Neda:

"Stop it. I'll let you know when I'm ready to talk."

There's a knock on the conference room door. And I wonder if there's any chance at all it's a kid I used to bully in grade school who's come back for revenge. And I laugh at myself for even *thinking* I might be so fortunate.

***

The average height of the members of our Jump Team is around six-foot-three.

The average weight is about two-twenty-five.

Those averages are about to go down.

Significantly.

Caleb is standing beside Patrick in the doorway of the conference room, the top of his head even with Patrick's shoulder. It's worth pointing out Patrick is maybe five-eleven. In heels. And no, Caleb is not bent over or hunching. The suit he's wearing, it would be snug on Neda.

This is awkward. Not so much Caleb's diminutive size; more that Patrick introduced him to me several seconds ago and I've yet to respond.

"Zero," says Patrick, "everything okay?"

Obviously not, Patrick. You aren't shouting.

I apologize, claiming something I was just reading distracted me, then stand up and extend my hand across the table. "Caleb, it's great to meet you. Looking forward to working together. Fynn has nothing but good things to say about you."

"Likewise," says Caleb, shaking my hand. He may be only five-two, but he has the grip of a blacksmith. "Ms. Cavanaugh says I'll be learning from the best."

We'll have to improve his ability to lie if he's going to succeed in the field.

I thank Caleb and ask him to have a seat so we can get started. Patrick clasps his hands together like a proud matchmaker. "I'll leave you guys to it!" he shouts before stepping out and shutting the door behind him.

"I apologize for the inauspicious workspace," I say.

"No need," says Caleb as he looks around with blue eyes too big for the rest of him. He loosens his tie and says, "I'm used to sitting in interrogation rooms. Some are half this size."

That must be why the FBI hired this guy in the first place. He was literally a good fit.

"How long were you with the bureau?" I ask.

"Three years," say Caleb. He shifts in his seat and runs a hand over the top of his wavy, dark brown hair, mussing his side part in the process. "It was a good experience, but I needed something more. Too much deskwork involved."

I tell him the only time he'll be sitting on his ass in this job is on planes. And he says, "Good. That's why I'm here."

There's got to be something more to it than that, but this isn't a job interview. There'll be plenty of opportunities for me to uncover his flaws without having to ask him about them. A few days in the field with the likes of Barrett and me, and Caleb will feel a lot more comfortable revealing how fucked up he is.

For now, I just need to make sure he can be a good pedophile.

"Fynn likes for me to start by going over a bunch of facts and statistics," I say.

Caleb nods and says, "Sounds good."

It's not.

Reading what's on my laptop screen, I say, "Trafficking women and children for sexual exploitation is the fastest growing criminal enterprise in the world."

I say, "Over two million children are subjected to prostitution in the global commercial sex trade."

I say, "The average age of a victim is eleven to fourteen."

I say, "The average life span of a victim is seven years, with many found dead from assault, abuse, HIV and other STDs, malnutrition, drug overdose or suicide."

The reaction I'm looking for at this point is calmness. Perhaps with a hint of disdain. The reaction I'm looking *out* for is anger, which is the natural reaction and thus unacceptable. I'm also looking out for sadness, especially tears. Tears are completely normal. This job is not.

Caleb, he's nodding his head and pursing his lips. This shows he's already aware of the horrors, perhaps even prepared for them. He's not pleased, but also not about to throw the table through the wall. Or cry.

Promising.

Now let's see how he does with the video portion.

Here is where I'd normally ask a trainee to stand up, walk around the table and take a seat next to me. But I don't want to be further distracted by Caleb's stature, so I get up with my laptop and come to his side of the table. By having him stay seated, I can imagine he's five-eight or five-nine. I just won't look down to see if his feet are touching the carpet.

I point to my screen and say, "We're going to watch a short documentary that OE produced a few months ago but has yet to release."

Again, Caleb says sounds good. Again, it's not. What I'm about to show him is so poorly filmed and edited, it somehow makes sex trafficking look worse than it is. But that's fine for our purposes here.

This is where some trainees buckle. This is when they start

having second thoughts about what they've signed up for. It's one thing to love OE's cause on paper, to get inspired by our mission statement. It's another thing entirely to peek behind the curtain and see the faces. Even when the faces are pixelated to protect identity. Or what's left of it.

We've had former homicide detectives fail to show up to the second day of training.

I've seen three-hundred-pound UFC fighters cover their eyes and sob before the opening credits have finished rolling.

Three minutes into the video, I glance at Caleb. He's fully engrossed in what he's watching. And what he's watching is a nine-year-old from Myanmar lying in a hospital cot a day after having her dislocated jaw wired shut.

Five minutes in, Caleb is quietly jotting down notes as a pimp caught on a hidden phone camera is bragging about how many virgins he's able to bring to the next night's party.

At the ten-minute mark, as the video is ending, Caleb closes his eyes and takes several deep breaths.

I've seen this before with trainees.

"It's okay, man," I say as I pat him on the back. "Should I grab the trash bin?"

With his eyes still shut, Caleb says, "I'm good" and continues breathing deeply.

"It's okay, man. No shame. What you just watched is too much for most people."

Caleb says nothing. Just long inhales followed by longer exhales. Hands in his lap. He looks too serene to vomit, but I get up and grab the bin from the corner anyway and place it by his chair.

"Do you need anything else?" I ask, wondering how I'm going to break it to Fynn that her golden boy isn't cut out for the job.

Caleb takes a couple more deep breaths, and opens his eyes. He says, "My apologies, I was just—"

"No need to apologize," I say. "We can take a break if you want."

He shakes his head and goes, "That won't be necessary. I just needed to get that little meditation out of the way. You know, send my intention out into the universe."

Now it's me who might need the trash bin.

Caleb points at my laptop screen and says, "Those traffickers are in pain, and they haven't learned how to respond to that pain with mercy and empathy."

He says, "The intention I sent out was for them to recognize this. To help them ease their suffering, and that of the girls."

Oh shit.

It's more serious than I suspected.

Caleb isn't an alcoholic or a drug addict or suffering from PTSD. He isn't depressed or bipolar or a masochist.

He's a Buddhist.

I can overlook a lot of things in a Jump Team member, but total enlightenment may be where I have to draw the line.

CHAPTER EIGHT

I'm sitting on my couch with my older brother, Hank. Only he's no longer older. He always had four years on me. Now I've got two on him.

Still, it's his birthday today. Even if it doesn't count.

We've just started watching Hank's favorite movie, *Harold and Maude*, on the widescreen. The two glasses of whiskey on the coffee table, one's for me and one's for Hank. I can't let something as trivial as ashes get in the way of tradition. Some people might say drinking with him like this is offensive, considering how he lived. Hank would tell those people to fuck off. Besides, it's not like I'm going to get as drunk as he was when he crashed. I can't, I've got to catch a flight to Mumbai in a few hours. That and, due to the acetaminophen in oxy, too much liquor is bad for you. Murder on the liver.

On the TV, Bud Cort hangs himself and his mother tells him he's not amusing. Hank and I laugh and Hank takes another sip. Me, I've had enough. Hank says to me, "Minus five for being a pussy." Sibling rivalry never changes, even when your brother's dead.

What I miss most about Hank is everything. Fortunately for me, I don't need a photo album to remember him as he was. I can just look in the mirror. From the time I was about sixteen right up until the end, Hank and I could pass for twins. We shared the same square jaw, slightly hooked nose, thin lips, heavy lids, hazel eyes and—before I shaved my head eight years ago thanks to Grandpa Isaac's receding genes—the same dark brown wavy hair. Height-wise, he was just a thumb's width taller than me at six-four, but I had about ten pounds on him throughout most of our adult lives. Hank was never much for working out, and muscle weighs more than whiskey.

Bud Cort drowns in the backyard pool and his mother rolls her eyes at him while continuing the breaststroke. Hank laughs harder than I do, then gives me more shit for not keeping up with him drink-wise.

Despite him being four years my senior and partying like a rock star's rock star idol, Hank never showed his age. My first fake ID wasn't fake. It was Hank's "lost" ID. His present to me on my eighteenth birthday. You know someone loves you when they're willing to spend an entire afternoon at the DMV just so you can drink illegally.

There were only two times in our adult life when Hank and I didn't really look much alike. The first was when I had a mullet haircut and acne all over a face bloated by beer my sophomore year of college. The second was six years ago when Hank went through the windshield of his Nissan. The latter I know because I'm the one who had to identify the body.

It was like looking into a shattered mirror.

Bud Cort falls in love with Ruth Gordon, four times his age, at a funeral after witnessing her steal the minister's car. Hank laughs so hard he spills some of his whiskey on the strawberry stain on my sweatpants and doesn't apologize. But hey, it's his birthday. Besides, now we're even for me knocking over his urn while toasting to him during last year's celebration.

I excuse myself and head to the bathroom to take a piss. While washing my hands afterward, I see what Hank looks like two years older and totally bald. I stagger back to the couch and we both start laughing. Not at any of the crazy shit Bud Cort and Ruth Gordon are doing; rather at some of the crazy shit Hank and I did. Like when we stole a case of beer from the Crowley's garage when I was ten and Hank was fourteen. Or when we stole a bottle of Jack Daniels from the Gibson's garage when I was eleven and Hank was fifteen. Or when Hank got me high for the first time when I was twelve and he was dealing.

Good times.

See also: Early warning signs.

As much fun as we had as kids in Chicago, the best memories were much more recent. Six months after Neda and I moved to LA for my OE job, Hank moved out to nearby Anaheim to take a job with a big construction firm. It was the first time he and I had lived in the same time zone in nearly two decades. He'd come over for dinner a couple of times a month. We'd grab drinks and shoot pool as much as my crazy travel schedule and Neda would allow. He even accompanied me on one of my OE missions. Not to participate, just to see the sights. He'd only been out of the country twice before—to Canada, which doesn't count, and to Canada again. I'll never forget the look on our face when I told him I was taking him to Bangkok.

Despite knowing what I did for a living, Hank spent most of the Bangkok trip in the bars on Soi Cowboy, the city's brightest street and most renowned red-light district. This was sort of the equivalent of Elliott Ness' brother going to Chicago to party with Al Capone.

Hank did swear up and down he didn't lay a finger on any of the young dancers in the bars. Said he was too busy falling in love with one of the bartenders, who, he pointed out, was clearly of age and then some. He said they made sweet love in a cramped storage closet during her break. He said it was special. He said she could be the one.

One month and two Anaheim girlfriends later, he was gone.

And here I am, toasting a silver and sapphire blue ceramic container, trusting as I have for six years that the Eden Funeral Home got things right. That there were no mix-ups in the crematorium. I don't like drinking with strangers.

"Here's to you, big brother," I say, holding my or Hank's whiskey in the air. "Miss you, man. The good news is, you're not missing anything. Things are total shit." I clink the glass against the urn and take two sips.

Ruth Gordon overdoses on sleeping pills and Bud Cort rushes her to the hospital but she dies, and neither Hank nor I laugh. My phone buzzes next to me on the couch. It's the only person whose call I'd accept right now. Hank's sister in-law.

"Neda, hi," I say, putting my drink down and sitting up straight, as if she can see me.

"Hi, Zero," she says like a cousin. "How are you?"

It's the first time I've heard her voice since she left five days ago. This, coupled with Ruth Gordon's death and my heartfelt toast, has me a little watery.

Pimps and pedophiles. Pimps and pedophiles.

"I'm hanging in there," I say. "You?"

"Same," says Neda. "I'm calling because … well, I know this day can be a little rough for you."

I tell her that's sweet but I'm fine. I say Hank and me, we're just hanging out before I head to the airport.

"Tell him I said happy birthday," says Neda. "And be careful with his remains this time."

I tell her that's some memory she has, and she says it was kind of hard to forget.

"So are you" is what I want to say, but I just go, "When are you coming h—"

"Please don't, Zero. Not now. Let's keep today about Hank." In Neda's background my nephew or niece shouts something in three- or four-year-old, and my nephew or niece shouts something back. Neda says, "We can talk after your trip."

I tell her I'm going to hold her to that. She tells me to be safe, wherever I'm going. I say, "Mumbai" but she's already clicked off the call.

The guy who used to be Cat Stevens sings as all the people who made *Harold and Maude* roll off the screen. And Hank takes a big birthday swig straight from the bottle.

CHAPTER NINE

I'm the best version of myself at thirty-five thousand feet. On the ground, I'm a shitty husband and a masquerader. Up here, I'm a god. Above it all. Suspended. Sometimes I even smile at other people, provided they aren't blocking the aisle when the flight attendant's coming through with the drink cart.

You can keep your tropical island vacations and your yoga retreats and your quiet moonlit strolls. Give me a pressurized cabin.

But something tells me the inner peace I generally experience seven miles over an ocean isn't going to happen this time. Not with the Little Buddha sitting right next to me.

Caleb made it through the four days of training. During our time together, he exhibited a tremendous level of warmth, openness and emotional intelligence. Still, I just couldn't bring myself to cut him. Figured I had to at least give him a shot to prove he can be a depraved son of a bitch when he has to be.

We've only been in the air for an hour and he's already on my nerves, what with his interest in getting to know me better and his polite offer to share a sandwich he prepared at home.

"You sure you don't at least want a bite?" he asks, holding up half a baguette filled with Portobello mushrooms and some veggies I'm sure he grew organically in a community garden that donates half its harvest to the homeless.

"Nah, I'm good, thanks," I say. "They'll be serving dinner shortly."

"I know," says Caleb, "but the vegetarian options on planes typically leave a lot to be desired. I always come prepared."

I pat my jacket pocket and think, "Me too."

Caleb swallows a nibble of his plant sandwich and asks me to tell him more about my time at the agency. The question irks me, but at least he had the sense not to say "CIA" on a packed plane.

I tell him there's not much to tell, that I was there only a couple of years.

"You didn't enjoy the work?" he asks.

I motion to the flight attendant to get me a refill. Then to Caleb I say, "The work didn't enjoy me."

"I know what you mean," says Caleb, staring straight ahead and nodding as he takes another bite of garden.

"You *do*?" I ask. "I heard you were somewhat of a wunderkind with the FBI. Rapidly rising through the ranks in your, what, late-twenties?"

Caleb wipes a piece of some leafy green from the corner of his mouth, then says, "I'm twenty-six. And don't believe everything you've heard."

I don't.

He says it's true he progressed quickly at the bureau, but that one day he woke up and knew he was on the wrong path. Felt there was no way he could continue.

Finally I got this guy talking about himself instead of me. Now if I can just get him to stop talking altogeth—

"But back to you," Caleb says.

Shit.

He says, "I think I interrupted you before."

He didn't.

He says, "You were about to tell me why things didn't work out at the agency."

I wasn't.

The flight attendant returns with my refill. Saved by the bourbon. Surely Caleb knows it's rude to interrogate a man while he's enjoying a—

"So?" he says. "Please, I'd love to know more about your path."

Someone needs to teach this Buddhist some manners.

I realize Caleb isn't going to let up until I give him something, until he feels we've bonded. I fear he views me as a mentor. Respects me as a leader. Admires me. Fortunately, I know how to put an end to all that.

I'll tell him the truth.

"The agency decided it no longer needed my services," I say, pausing to knock back my bourbon, "after I conducted an unsanctioned secret experiment."

The guy sitting across the aisle shoots me a look. I give him a thumbs-up and he goes back to reading the in-flight magazine.

Caleb says to me, "You're pulling my leg."

I say I never joke about unsanctioned secret experiments.

Then, in a whisper so that Mr. 37-F won't get distracted from "25 Amazing Things to Do in Jaipur," I tell Caleb it all started when I gave a terrorist a cookie.

Caleb cocks his head.

I whisper, "Laced with psilocybin mushrooms."

Caleb goes, "Ah." Then scowls.

I ask him if he remembers Aafa Abdul Jabara. Caleb thinks for a moment and shakes his head. I say, "He made big news back in 2005 for plotting to blow up a shopping mall in DC."

"Because you gave him mushrooms?" Caleb asks.

"No," I say. "I gave Aafa the 'shrooms just *after* he'd been arrested and detained.

Caleb cocks his head again.

I tell him I'd been reading how psilocybin, as well as MDMA, had been used to effectively treat patients with post-traumatic stress disorder, depression and a variety of forms of psychosis. How such substances could unlock the mind and bring about incredibly positive transformations.

Mr. 37-F looks over again. I point to his magazine and tell him there's a piece on the history of Bollywood on page sixty-seven he shouldn't miss.

Caleb takes a sip of his cranberry juice and says, "I've heard that about psychedelics. I think I'll stick to meditation."

Caleb asks how things went with Aafa, and I say great. I explain how, half an hour after eating the cookie, he started dancing and twirling around the interrogation room, commenting on all the beautiful colors, asking me and my colleagues if he could hug us even though his hands were bound behind his back. "With all that joy and love he was exhibiting, my colleagues suspected something was horribly wrong. They didn't know about the cookie."

Caleb wraps up what's left of his sandwich and is all ears. I tell him how, with the help of a guard friend of mine, I tested the cookies out on three other radical extremists who'd been detained. And how two of them, while tripping off the charts, no longer wanted to kill in the name of Allah—they wanted to kill because each was convinced he *was* Allah. "You'd be surprised how many tasers and tranquilizers are required to bring down God. Twice."

"Well," says Caleb, "at least you had good intentions."

I tell him my good intentions got me booted from the agency the second my director got word, and add that I was lucky to only be fired. "I singlehandedly tried to put an end to radical Islamic terrorism, and made it worse," I say, ignoring the stares of Mr. 37-F. "I could easily have been incarcerated. Or committed."

What I don't bother telling Caleb is my little failed experiment was just one of a series of snafus I either orchestrated personally or was directly involved in during my stint with the CIA. He'd only want to hear about them, and with just ten hours left on this flight, there isn't time.

Besides, he just slipped on a sleep mask and reclined his seat. Apparently my biggest humiliation to date makes for a good bedtime story.

With the cabin quiet and dark, I should be experiencing the bliss of nothing to do at six hundred miles per hour. But I don't. Instead I feel like myself. Fortunately, I have the antidote.

From the front pocket of my windbreaker I pull out a fifty-count gel-cap ibuprofen bottle. The expiration date is so long ago, the numbers no longer exist. That's okay, neither do the gel-caps. I twist off the cap, tap three white tablets into my palm, and knock heads with Caleb as everyone on board gasps.

The plane drops somewhere between a hundred feet and a mile. The windows become the floor and the ceiling for a few seconds or a minute. However long the screaming lasted. The screams revealed there are no atheists on this flight.

"Sir!" a ghost-pale flight attendant shouts at me from her jump-seat. "Please sit down!"

And gripping my armrest and that of 37-F across the aisle, I go, "Don't worry, I just have to—"

"You 'just have to' SIT DOWN!"

Caleb reaches from his middle seat and tugs at my sleeve. "It'll be okay," he says, motioning for me to do as the flight attendant demands.

It won't be okay. Fucking clear-air turbulence stole my drugs.

After sitting down and fastening my seatbelt, I scan the floor and the seats and the hair of the passengers around me for even just one or two of my fourteen tablets, but there are only empty cups and ice cubes and strands of pasta. Chicken and lime wedges and tiny red plastic swords. And even though the plane has leveled out, everyone is still swearing. Or crying. Or praying. A mother bleeding mascara is clutching her infant like it's the last piece of the world. A couple grayer than God's parents are gritting their dentures as hard as they're gripping each other. Everyone's looking out for their loved ones. No one's looking for my oxy.

This is what you get when you fly coach.

Caleb sees me holding my cap-less empty ibuprofen bottle and goes, "Relax, I have some Advil."

"I don't need Advil," I say as all of my fingertips scratch the inside of my windbreaker pockets for a fix.

Caleb points to the ibuprofen bottle and asks, "Then what was in there?"

"Nothing," I say, jamming my hands into the crack between our seats, sweating like we've already arrived in Mumbai.

"You must need nothing pretty badly to have jumped up like that when we were still bouncing around," says Caleb.

I lean over and search his crotch.

"Are you going to be okay without it?" he asks. "It's not like blood pressure medicine or anything, is it?"

I shake my head and thrust my hand into my seatback pocket, and then into Caleb's.

"Sleeping pills?" he asks.

I shake out the in-flight magazine and the barf bag and the safety instructions.

"Xanax?" Caleb asks. "Valium?"

I check the four pockets of my jeans and then run my index finger under the fold of my fly. Mr. 37-F and the guy sitting to Caleb's left both keep looking over at me. They're concerned about my fidgeting. They should be more concerned about possible damage to the landing gear.

Caleb places his hand on my shoulder and says, "You know, we actually create more suffering for ourselves by trying to mask our pain."

I stick half my hand down the waistband of my jeans and dig around inside.

Caleb says, "We suffer by constantly seeking pleasure. Pleasure is impermanent, so trying to cling to it only causes pain."

I assume the crash position and, with my head between my knees, look under my seat and the one in front of me.

Caleb says, "We will never be happy until we stop trying to be."

Listening to him, I'm now thinking fuck the pills. Instead, I search for the nearest emergency exit and wonder if I'd be able to drag Caleb to it before an air marshal intervenes.

CHAPTER TEN

The street we're on, it looks like it's been experiencing clear-air turbulence for decades. There's more broken glass and discarded plastic than there is dirt and macadam. But this doesn't seem to bother any of the junkies, roaches or rats Caleb and I are doing our best not to step on. To improve the smell here, you need only piss or shit yourself. Think of the opposite of a Norman Rockwell painting. Think of the inverse of Disneyland.

Tourists come to the Kamathipura district of Mumbai for one reason and one reason only: To arrange for sex with young Indian and Nepalese girls kept in wooden cages in one of the district's various brothels. If you're not into that sort of thing, best to stay away from Kamathipura and stick to Mumbai's lovely temples and bazaars.

This time around, I'm the fixer—the guy who comes in a day before the rest of the gang and plans the party. Caleb, he's here to see if he'll *still* be next week. A couple hundred feet from our destination, I turn to him and go, "You ready?"

He takes a deep breath and nods.

While walking, I pat the chest pocket of my yellow and blue floral Tommy Bahama shirt to make sure my third nipple is still there. My third nipple is the last of three oxy I found the second the flight attendant turned off the seatbelt sign. The other two I chewed in the lavatory, and when I returned to my seat, everything Caleb was saying about the futility of clinging to pleasure and masking pain sounded wonderful.

But that was fifteen hours ago.

The key when approaching a pimp is not to. You let him come to you. You just walk down the street looking eager yet a little confused and scared. As a stranger in a place like Kamathipura, a pimp knows why you're there, but he doesn't want you to know exactly what you're doing or exactly who he is. Appear too confident and comfortable, and your cover is blown. You are a perverted coward with no shred of decency, so for God's sake act like it. Think of the opposite of Superman. Think of the inverse of John Wayne.

And remember you have a shit ton of money.

"Hey misters," a gangly kid with cystic acne calls out to us. He's wearing white denim jeans, an untucked gray T-shirt and brown flip-flops. Above his upper lip is what some might call a mustache. Dolemite he's not. "You are looking for girls?" he asks.

"Yeah," I say, feigning a nervous smile. "Young ones."

"I have virgins," says the kid. "I have girls used only two, three times. I have anything you want, friend."

What's nice about Indian pimps is their English is almost perfect. Makes it easy to understand every heinous word.

The kid points to the three-story building behind him, but we can't see anything inside because the windows are boarded and, just to be safe, over the boards are iron bars. Think of the opposite of any place you'd send your daughter. Think of the inverse of any place you'd send *anyone's* daughter.

The kid runs his fingers through his greasy black mop and goes, "You come look?"

"We don't need them right now," I say, patting my third nipple again. "Me, my friend here and several of our associates are having a private party tomorrow night. We would like to have ten of your girls there."

"*Ten* girls?" says the kid, dollar signs replacing his pupils. "You guys are real players."

I say just some hard-working gentlemen looking to have some fun.

Caleb nods and smiles. It's a very special moment for him. You never forget your first pimp.

The kid looks Caleb up and down, seemingly unfazed by how small the distance is between the up and the down, then looks back at me. "Where is this party, friend?"

"Bandra West," I say. "We're renting a house there."

And the kid's all, "Bandra? Whoa, you guys are *definitely* players."

More than he knows.

"So," I say, "is that something you can help us with?"

The kid scratches the three hairs of his 'stache and says, "Wouldn't be cheap. Bandra is forty-five minutes from here by car."

I tell him I don't think money will be a problem.

Eyeing my TAG Heuer-ish watch, the kid goes, "Why don't you bring the party here? Easier for everybody."

I say we would but the gentlemen who'll be joining us like to keep things as discreet and as private as possible.

"We are discreet and private here, friend," says the kid as he fingers one of his face craters.

"I'm sure you are," I say, "but I'm afraid our associates won't have it any other way."

The kid presses the pad of his index finger against his nostril and blows a wad of snot out. The wad lands next to a cockroach, which the kid assassinates with the heel of his flip-flop.

All you can do in a situation like this is caress your third nipple. And start to walk away.

Five steps into our retreat, the kid calls out, "Hold on."

Even before Caleb glances at me I'm mouthing "not yet" to him as we continue walking.

The only sounds are muffled shouts coming from one of the rooms of the boarded and barred brothel. And flip-flopping footsteps behind us. And Caleb gulping.

"Hey misters," the kid calls out again, "where you going?"

Without stopping or turning around, I tweak my third nipple and say, "Sounded like we were done."

And the kid goes, "I didn't say no yet."

The kids never do.

I turn around and, while walking backward looking at the kid, I say "So, how much?"

"Give me a second," he says, both hands beckoning for us to halt.

I stop, so Caleb does too.

The kid says, "One thousand rupees a girl and two thousand to rent a van." He says, "Two hundred for petrol and another thousand for the extra time the girls will be away from home." He scratches a molten scab on his cheek and says, "That comes out to ..."

"Thirteen thousand two hundred rupees," says Caleb.

The kid glares at him. "Thank you for that, friend."

I taught Caleb a lot last week, but guess I forgot to mention you never interrupt a pimp when he's doing math. Especially in India.

I say, "How about we make it an even thirteen thousand, paid in full tomorrow night."

The kid grins. "You got it, boss."

I'm not sure if going from friend to boss is a promotion or not. All I care is we have a deal. The kid's grinning because he has charged us way too much. I'm grinning because we'll never have to pay.

All that's left to do now is talk specifics about the girls we want. It's the easiest and the hardest part of my job.

"These girls do everything, right?" I ask the kid, hoping I didn't just crush my third nipple with my thumb.

"Yeah, boss."

"Oral?"

"Yeah, boss"

"Anal?"

"Yeah, boss, anything you want. Just no hitting, punching or cutting."

Of course not. That's *his* job.

"And these girls, they're hot?" I ask.

"Very." He points to the boards and the bars behind him again. "I can show you some now, if you want."

I tell him that won't be necessary. I say we trust him.

Caleb clears his throat. "And you'll include some virgins?" he asks, rubbing his hands together. Practically drooling. Making me proud.

"Yeah," says the kid. "But just one or two. You want more, it will cost extra."

Caleb glances at me and I nod. And he goes, "One or two will be fine."

After giving the kid our address in Bandra and thanking him for being such a gracious hustler, Caleb and I start to make our way out of Kamathipura, morphing back into ourselves, remaining silent.

In one of the narrower alleys, a man who looks like Gandhi exhumed is propped up against the rusted corrugated metal of a shuttered garage. Beneath him is a sheet stained with weeks of what's gone into him and what's come out. He sees us through closed lids and holds out his palm, which is barely attached to what's left. What's left is black and blue and bones. What's left is nothing I look in the eyes. Caleb steps around him. I take four hundred rupees out of my wallet and drop the money into his hand, thankful that the weight of the paper bills didn't shatter his wrist.

I wish the junkie luck and pledge allegiance to my third nipple. Caleb, watching all of this from a few feet away, chooses his words wisely and says nothing.

"Not bad back there, rookie," I say to him, my thumb pointing past the junkie, in the direction of the pimp.

"Thanks," says Caleb. "I was surprised how young and scrawny the guy was. Guess I was expecting someone, I don't know, more menacing."

"You don't need to look menacing when you're concealing a Glock in your back pocket," I say. "Or when you have two or three guys with much bigger guns watching your back through a hole in a board."

Two rats dart out of a cluster of trash, and Caleb says, "You didn't mention there'd be weapons involved."

"There weren't," I say. "That's how you know we did well."

Caleb stops walking and closes his eyes.

"It's okay," I say, "You weren't in any danger."

Caleb clasps his hands together in front of his chest and inhales through his nose for several seconds, then exhales for several more.

"Oh," I say. "This again."

And not the squeaking of rats or the moaning of junkies or the smell of rotting mutton curry and urine can distract Caleb from his standing meditation. I give him a few seconds and then ask, "What's the 'intention' this time?"

Caleb takes and releases two more breaths, and without opening his eyes he says, "That everyone—you, me, the pimp, his colleagues—that all of us be filled with compassion and generosity."

I say, "I think you may need to close your eyes a little tighter."

And Caleb just continues meditating.

I say, "It's okay to despise people who continually perpetrate unspeakable acts."

Caleb, eyes still closed, says, "If you continue to despise, the world will continue to be despicable."

And I just laugh. I mean, get a load of this guy. Telling me there's no room for hatred. Trying to take all the fun out of this job.

***

There are three major rules to remember in the minutes leading up to a sex party:

1) Don't go in angry.

2) Don't go in drunk.

3) Don't go in high.

I need to add another one to the list:

4) Don't check your phone.

I just did, and there's an email message from Alice saying she's attached a new photo of Sung. Going forward, I'll remember:

5) Don't open any attachments.

Sung is standing beside an easel smiling, almost laughing, as she points her paint-covered finger to a pink and tan and blue mess. Next to the mess, scrawled in red, are letters spelling my fake name. Bob.

I would have been much better off breaking one of the first three rules. Anger, alcohol and drugs are easier to suppress than this.

"You look like someone just ran over your puppy," says Barrett as he checks the gold-painted cuff links on his twenty-five dollar two-hundred dollar shirt. "Why so glum all of the sudden? Trouble at home?"

It's not unusual for Barrett to be right about the wrong thing.

I tell him everything's fine, then power off my phone. It goes into the back pocket of my forty-dollar five-hundred dollar pants while I regroup. Don't want to be the one who puts us all at risk of not getting arrested.

After a shot of Crown and some creative visualization, I'm back up to a seven or eight on the jet set pedophile scale. I pour another Crown, but don't drink it. Time to check in with Caleb once more before the curtain rises.

My black not-exactly Ferragamo oxfords clip-clop atop the ceramic tile floor over to the oak dining table where Caleb's thankfully not meditating. I go, "You all good?"

Caleb straightens his tie, then claps and says, "Fuckin' ay right I am." His eyes look like he's on steroids and cocaine. He grabs a bottle of Kingfisher from the table, takes a big swig and, channeling our forty-fifth president, shouts, "Let's get some pussy!"

At least *one* of us had no trouble getting into character.

Over on one of the couches, Drew looks up from the copy of *Playboy* he's not reading and gives Caleb a subtle nod. Drew knows not even he showed this much potential in his inaugural outing.

Into Caleb's ear I say, "Doing great, man. Just take it easy with that beer. Think of it more as a prop."

Caleb lifts the bottle to his lips, tilts his head back and starts guzzling.

If there's one thing I hate more than enlightenment, it's insolence. "What the hell—"

Caleb holds up two fingers to shush me as he finishes swallowing. Then he burps and goes, "Relax, it's just water."

Outside an engine backfires. I clip-clop over to one of the narrow floor-to-ceiling windows near the front door and wait with the curtain cracked. Two sips from my prop whiskey, and a filthy white minivan with tinted windows comes sputtering up the long driveway. The kind of vehicle your mother told you never to hop into. In our line of work, a ticket out of Hell.

"It's go time," I announce to the room. "Everyone act unnatural."

But we have a problem. I'm starting to feel like myself again. And it's all Sung's fault.

The sputtering engine stops, and I'm down from an eight to a seven on the scale.

This is no time to forget how to gawk at children and convince their boss you want to defile them. I knock back the rest of my prop beverage and set the empty glass on an entryway table. If Caleb asks later, I'll say it was apple juice. Or I'll just tell him to do as I say, not as I do.

I hear the driver and front passenger doors open and shut in rapid succession, and I'm down to a six.

This can't be happening. There's no way I've lost the gift. You look *one* lousy orphan in the eyes, and there goes your career? You show a *single* lapse in inhumanity, and everything turns to shit?

The side of the minivan slides open, and I'm at a five.

The side of the minivan slams shut, and the countdown continues.

A parade of stripper heels clatter against the stone walkway.

Three.

A girl cries.

Two.

A man shouts, then a girl cries louder …

And I'm back up to a four.

I peek out the window again. The man shouting is the gangly kid from yesterday. The girl crying is nobody I want to know. The kid towers over her on the walkway while a dozen other girls stand waiting, their heads down.

Five.

A brute as thick as Barrett stands near the entrance with folded arms, keeping his eyes on the girls. Ready to pounce on any runners.

Six.

The kid barks at the crying girl and slaps her across the cheek. Then backhands her other cheek.

Seven. Eight. Nine.

The girl stops crying.

And ten.

The doorbell rings.

The fixer always greets the guests of honor. It puts the pimps at ease to see a familiar face. I undo the two latches on the door.

"Right on time, guys," I say, smiling at the kid and his partner, the Hulk.

"Any trouble finding the place?" I ask.

"Not at all," says the kid, stepping forward to peer into the house.

I tell him he's welcome to have a look around before he brings in the girls.

He shakes his head and says that will not be necessary. Then he says, "But please remind your friends to behave themselves" as he waves the girls in.

Behave ourselves. He's not asking us to say please and thank you. He's not asking us to raise our hand if we have a question or to remember to put the toilet seat back down after using it. He's merely asking we return the girls without any serious lacerations, abrasions, contusions, concussions or fractures.

In other words, he's asking way too much.

We don't do returns.

As the girls enter, Barrett, Drew and Dax gather in the center of the great room, looking as nefarious as they need to. I clip-clop backwards to join them there. Caleb's in the kitchen refilling his beer in the sink. I'm just happy to see he hasn't cracked under the pressure and run and hid. Or worse, started meditating in plain sight.

The kid and the Hulk prod the girls toward us. Their bright orange and red and yellow and blue and purple saris are perfect distractions. The stunning colors make it easy for us not to look into their eyes. Make it easy to ooh and ahh and overlook their age and the agony hiding behind the opium.

Caleb struts over from the kitchen and, placing the tip of his pinky and thumb into the corners of his mouth, wolf whistles at the girls. A few of them giggle. Whether they're entertained by the shrill sound of approval they just received or by the fact that it came from a grown man shorter than they are, it's hard to tell.

To top things off, Caleb grabs his crotch and winks at them.

He may be the best I've seen.

One of the girls approaches me and squeezes my bicep

through my almost Armani shirt. She says, "So big and strong."

"Hey, beautiful," I say, pinching the fabric of her yellow sari. "What's your name?"

And she tells me and I don't listen.

In other words, I've still got it.

There's nothing better than being the bad guy. Long enough to do some good.

In come the cops to arrest us, and I couldn't be happier.

"On the ground NOW!" one of the officers shouts, his hands on a nine millimeter. I lie prone on the floor and put my hands behind my back, trying my best not to smile. Most of the girls are screaming and crying right now, so it makes things a little easier.

As my cuffs go on, I look over at Caleb. He's spitting on the floor and telling the cop to fuck off. He may be overdoing it a little, but it's okay. I'd rather see him accidentally get charged with resisting arrest than hear him invite the officer to tea.

Barrett and the boys are also watching Caleb's performance, and look as impressed as I am. Trouble is, we don't *want* to look impressed right now. Sure, both the kid and the Hulk are already down and cuffed, but still, we owe it to them and ourselves to seem just as put out as they are.

As they're yanked to their feet by two of the officers, Caleb—still lying on his stomach like the rest of us—arches his neck back and head-butts the ceramic floor. "Fuck this!" he shouts.

Even the two pimps on their way to decades in prison seem worried about him.

With the girls evacuated and the kid and the Hulk removed from the premises, the remaining officers help us to our feet and remove our handcuffs. After thanking one another and congratulating ourselves on a successful mission and yada yada,

I walk over to the bar and grab the half-empty bottle of Crown.

"No sense in letting this go to waste," I say and take a swig. Then with my back to the guys I call out, "Anybody else want a bottle of something for the road?"

Nobody answers. They're too busy staring at Caleb, who's standing in the middle of the great room. With his eyes closed, his breathing slow and controlled.

"Hey, kid," Barrett calls out, "You okay?"

Caleb doesn't respond.

Barrett looks at me and shrugs.

"Don't worry," I say. "He does that from time to time. I should have warned you."

CHAPTER ELEVEN

It's always nice to arrive home after a stressful mission and a long flight. Except when your wife isn't there anymore to yell at you for waking her or for not waking her.

Or when there are obvious signs of forced entry.

My front door is slightly ajar and shows crowbar damage. Judging by the leaves and other outdoor debris on the laminate floor of the entranceway, this happened at least a day ago. Surely the culprit is long gone. At least that's the wager I'm making at one thirty in the morning.

The key to clearing your house after a break-in is not to. Unless you're packing a loaded semi-automatic handgun, have extensive training on house-clearing, and have a blood alcohol content of zero percent, you're out of your element.

I have none of those things.

But I have oxy in the house.

I drop my valise on the welcome mat outside, shove the door open the rest of the way and rush in. Past the broken sideboard drawers lying in the foyer. Past the open dining room cabinets and the shards of glass and stoneware littering the floor. Through the living room, dodging the books and plants and knickknacks strewn about. Up the stairs and down the hall past whatever happened inside the master and the guest bedroom. And into the study/gym/storage room, where I trip over one of my barbells and fall face-first in front of the closet with its bi-fold door ripped off its tracks.

The flashlight.

It's always covered by old sweaters inside a box I keep under a box of old trophies I keep under a box of old textbooks. But right now the textbooks and the trophies and sweaters are out of their boxes and all over the closet floor. The flashlight, it's lying atop a sweater I haven't worn since some Christmas last century. The important part of the flashlight is, anyway. The part without the light. The part where the batteries go and haven't been for years. The part where the sandwich-sized zip-lock baggy goes and now is gone.

The part I just fastballed through the drywall.

This is a good time to curl up on the floor next to my bench-press bench, sweat like I'm still in Mumbai, and fight to catch my breath. Were someone to walk in right now, they'd think I'd been training too hard.

I pull out my phone to text my dealer, but look at the time.

I throw the phone against a stack of boxes of who cares, but then remember I have to call the police.

After crawling to get the phone and dialing 911, I tell a woman's voice my house has been burglarized. She asks if I'm in the house and says not to be. I tell her the thief is long gone and she says get out of the house and stay out. She asks for the address and says officers will arrive shortly and again urges me to leave the house immediately. I say sure thing and hang up and go downstairs for a drink. The crook was nice enough to leave my mini-bar untouched. The bourbon mixes well with the wreckage all around me.

Waiting for the cops, I'm thinking what the hell kind of burglar breaks into an LA home under two thousand square feet. A home with no privacy fence or tall vegetation to obscure things from neighbors. A home with a six-year-old Jetta parked on the driveway. A home without a security company sign out front advertising things of value inside. There's no mistaking my house for that of a celebrity or a professional athlete or a plastic surgeon. Sure, I occasionally wear what look like thousand-dollar suits, but never anywhere near this neighborhood.

Shit. My suits.

I jog back upstairs expecting the worst. The suits may be knock-offs, but they were custom-made by some of the finest dirt-cheap tailors in Southeast Asia. Replacing them would require a flight to Bangkok or Jakarta or Hong Kong, and none of those places are on the schedule again any time soon.

I enter the master and step over and around all the shit pulled and thrown from our nightstand drawers—Neda's lotions and tea candles and self-help books, my ear buds and ibuprofen and grip strengthener—then stop at the entrance of the walk-in closet. I don't want my dirty shoes tramping on all the dresses and pants and gowns and skirts and blazers and blouses and panties and boxer briefs and coats.

Down on my hands and knees I search for matching sets as an approaching siren reminds me to hurry. How humiliating to get shot by cops in your own house.

It appears all my sex tourist costumes are accounted for. Still, seeing them off their wooden hangers and crumpled up is unsettling. The siren times me as I run back downstairs, hoping my homeowner's policy covers dry cleaning.

The siren tells me I have less than a minute for another drink, but not out of a glass. I down a shot or two of bourbon from the bottle, then slip out the front door like a criminal, grab my valise, have a seat on the trunk of my Jetta and, with my head raised and my hands in clear view, wait for the headlights to hit me.

The patrol car rolls up and cuts the noise but keeps the hood-top LED going. With both arms I wave at the vehicle like I'm flagging it down. A male and a female officer step out and I thank them for coming so soon. Mr. Cop heads into the house. Ms. Cop stays outside with me.

"Yes, I'm okay, officer."

"No, nothing of real value."

"Yes, the house was locked."

"Yes, I'm sure. See how the door is broken?"

"Sorry, I wasn't aware I was rolling my eyes."

"No, nobody was home at the time of the break-in."

"Yes, I'm married. No, no kids."

"My wife? She's been visiting family while I've been out of town."

"I don't know when exactly the break-in occurred. Like I said, I was out of town."

"Sorry, it's just sometimes my eyes do that when I'm exhausted."

"No, I haven't asked any neighbors if they saw or heard anything suspicious. It's two in the morning."

"Yes, I have been drinking."

"Why was I out of town? Business."

"What do I *do*? It's complicated."

"No, I'm *not* trying to make this difficult."

"Okay, fine. I travel around the world rescuing victims of child sex trafficking."

"No, I'm *not* kidding."

"No, I'm *not* on drugs."

"I agree, I really do need some sleep."

"At a motel, I guess. Until the door gets fixed."

"Yes, thank you. A ride to the La Quinta later would be greatly appreciated."

Over Ms. Cop's walkie-talkie Mr. Cop says all clear. Ms. Cop says roger that and tells me to follow her inside.

Mr. and Ms. Cop do a final sweep of the house while I wait on the living room couch, furious I can't report the most important thing that was stolen. They finish up and we exit, leaving several inside lights on to, as Mr. Cop explains, deter any additional burglars. Ms. Cop says they'll do a few drive-bys later just in case, then hands me the card of a police-vetted home repairman and locksmith, and urges me to call first thing in the morning.

Before climbing into the backseat of the patrol car with my valise, I wave to several neighbors peeking through their windows in pajamas at the red and blue lightshow. None of them wave back.

"Buckle up," says Ms. Cop through the Plexiglass partition and I fumble with the seatbelt as we reverse out of my driveway and head for the motel.

The darkened strip malls and Starbucks roll by and I'm starving. The only thing open is a donut shop. And while I'd love a donut, asking the officers if we can stop for one might be construed as offensive.

I pull out my phone to see if Neda has responded to the text I sent earlier informing her of the break-in and telling her not to go near the house until further notice. But of course she hasn't answered. She's dead asleep, it being a school night and all.

While I have my phone out, I check my email.

Two new messages. Both from Alice.

The first one says she's done some initial research into Cambodian adoption like I asked. She says it's possible but improbable, and that the process takes some time. She says it would require me to prove I can provide a stable home environment, preferably cohabitated by a spouse or partner to ensure additional support. She says a pet would help. She points out that my profession, with all the travel involved and the dangerous nature of the work itself, would likely reduce the chances of an adoption being approved. Significantly.

In the second email message, she says she forgot to mention one other thing: Both myself and spouse or partner would need to pass a physical examination.

And a drug test.

"Everything okay back there?" the female officer asks through the partition.

It's a perfectly reasonable question, seeing as how she just heard me mutter "fuck" and turned to catch me biting my own forearm.

***

The silicon earplugs are no match for Room 27. I've been waiting for some other schmuck to complain to management or call the police, but I'm probably the only schmuck situated anywhere near the party or the dance-off or the virgin sacrifice next door.

The clock radio says I've got only about an hour and a half to sleep. I hop out of the bed and drop to the floor for a set of pushups in my white tank top and navy sweatpants. While pumped pecs and triceps won't do shit to stop a bullet, the Taylor Swift or Katie Perry song buzzing the walls tells me the party people are unarmed.

A warm, dry Santa Ana breeze greets me on the motel sidewalk. The Taylor or Katie song is now a Kenny Chesney song, causing me to question the gun situation inside.

Three hard knocks on the door. No response. Not even a momentary lull in the shouting and the stomping and the laughing.

I rear back to pound the door again and a male voice on the other side shouts, "Damn it, Eric! I told you not to forget the room card!" The door opens to a guy about a foot shorter and three decades younger than me, wearing a red hoodie with the hood up. He smiles and shouts over the music, "*You're* not Eric."

"And *you're* not quiet," I say, arms flexed across my swollen chest. The smell of nightclub mixed with disinfectant mixed with onions seeps out of the room.

"Aw, my bad, dude," says the kid, playing tug-of-war with his hoodie string. "We'll dial it down."

Hoodie heads back into the room to lower the volume, but leaves the door wide open. I try not to look at two girls in T-shirts and panties bouncing on one of the beds. Black Panties catches me and shouts, "Hi!" then bounces off the bed and blows the landing, nearly cracking her skull against the bottom of TV stand. White Panties continues bouncing, eyes closed, smiling like she just got out of surgery.

Black Panties pops up from the floor and dances over to the doorway. "Wow, you're big!"

Hoodie joins her near the door, taps her on shoulder and goes, "Shhh! We woke this dude up."

Keeping her glassy green eyes on me, Black Panties tells Hoodie not to shush her, then tells me it's her birthday. Hoodie looks at me, shakes his head and mouths, "No it's not." I say happy birthday anyway, and they both double over laughing.

"Come party with us!" Black Panties yells despite the music being barely audible.

Hoodie says to her, "The man wants to sleep."

Black Panties pouts and huffs. "But it's my—"

"It's NOT your birthday!" Hoodie shouts, then snorts. And he and Black Panties double over again.

I shake my head and turn to go back to my room, but notice a small table in the corner of theirs. Spread out on it are several fifths of various liquor.

And a ton of pills.

Hoodie stops laughing and says, "Sorry about all this dude. We'll let you sleep."

"Actually," I say, my eyes fixed on the table. "I'd hate to be the guy who ruins a birthday party. Mind if I pop in for a sec?"

Hoodie says, "Sure, dude! But just so you know, it's not actually anyone's birth—"

"Of course it is," I say, and step into the room.

Black Panties shouts, "Yay!" and claps, then announces she has to pee and skips to the bathroom.

White Panties has stopped bouncing. She's sprawled out supine on the bed and struggles to catch her breath. En route to the small table, I smile and wave at her. She greets me by picking her nose.

"Help yourself, dude," says Hoodie as he trails me to the table. "We got all types of shit."

I nod and lick my lips. "You sure do."

Hoodie points to a dark blue round pill. "MDMA," he says. "This will help you see all the beauty in everything while also amping you up." He says, "It's a sort of psychedelic amphetamine."

"I'm familiar with it," I say, and tell him no thanks.

He points to a cream-colored tablet and says, "Ketamine.

This will put you in a trance-like state. Really popular on the party scene." He says, "And when mixed with MDMA, you'll understand true bliss, but probably won't remember shit afterward." Then he points at White Panties, who is now doing snow-angels atop the bedspread, and says, "That's the combo she's on right now."

I go, "Enticing, but I think I'll pass."

I go, "You got any painkillers?"

Call me old-fashioned. Call me unadventurous. Call me a creature of habit.

Hoodie laughs, then yells to Black Panties in the bathroom, "Dude here wants to know if we have any painkillers!"

Black Panties shouts back, "Shhh, I'm pooping!"

Hoodie says to me, "Yeah, we got painkillers."

He points to the three unlabeled vials on the table and says, "Morphine, tramadol and oxycodone. Take your pick."

I tap the cap of the third vial.

Call me monogamous.

Hoodie twists the cap off the vial and slides two tablets onto a piece of La Quinta stationery that's lying on a small plate. When I reach for the pills, Eric blocks my hand and says, "Let me crush 'em for you."

I tell him I normally just chew them.

Hoodie goes, "Ever snorted?"

I shake my head.

"Oh man, dude," says Hoodie. "You've gotta give railing a try."

I'm not one to succumb to peer pressure.

"Fine," I say.

The toilet flushes, and out of the bathroom comes Black Panties. "Miss me?" she shouts, then grabs a bottle of vodka from the table, takes a swig and flops onto the bed next to White Panties, who's now doing yoga.

Hoodie folds the stationery over the two pills, takes a spoon from the table and presses down hard on the paper, rolling the spoon over it several times. He then carefully unfolds the paper and, with a Target credit card, scrapes the powder onto the small plate, using the edge of the card to create a fine, neat line.

Hoodie picks up the plate and holds it in front of me. "Captain," he says, "you're cleared for takeoff."

I admire the pretty little inch-long line for a moment. Hoodie goes, "It's easy, man. All you do is—"

"I know what to do, champ," I say.

And just like the cokehead RA of my dorm taught me in 1980-something, I turn away and exhale, bring my face toward the plate, press my index finger against my nostril and, with my other nostril practically touching the line, sniff short and hard.

Burns more than I remember coke ever burning. Not enough to cry about, but tell that to my tear ducts.

Hoodie grins and goes, "Nice, dude."

Over on the bed, Black Panties shouts, "Woohoo!"

White Panties says nothing and just moves from bridge pose into happy baby.

I use the front of my tank top to dab my eyes and my nose. Hoodie says, "Fight the sting and keep sniffing it in." He says, "Don't blow your nose or you'll lose some of the high."

I thank him for the tip and say I need to head back to my room.

Hoodie goes, "You sure, man?" and I nod.

Black Panties shouts, "No! Boo!"

White Panties transitions into corpse pose.

On my way to the door, my nose and eyes stop running and

the first wave of wonderful rolls in. I sit down on the edge of the unoccupied bed. Hoodie laughs and goes, "That's it, dude, there's no rush."

Now the bedspread. It's cool on my shoulders and the ceiling is up there and my skin and my muscles also the inside of my bones are all yes.

The question is, where'd the sun come from and who's this hovering over me?

CHAPTER TWELVE

Talk about your upgrades.

From a bug-infested mattress to a five thousand dollar fully-adjustable bed. I don't even have to leave it for nourishment. Just lie here while all the fluids I need continue to be pumped straight into my veins.

Plus all the fancy machines pinging and beeping along with my every breath and movement. I'd enjoy it all a lot more if my every breath and movement didn't feel like I shouldn't be breathing or moving.

A nurse peeks into the room, then turns around and calls out, "Dr. Brooks, Mr. Slade is awake now." She turns back to me and says, "The doctor will be in to speak with you in just a moment. Can I get you anything?"

"Some water would be great," I say. "And my pride."

The nurse smirks and says, "I'll be back with the water."

For pride, you need a prescription.

The clock on the wall says three fifteen, and since the sun is coming through the blinds, I know it's p.m. Otherwise it would be a fifty-fifty guess.

Standing in the doorway now is a black woman wearing a white lab coat over a light blue oxford shirt that's neatly tucked into khaki pants. She pauses to review whatever is clipped to the clipboard she's holding. If she were smiling, she'd be an award-winning pharmaceutical commercial.

"Good afternoon, Mr. Slade," she says as she enters the room, stopping a few feet from my high-tech bed. "I'm Dr. Brooks, head of emergency medicine here. I treated you when they brought you in this morning."

I nod, then shake my head and say, "I don't remember much since the ambulance ride. Or before it. And the back of my eyes hurt."

Dr. Brooks purses her lips. "Well, none of that's surprising, considering what we found in your system."

I blink twice in slow motion and go, "Would you mind elaborating?"

Dr. Brooks says we'll get to that in a minute. She says, "First I'd like you to answer some questions for me."

The nurse from earlier enters holding a lidded Styrofoam cup with a straw sticking out of the top. "Pardon me, doctor," she says, then places the cup on the bedside tray table and leaves.

Careful not to twist or yank the IV tube stuck in my right arm, I reach for the cup and take a long sip through the straw. Like scalding coffee, the ice-cold water burns my throat and stomach.

Dr. Brooks asks if I'm ready to begin and I give her a thumbs-up while taking a much smaller sip of water.

"Okay," she says. "Do you know where you are?"

"The hospital," I say, hoping to at least get partial credit.

"Do you know *which* hospital?"

Pass.

"That's okay," says Dr. Brooks as she jots something down on the clipboard. "Do you know what day it is?"

I say, "Tuesday," only more in the form of a question than an answer.

Dr. Brooks says, "Good. Tuesday the …"

I scratch my eyelid. "Uh, Tuesday the … fifth— no, the *six*teenth."

"Okay," says Dr. Brooks. "The sixteenth of …"

"May," I say, then throw in the year just to show off.

Dr. Brooks nods. "And finally," she says, "who is the current President of the United States?"

I tell her I never talk politics in the hospital, and she just stands there holding her clipboard, waiting.

I go, "If I don't say his name, it's like it never happened."

Dr. Brooks rolls her eyes and shakes her head while checking off something on the chart. Then she says, "Regarding the one question you missed, you're in the intensive care unit at Providence St. Joseph Medical Center in Burbank."

I look around the room and nod. "Seems like a nice place."

Dr. Brooks asks if I know why I'm here.

I pause to think, then shrug and say, "A reaction to some medication I took?"

Dr. Brooks says that's one way to put it. "Mr. Slade, we found trace amounts of a powerful opioid in your system."

I tilt my head and go, "Huh?" then close my eyes and nod. "Ah, I forgot about the oxycodone I took for my stiff—"

"Actually, I'm not talking about oxycodone," says Dr. Brooks. "We found *plenty* of that in your system, but we'll come back to that later." She says, "The opioid I'm referring to—the one that landed you here and almost killed you—is fentanyl."

"Fentanyl? I've never taken that in my life."

And Dr. Brooks says, "That's what *most* people who take fentanyl think."

***

Turns out not everyone in the illegal narcotics business is a good person.

While the vast majority of drug cartel members and cartel middlemen and dealers and dealers' dealers can be trusted to supply a clean product, there are always going to be a few bad apples who spoil the bunch and land your ass in the ICU.

This probably wasn't Hoodie's or Black Panties' or White Panties' fault. Doubtful they knew the oxy they offered me was laced with fentanyl, at least not based on what Dr. Brooks is telling me.

She says a rapidly growing drug-distribution network is feeding fentanyl to the Americas. She says cartels, particularly in Mexico, get the fentanyl in powder form from China for cheap. "They add it to pills they press and then sell them as regular oxycodone or hydrocodone to dealers, who sell them to unsuspecting consumers."

Dr. Brooks says fentanyl is fifty times more potent than heroin. So consumers keep going back to their dealer for more of the best "oxy" they've ever had.

Until they die.

"Isn't killing customers generally bad for business?" I ask.

Dr. Brooks says the enterprising folks behind fentanyl view a few hundred overdoses a year as more than acceptable. "For every customer who drops dead, thousands more are just getting hooked. And getting their friends hooked, as well."

Dr. Brooks says I'm one of the lucky ones. Lucky because I nearly died the first time trying this drug. Most people, she says, the *un*lucky ones, have wonderful first- and second- and third-time experiences with fentanyl. And then they're in it for good.

I, on the other hand, got to learn firsthand the devastating nature of fentanyl before I could enjoy all that it has to offer.

Dr. Brooks says I should count my blessings. She says respiratory failure saved my life.

To get over an event as stressful as a near-death experience, I'd typically text my dealer. But a voice is telling me that may not be the best idea.

It's Dr. Brooks' voice.

"I can't emphasize enough how important it is for you to quit using any kind of prescription painkiller that hasn't been ordered for you by a physician."

I nod and say I understand. And I'm thinking how Dr. Brooks is a physician.

She says, "You truly dodged a bullet this time. All it takes is another tiny pill containing even just a touch of fentanyl, and you could easily die."

I nod again, thinking don't make me beg for it.

Dr. Brooks says, "Now, quitting painkillers cold turkey can be dangerous, resulting in serious withdrawal symptoms."

We certainly wouldn't want that.

"Severe nausea and vomiting and diarrhea," she says. "And profuse sweating and abdominal cramping. Also, extreme anxiety."

She's made her point.

"Which is why I'm going to give you something."

Whatever she thinks is best—she's the doctor.

"A prescription."

Go on.

"For Suboxone."

Boom! Wait, what?

"Suboxone contains a combination of buprenorphine and naloxone. Buprenorphine is an opioid medication."

Okay. Never tried it, but I'm open to new—

"And naloxone blocks the *effects* of the opioid medication, including pain relief or feelings of well-being."

I try to nod but can't. The muscles required to do so have gone flaccid.

"I don't understand," I say. "Why would you prescribe me that?"

Dr. Brooks steps forward and sits down in the chair next to my bed. "Suboxone," she says, "is used to treat opioid addiction."

I say, "But I'm not an addict."

I tell her if she had any idea about the kind of work I do, she'd understand why I occasionally take a painkiller.

Dr. Brooks tells me she sees exit wounds and avulsions and massive chest trauma and severed limbs and dying children on a daily basis, so she understands the desire to reduce job stress. "But there are much safer, more effective ways than popping pills," she says.

I tell her I have it totally under control.

"Mr. Slade," says Dr. Brooks, "there was fentanyl in your nasal passages. That is not a sign of somebody who has things under control."

Fucking Hoodie and his recommended delivery system.

I tell Dr. Brooks it was the first time I ever snorted pain meds and that I only did it to shut up a friend.

"And where was that *friend* when the paramedics arrived?" she asks, looking inside a folder under the chart she's holding. "Their report says you were in your motel room alone and unconscious when they got there."

I point at the folder, shake my head and say, "The report is wrong. I was in the room next door with some acquaintances."

Dr. Brooks shifts in her seat as she peeks inside the folder again. "Says here the front desk clerk at the motel said you were in the same room you paid for and checked into."

I go, "That's impossible."

And with Dr. Brooks staring at me, tapping her stupid pen on the stupid folder, I remember the door. The one I left ajar before the little party.

Up until now I assumed Hoodie had called in my OD *and* stayed with me until help arrived. I even imagined Black Panties and White Panties crying while stroking my hair and praying for me to come to.

Turns out they just dumped and abandoned me after alerting 911.

No use explaining any of this to Dr. Brooks. Her knowing I was carried to my room by three kids less than half my age isn't going to convince her I don't have a problem.

So I just say, "Last night is not how I usually roll."

And Dr. Brooks says judging from my blood and urine, I roll like this often enough. Then she rests her hand on my shoulder and tells me I'm not alone. How there's nothing to be ashamed of. How nearly five million Americans are addicted to prescription painkillers. How there are support groups all over the city that can help. She says, "I strongly recommend you give one of them a go."

I bristle over being lumped in with nearly five million losers, and Dr. Brooks says there are substance abuse counselors on staff I can talk to if I'm not comfortable speaking with her. Then she asks why I'm laughing.

"Sorry, doctor," I say, trying to wipe the smirk off my face. "I get that you're just doing your job, but, um, I don't need to talk to a counselor."

Dr. Brooks nods in disagreement.

"Also," I say, crunching my knuckles, "I don't need to be on any Suboxone."

Dr. Brooks stands up, sighs, and says she can't make me do anything once I'm released later today, but adds that she seriously hopes I'll reconsider her recommendations. Then she leaves.

I grab the remote control for the robot bed and press the recline button until I'm lying almost completely flat. Amidst all the beeping and the pinging and the vitals flashing, I lift my arm with the IV tube running from it, bring my hand to my face, then use the middle finger to dab what just dropped from my tear duct.

***

Neda. She's standing right where Dr. Brooks was half an hour ago. And just like Dr. Brooks, she's concerned about me.

"Zero … what in the *fuck* is the matter with you?"

The beeps of the heart monitor accelerate. I tell her it's great to see her, that I've missed her.

She repeats the question with her eyes. As I open my mouth to give an answer, like I have one, she grabs the chair behind her and drags it close up to the side of my bed. She sits, then stands up again and says, "Do you have any idea what it was like to wake up this morning to a message from you telling me our house was broken into, followed by another message from the hospital saying you were in the emergency room?"

"So sorry," I say. "Things went a little sideways last night."

She sits back down and rakes her fingers through her hair. "A little sideways?" she says, her Farsi accent coming through like it does whenever she's furious. "An overdose is not a little sideways!"

An orderly peeks his head into the room and asks if

everything's okay. Neda and I give contrasting responses, hers drowning out mine, and the orderly ducks out.

I say, "I don't know what the doctor told you, but she doesn't—"

"Save the bullshit for someone else, Zero," says Neda, arms folded. "Dr. Brooks and I chatted during my entire drive here. She says lab tests don't lie. Lying, that's *your* job." Then she asks me why I didn't answer any of her texts or calls this morning. I tell her my battery died, and she goes, "See what I mean?"

"Not really," I say.

She shakes her head, grabs my fully charged phone from the small table by my bed and holds it up to my face. "Lies!"

Then she starts crying.

"Baby," I say, reaching out to her, my IV tube coming along for the ride. Neda nudges my hand away, stands up and goes, "How could I have not known about this?"

"About what?" I ask, and with a quick glare Neda slaps the words back into my mouth. She looks off into space and says, "Am I really *that* clueless? I mean, I knew you *drank* a little too much, but *pills?*"

I start to tell her it's no big deal, but decide it's better to keep my teeth.

Neda looks at me and shakes her head, then scoots her chair in closer. She smells like lemon oil and goodbye. "Where do you even *get* them?" she asks. "The pills."

I say from a guy in Inglewood, not far from LAX. Neda scoffs and says, "I can see how that would be convenient for you."

I point out he's not the one who gave me the fentanyl. I tell her he's a good guy, a trusted supplier. Neda scoffs even louder and suggests nominating him for drug dealer of the year.

"How long have you been using?" she asks, shaking her head again, like the question can't be real.

I say, "Using? Baby, that's a term for addicts, and I'm not—"

"Shall we look at the lab results?" Neda snaps. She leans in closer and smells so nice and says, "How long?"

I shrug, but Neda's eyes say think harder.

"About a year after starting at OE," I say. "Not long after Hank's accident."

And Neda says, "Jesus," like she's converted. "What's that, six years?"

I nod. And there goes Jesus again.

"Baby," I say, "the fact that I've been taking the stuff for six years is proof I'm not an addict."

Neda slaps her palm over her face, and I say, "No, no, listen." I tell her an addict can't use for that long and get away with it. I tell her the reason she had no idea I had a problem is because I have no problem.

Neda yanks her hand from her face, "Yeah?" she says to me. "Really? Look around, Zero." She stands up from the chair and says, "That's a hospital bed you're lying on."

She points at my arms and says, "Those are tubes coming out of you."

She points at the monitor and says, "Your heart stopped a few hours ago. Your *heart*, Zero. It *stopped*."

Then she smiles at me, her tears turning the floor into a safety hazard. "So guess what? You *didn't* get away with it, and you *do* have a problem!"

A nurse peeks in and asks if everything's okay. Neda says yes and apologizes for the noise. "Just having a little argument." The nurse says, "Oh, I don't care about that—I'm wondering what all the beeping's about." And I go, "It's all related." The nurse checks my monitor, tells Neda to go easy on me until I get home, then disappears from the doorway.

And Neda starts doing her best Dr. Brooks impression.

"You need to get help," she says as she reaches for the same hand she knocked away a few minutes ago. "You need to do a program."

I tuck my lips in to keep from laughing, and Neda squeezes my hand. I say, "Sorry, I know none of this is funny, but I don't need any program."

Neda says the lab tests and the doctor and the tubes and the monitors beg to differ.

I tell her I don't have time for twelve steps. That it won't work because of my travel schedule, plus there's too much God. "Also, I'm not an addict."

Neda says if I don't join a program, I can forget about us.

And I say I thought she already had.

Neda clenches her jaw. Hot air from her nostrils warms my sheets. She says, "I wouldn't be here if that were the case, idiot."

CHAPTER THIRTEEN

Liza fell down the stairs at a stranger's house in Van Nuys while trying to find the bathroom.

Jerome is finally eligible for a new liver.

Annette hasn't seen anyone in her family besides her cousin Spike in over three years.

Paco just finished constructing another model airplane, without sniffing any of the glue.

These people are standing here telling me all the intimate details of their lives. And I've yet to meet them.

Nigel can no longer speak, but his sister Gwen tells us he passed his driving test last week.

Kelly is dropping her rape case.

Estrella loves Jesus again.

And now it's my turn.

At least that's the look most are giving me. The unspoken consensus seems to be if black-and-blue Liza and her crutches and her stitches from chin to ear can stand at the front of the room to tell us everything, surely I can say my name and a few words.

"So, nobody else then?" asks the group leader, Reginald, as he rises and rises and rises from his seat in the first row. Reginald is Barrett-big. He peers straight at me sitting alone in the back row and says, "I see a few new faces tonight," but he sees only mine. He says, "We'd love to hear from some of you." Some of you is no one but me.

At about six-six and pushing three hundred pounds, with a giant black shaved head etched with pinkish-gray scars, Reginald doesn't realize his tactics aren't going to work. It takes a lot more than scarred brawn and passive-aggressive stares to press me into action. Now, if Reginald hints he has little girls locked in crates in the basement of this church, then we can talk. Until then I'll just sit back and ignore him, along with the nausea creeping up from the fake opioids Neda's making me take.

For relief from Reginald and the sick rising inside me, I look to Jesus. It's hard not to. There are seven or eight of him hanging on the walls. He could be my ticket out of here. Surely my Muslim spouse won't force me to return after hearing about the Christ-chic décor.

"Remember, everyone," Reginald says to me, "the smartest thing an NA member can say is 'help me.'" He looks down and runs a finger along one of the scars on his scalp. "NA is not for people who need it and NA is not for people who want it," he says. Then he looks back up and goes, "NA is for people who *do* it."

Jerome turns around in his second-row seat, his eyes following the laser pointer shooting from Reginald's sockets toward the back of the room. Maybe Jerome should worry a little less about me and a little more about putting some skin on those bones. Or about how far down he is on the liver list.

I look at a Jesus and tell him to apologize to Jerome on my behalf.

Addressing the group, Reginald tells me, "Whatever you put

before your recovery, you shall surely lose."

And here comes the headache—the one Dr. Brooks told me to expect if I'm doing things right. That the room reeks of bad decaf mixed with stale baked goods mixed with Lucky Strikes isn't helping.

Paco stands up in the third row and takes half a step toward the front before Reginald reseats him with a single finger. "Let's just make sure everyone's had a chance to go before any encores," Reginald tells Paco without looking at him. Then he starts real slow up the aisle that splits the room.

"Untreated addiction will soon make your past your future," says Reginald, with several of the attendees joining in at "make."

My headache and nausea are bad enough without the chorus. And then there's Nigel. He may not be able to speak, but his constant nodding is deafening.

Reginald continues inching up the aisle. Getting larger.

"Addiction is the only disease that tells you you're all right," he says.

He's halfway up the aisle and fuck it.

I stand. I stand to show him he's not the only big bald dude up in this joint. And to make Neda stop shouting. She's loud for someone not here.

To the nearest Jesus, I say, "Hello. My name is—"

"Sorry, sorry," says Reginald as he shows me all the calluses on his palm. "Would you mind going up front for this?" He tells me that way everyone can see me without having to turn around in their seats, and I'm thinking it didn't seem to bother anyone before. Or now.

Reginald walks me down the aisle like he's giving me away, and I try to smile through the gut churn for the benefit of the onlookers.

We get to the front and the least they could do is put a podium up here. Or something else to hold on to. Reginald takes his seat, and his calluses invite me to please continue.

"Hello, my name is Zero." My hand searches the pocket of my windbreaker as I pause to swallow. "And uh, yeah, so uh, some doctor—well, she and my wife—they think I may have an issue with, uh …"

Jerome or someone in the front row says, "You got this." Hard to tell with my eyes closed.

"Excuse me a sec," I say to the floor before turning around and stepping behind a large reversible chalkboard, the kind you can flip from one side to the other. Out of my jacket pocket I pull a plastic shopping bag and snap it open. Sweat drizzles into it from my face.

"We've all been there, Zero," Reginald calls out. "No need to hide."

I'm invisible from the waist up.

The backside of the chalkboard says bible study every Thursday at seven.

I pray for no holes in the plastic bag. And then fill it with the partially digested blueberry muffin and coffee I had six or seven shares ago.

The room erupts in silence.

Neda says it's no excuse. She tells me to keep going.

"Painkillers," I say from behind the chalkboard before spitting a mouthful of bitter into my sagging baggie. "My wife and doctor think I have an issue with painkillers."

A handful of voices mutter, "Welcome, Zero."

Behind me and the chalkboard there's no door to escape through.

"Come on out," Reginald says to my legs and feet. "Nothing to be ashamed of, man."

I clear my throat and spit into the bag again, then wipe my mouth on the sleeve of my windbreaker. "What should I do with the—"

"Just leave it," says Reginald. "Don't worry about it."

I tie the ends of the plastic bag together, set the bag on the floor, and ask one of the Jesuses to apologize to the janitor on my behalf. It's time for my upper body to reappear, but tell that to my feet.

They say the first step is the hardest.

"Sorry everyone," I say to the floor as all of me emerges from behind the chalkboard.

"Don't worry, we've seen much worse," says Reginald. I look up and everyone's nodding. Reginald says, "That took guts," and everyone nods again, missing what to me sounded like a bad joke.

I start to slink back to my seat, but Reginald asks me to hold up. He says, "I get why you don't want to use your real name, Zero, but may I suggest choosing one a little less self-deprecating."

"Zero *is* my real name." And everyone giggles. Everyone except Reginald. He just sits there with his arms folded, his biceps crowding the room.

"Okay, *Zero*," he says. "Anything else you'd like to share today?"

"No thanks," I say and continue up the aisle, smelling like Folgers and blueberries and bile, begging every Jesus on the wall to teleport me out of here.

Reginald turns in his chair and says, "Before you sit down, let me ask you something else real quick."

I stop, bite the inside of my lower lip, and turn to face him.

And Reginald goes, "Do you agree with the doctor and your wife?"

Some saint on the wall tells me to be honest, so I tell Reginald, "Not really."

Jerome and Annette and everyone shake their heads. Paco drops his, probably upset he lost his second share to nothing worthwhile.

"So," says Reginald, "you don't think you have an addiction."

Dr. Brooks wasn't kidding about the headaches. I rub my temples with both hands and give Reginald the same answer as before. He nods, then stands up—arms still folded—and goes, "So then why are you here?"

Everyone and all the Jesuses look at me like parents waiting for their toddler to walk to them for the first time. Reginald says, "It's cool, man. I'm not here to try to force a confession from you. I'm just here—*we're* just here—to help you if you want to be helped."

And despite Neda nudging me in the ribs, I just shrug.

"Can you be a little more specific?" asks Reginald.

I open my mouth to say nothing. After a quiet bile burp, I shrug even harder than before.

"Well, then," says Reginald, "go on home and think about it some more."

"Fair enough," I say, then turn and resume my long-awaited trip up toward the exit. As I pass mute Nigel, he says how sorry he feels for me.

I'm at the doorway and Reginald, almost yelling, says, "If you're not moving away from your addiction, you're moving closer to it." But I can't hear him.

A few steps into the hallway, there's Neda again.

"Please, don't half-ass this," she whispers with all her might.

I'm too tired and too sick to argue with her. And with Dr. Brooks and Reginald and all those people inside. And Jesus, Jesus, Jesus.

"Forget something?" asks Reginald as I march back into the meeting room. Everyone turns in their seat like I'm getting married again. Nigel smiles at me and I tell him to keep it down.

"My name is ... Bob," I say, looking Reginald and everyone in the eye. "And I'm an addict."

"Welcome, Bob!" shouts the world as I run to the snack table on the side wall and puke a bunch of nothing into the trashcan.

CHAPTER FOURTEEN

One of the girls on the couch picks her nose and wipes her finger on the tattered jean shorts she's barely wearing. If I had to guess, I'd say she's twelve. Thirteen, tops. Out of her purse she pulls a plastic bag. Out of the plastic bag she pulls a small rag that reeks of gasoline. Just as she lifts the rag to her face, one of the pimps shouts, "Luiza! *Pará-lo!*" The girl startles, then sneaks a quick sniff before stuffing the rag straight into her purse.

She looks at me and in a heavy Portuguese accent says, "I go sex you," as her vacant eyes roll back in her head.

It's nice to be working again. Being surrounded by pimps and prosti-tots helps to instill a sense of normalcy.

The Suboxone is managing my withdrawal symptoms just enough to keep me functional down here in Rio. The faces of the Lost Girls are more than enough to make me forget whatever the Suboxone isn't managing.

Caleb, in what has quickly become typical Caleb fashion, returns from the kitchen with a fake beer and shouts something disgusting and objectifying in the girls' native language. Good to see he isn't suffering a sophomore slump.

The girls—the ones who are wasted on gasoline and glue—

titter over whatever Caleb just spewed in Portuguese. I'm a little jealous. Not of the girls for being high. Inhalants have never been my bag. No, I'm jealous of Caleb. For his ability to become the very antithesis of who he is. Pretending is one thing. Pretending I'm good at. Becoming, that's something entirely different. It takes tremendous self-control to relinquish control of yourself.

I lean back on the couch and take everything in, realizing how lucky I am to even be here. Smiling at how smoothly everything is going. There's Barrett, whispering into the ear of an eleven-year-old who's wearing a bikini sized for a nine-year-old. There's Malik, laughing as two tween girls in front of him twerk along to the Brazilian hip hop music we have pumping through the house's speakers. There's young Caleb, using whatever new phrases he learned from his Rosetta Stone CDs on the flight here to flirt with a girl young enough to be his daughter.

And there's the pimp who earlier yelled at Luiza. He was just grinning, even swaying to the music a little, while looking at his cell phone.

But not now.

Now, he's holding a gun.

"Whoa, whoa!" I say, holding my hands out to the side, motioning for the pimp to pump the brakes.

Everyone else in the room looks at me, and then at what I'm looking at. Several of the girls scream. The pimp, lifting his pistol toward the ceiling, shouts, "*Cala a boca!*" and the girls cover their mouths and cower. I couldn't have learned "shut the fuck up" any quicker from Rosetta Stone.

"Take it easy, sir," I say to the pimp. I think his name is Dimas, but I figure I'll keep things formal for now. "We don't want any trouble."

The other pimp, who moments earlier went to the fridge for a beer, looks just as confused as Barrett, Malik, Caleb and me. The difference is, his confusion is genuine. Me and the guys, we already know what's up. Well, maybe not Caleb, but he'll get there.

Barrett slowly stands up from the couch. Dimas points the gun at him and says, "Down."

"Is there a problem?" Barrett asks as he retakes his seat. "Did we do something wrong?" Being as large as he is, Barrett's quite convincing when playing dumb.

Just not at this moment.

"Don't fuck with me," says Dimas, wagging the index finger of his free hand at Barrett.

The other pimp sets his Heineken on the marble countertop and shouts something at Dimas in Portuguese. Judging from his anxious tone, and from how his shoulders are raised and his hands turned upward, he just asked Dimas either what the hell is going on, or why Dimas couldn't wait until he'd finished his beer.

Dimas shouts something back in Portuguese. Based on the other pimp's clenched jaw and how he's now glaring at us while gripping the jagged half of the bottle he just smashed against the countertop, he's been clued in. Either that or he forgot to take his meds. Or both.

The good news is these two are now speaking in English, which leaves all guessing aside.

"You guys are fucking dead!" shouts the pimp with the broken bottle as he starts toward us in the center of the parlor room, stopping after a few steps only because Dimas just told him to.

With his revolver, Dimas motions for the three girls who are still frozen on the couch to join the other five who have since run and huddled together in the corner. He then points at the girls and says to us, "You should have just fucked *them*. But instead you decided to fuck *us*."

The worst thing about all of this isn't that a crooked cop tipped these two pimps off. Been there, done that.

It's that these two pimps aren't running for the door.

Whoever tipped them off must have had enough pull to cancel the whole sting, and these two know it. This means the cops aren't coming to arrest them or gather the girls. And if the cops *do* come, it won't be until later, and only to put up yellow tape and outline four bodies in chalk.

I'm in no mood to be executed. This isn't last week.

To Caleb, who's still standing with his fake beer, Dimas says, "You, drop the bottle and sit down with your friends."

Caleb sets the bottle on the end table of one of the couches, the one where I'm seated, but doesn't sit down. Instead he presses his hands together in front of his chest and bows, first to Dimas, then to the other guy.

The two pimps look at one another and laugh.

I slap the cushion next to me and say, "Caleb, sit your ass down."

"Better listen to your friend, little man," says Dimas.

The patience Dimas has exhibited thus far is a good sign. He could easily have fired off four rounds by now. I'm thinking as long as we cooperate and don't do anything to aggravate him further, he might just let us—

"This work you do," says Caleb, still standing, pointing over at the girls, "it's not your fault."

I never would have pegged Caleb as suicidal.

Dimas squints. The other pimp raises his eyebrow and cocks his head. Dimas goes, "What the fuck are you talk—"

"You are doing what you feel you must to survive," says Caleb, smiling.

I reach forward and tug on Caleb's belt, hoping to pull him on to the couch with me, but he wiggles out of my tenuous grip.

"Just sit!" hisses Malik from the other couch. Next to him is Barrett, who just shakes his head and groans.

To Dimas and the other pimp, Caleb says, "I can only imagine what life has been like for you two, what you've had to endure, what led you to this work."

Barrett stands up. "I apologize for our colleague," he says. "He—"

"Quiet!" Dimas shouts at Barrett, pointing the gun first at him, then at the couch. "Sit down!"

Dimas turns back to Caleb, takes two steps toward him, and says, "You know *nothing* about me, or about life in the favela."

Caleb, still smiling, says, "You're right. That's why I said, 'I can only imagine.' But I can also imagine a better life for you. And for your partner over there. And for all those girls trembling in the corner."

And this is where Dimas raises the revolver and shoots Caleb in the head. Or the heart. Or the crotch.

I'm sure of it.

It's why I'm ready to spring from this couch and turn Dimas into bone meal, if a bullet doesn't end me first.

But Dimas is holding the gun by his side, relaxed. His index finger isn't even resting on the trigger. He says to Caleb, "Yeah, little man? Well what makes you think I *want* a better life?"

"Because," says Caleb, "you and I are the same. We are both human. And I truly believe that humans don't want to cause harm."

Good idea, Caleb, dare the guy with the loaded gun to put a hole in your philosophy.

Caleb says to Dimas, "If you hurt someone, you hurt yourself a thousand times worse."

He says, "When you prick another person's finger, you bleed out."

He says, "If you keep somebody captive, you can never be free."

If Dimas doesn't shoot him now, *I* will.

Caleb says, "All pain and suffering can be overcome with empathy and compassion. For yourself and for others."

The two pimps laugh and sneer at Caleb, but don't say anything to silence him. It's hard to tell if they are just letting him ramble off his last words until they decide to turn out the lights, or if what he's rambling about is starting to resonate.

Caleb says, "I apologize for trying to trick you today, but I, along with my colleagues here, did so in an effort to end suffering and confusion."

We must have failed because I am currently experiencing both.

Caleb looks at Dimas, then over at the other pimp, then at Dimas again and says, "I ask both of you to forgive our deception."

The look of derision on Dimas' face begins to morph into one of contemplation. His partner, noticing this, loosens his grip on the broken bottle and softens his stance. Malik and Barret and I look at one another, baffled over what we're witnessing.

Caleb. The Pimp Whisperer.

Maybe instead of us running dangerous sting operations all around the globe we can just have Caleb record an MP3 file and email it to all the brothels.

"That gun you are holding," Caleb says to Dimas, "that gun is not you."

He turns to the other pimp and says, "That broken bottle in your hand, it's not you."

He points over to the eight girls sniffling in the corner and says to both men, "Selling those children to predators is not you."

And instead of killing all of us, the two pimps just stand there, listening. Hanging on Caleb's every word. Seemingly hypnotized. Being guided toward an improbable epiphany.

Caleb says, "None of this is you. None of it's your fault. It's all the product of tens of thousands of years of human suffering and confusion."

He says, "You have a choice. You can allow suffering and confusion to continue to rule human history, or you can look tens of thousands of years straight in the eye and say 'enough.'"

He says, "Dropping your weapons and letting the girls go, that would be the most powerful thing you will ever do."

Dimas, his eyes glassy, stares at Caleb in silence for a few seconds, then slowly turns to look at the other pimp, who's gazing up at the ceiling and swaying back and forth. Both are still holding their respective weapons, but neither seems prepared to use them. Neither seems prepared to do much of anything, really. Except stand there and smile.

I've seen this before.

In an interrogation room years ago.

These men haven't been transformed by Caleb's impromptu Buddhist sermon.

They're just high as shit.

And so am I.

I'd gotten so caught up in Caleb's monologue and how it was keeping us alive, I'd barely noticed the increased level of glue and gasoline fumes filling the room.

I look over at the eight girls in the corner, all of whom have stopped crying, and see them taking turns huffing rags, sharing five among the group. There's also a rag on the floor by the couch I'm sitting on, and here's one tucked in between a cushion and the back of the couch.

I'm pretty sure as long as I don't pick one of them up and hold it to my face, I still qualify for an orange key tag at my next NA meeting. Plus now I'll be able to share a story with the group about how harmful intoxicants *saved* my life.

Over on the other couch, Malik and Barrett are whispering to one another. I can't make out anything they're saying or tell if they're as high as me and the pimps. I turn back to Caleb, who, probably sensing he's close to converting the pimps, says, "You can change the world simply by changing your mind."

Caleb is too high to realize his Buddhism isn't what's taming the two men, and he's too Buddhist to realize he's even high. That's one of the biggest drawbacks of being enlightened. It ruins artificial euphoria.

That said, artificial euphoria ruins windows of opportunity. Two minutes ago, a man with a gun and another wielding jagged glass were ready to annihilate my crew and me. Right now, those same men are wobbling and giggling not ten feet away from me and I'm too damn happy to disarm them.

Still, I have to at least try. Let me just stand up here and—

"*Dimas, Cuidado!*" shouts the pimp with the broken bottle, but there's no time for Dimas to react to Barrett's bull charge. Like a Pee Wee league quarterback being sacked by an NFL linebacker, Dimas—with Barrett attached to his waist—flies five feet through the air and lands back-first on the hardwood floor.

Nice hit. But Dimas still has the gun.

Technically.

He lost partial grip of it when tackled and is now holding it upside down by the barrel. Barrett, still on top of him, reaches for the gun with his right hand while keeping Dimas pinned to the floor with his left arm and torso. Dimas evades the reach and rams the butt of the gun's grip into Barrett's nose, then knees him between the legs, incapacitating Barrett long enough to wriggle out from under him. Dimas gets to his knees. Flips the gun into proper position. And fires.

At Caleb.

I'm on top of Caleb now, looking him in the eyes, and *he's* asking *me* if *I'm* okay. *He's* telling *me* to hang in there. The guy just got shot and he's still putting others first. This selfless son-of-a bitch is starting to grow on me.

I'm not sure where he got hit, but there's blood all over him. His face. His neck, his white dress shirt. A lot of the blood got on my shirt, too. I say, "You're gonna be all right," and he shushes me. I say, "You ain't dying on my watch," and he doesn't respond.

What I don't get is why I'm now lying on my back with Caleb kneeling beside me, and he's tearing his shirt off. I say, "Just lie down and stay still," but he ignores me and slides the bloodstained shirt under the middle of my back.

Another thing I don't get is why that hurt so fucking much.

Barrett comes rushing toward Caleb and me with a gun tucked into his pants and blood trickling from his nose. Behind him Dimas is lying motionless on the floor. Barrett rips off his shirt and tosses it to Caleb before squatting down by my feet.

"How's he doing," asks Barrett.

I say, "He'll be fine. But make him lie down."

Barrett looks at me, perplexed, and then back at Caleb, who says either, "Right through the chest and out the back" or "Write two more checks out to Jack." I'm not sure which. It's getting more and more difficult to understand the nonsense coming out of Caleb's mouth. He's obviously delirious from the trauma.

Barrett asks, "You get hit, too?"

Caleb and I both say, "No." Then Caleb says either, "Must have just missed me exiting," or "Mustard's just good on eggs and things."

He's lost a lot of blood.

Yet still he insists on pressing Barrett's shirt against my chest.

And while I know I need to help out, first a nap.

Someone says something about an ambulance.

Someone says something about some towels.

Someone shouts something from the other side of the room.

There's warm breath on my ear, then whispering. Nonsense.

All I'm getting are children's screams bouncing off the rafters.

CHAPTER FIFTEEN

'

Beeping and pinging. Suction and hissing. Cinnamon and vanilla.

"Neda?"

It comes out as silence. Lips stuck together. Glass tongue.

Another "Neda?" comes out as sound.

"Zero?" and it's her with my eyes closed. I try to "Yes" and footsteps move away shouting "Doctor! Nurse! I think he's awake!" Footsteps come back. A hand hot on mine. Now on my cheek. Cinnamon and vanilla. Down my neck run raindrops.

My eyelids don't listen to me. Won't lift.

"Where?" and "When?" come out broken.

"Shhh, shhh, relax," says Neda and there's a finger on my cracked lips. "They're coming."

Footsteps and voices. Closer and Portuguese. I'm dead who knows how long.

Aftershave and then "Mr. Slade?" with an accent. Loud and slow. Says he's … silver? "Wiggle your fingers if you hear me."

Fingers and toes. Stiff like it's been years.

"Very good," says Silver.

An eye. And the other. And neither now because the brightness burns, but a glimpse of Neda. My reach for her gets nowhere. Squinting shows why. I've gone insane.

Silver sees me see the straps. Tight on my wrists. He says something about safety. About preventing … extubation? "We will remove them shortly."

My wrists?

I squint at Neda. She laughs a cry. Her hair. That's my favorite way to wear it so shiny and down. I open wider and her skin, yes. We're still young.

The bandages. The middle of me's a mummy.

A plastic hose, stuck to my hand. Another runs up to my face. In my nose maybe. My throat, something's down it.

"Can you speak?" asks Silver.

"Sort of," comes out scratched.

Silver looks at Neda and tells her it's normal. Something typical laryngeal something. Something anesthesia also. Looks at me. "Do you know where you are?"

"Here" comes out close enough, and Neda cries a laugh. In her eyes are emeralds.

Silver. "Do you know where 'here' is?"

Lids down and fingers and toes tickle the air to think. "Flew to Rio?" comes out even closer. Lids up and Silver smiles.

"So, Rio?" he says.

A nod. But barely. Neck stiff as fingers as toes. And these bandages.

"Very good," says Silver. Then Portuguese to the nurse.

Neda. Smiling like it's long before. Like outside the mosque we met.

The nurse undoes me. No longer a danger.

"Do you remember what happened to you?" asks Silver.

Neda. All this way. Wait, she lives with her sister now?

"Mr. Slade? Do you know why you are here?"

No, she came back. She came back before here. Said she'll stay if I keep going.

"Mr. Slade, it's okay if you don't remember."

The plastic hose. It goes from my hand on up to that bag of clear. And under these bandages is what happened but doesn't hurt.

There's a hole in me.

Looking at Neda, "I'm sorry" comes out just like that.

***

Slides are moving at warp speed. All out of sequence.

A dozen Haitian girls trembling [*click*] a morgue attendant showing me a photo of the tattoos on Hank's arm [*click*] a silhouette shouting at my mother [*click*] Sung too terrified to let go [*click*] me eating two oxy on a flight home from Lima [*click*] Neda walking out the door carrying a suitcase [*click*] two Ugandan girls with electrical burns on their thighs [*click*] my mother lying in a casket [*click*] me laughing with a Mexican pimp [*click*] me handing fifty dollars to my dealer [*click*] me handing a hundred dollars to my dealer [*click*] Sung too terrified to let go [*click*] Neda all red in the kitchen telling me it's over [*click*] a Laotian girl with a scar as long as forever on her face [*click*] me eating three oxy on a flight home from Kolkata [*click*] me handing two hundred dollars to my dealer [*click*] Neda screaming about the overdose [*click*] sirens blaring outside La Quinta [*click*] Sung too terrified to let go [*click*] Neda crying about the overdose [*click*] Caleb bleeding my blood [*click*] me eating four oxy on a flight home from Kampala [*click*] and on a flight home from Mexico City [*click*] and on a flight home from Phnom Penh [*click*] Sung terrified [*click*] Sung terrified [*click*] Sung terrified [*click*].

"Look who's awake again," says Neda as our eyes lock. Mine

roll away and return. Standing next to her is Silver, holding a folder. He's either still here or came back.

I smile and my upper lip splits without stinging. Hurts my throat some to swallow though. What was down inside there's gone now. What's under the bandages feels bigger.

Neda says, "You've been in and out all morning."

Silver assures her it's quite normal.

The clock on the wall gives me nothing to go on.

Neda moves cinnamon-vanilla close and lays her palm on the top of my head. Rubs it. The roughness sounds like days.

"How long?" I ask low and raw, and Neda asks how long what.

My eyes point to my bandages. "Since *this*?"

Gasoline [*click*] gun blast [*click*] the rafters [*click*].

Neda bites her lip and says, "Since Sunday."

I ask what's today and she says Tuesday.

"Tuesday?" The span jolts my wound. *Five* days?

Neda shakes her head. "No baby, *two*. Sunday to Tuesday." She looks at Silver like my math is his fault.

Silver assures her it's quite normal.

"And actually," he says to her, "it's only been about a day and a half." He peeks into the folder. "Let's see ... yes, he was admitted after six Sunday evening, and came out of the co—I mean, woke up this morning." Silver's accent, it's like an American commercial for a Brazilian beer.

He tells Neda I'm surprisingly alert, considering. He tells her me asking such relevant questions is a great sign.

He's saying all this like I'm not here. Like it's still Sunday or Monday.

I look at him and go, "So, a coma right?"

Silver steps closer to my bed and a laminated name badge

tells me I've had him wrong all this time. He, Dr. Silva, says, "Technically, yes, but only a light one. A nine on the Glasgow scale."

A nine sounds bad, but I'll take his word for it. Apparently comas aren't earthquakes.

"And a lot of the time," Dr. Silva continues, "you were unconscious due to anesthesia during surgery." He peeks into the folder again. "You were operated on for ... nearly ten hours."

Neda covers her mouth with both hands.

I look down at the bandages wrapping me from sternum to stomach.

Dr. Silva says, "You are actually a very lucky man."

My father's early departure [*click*] my brother's bloody windshield [*click*] my mother's rapid metastasis [*click*].

Dr. Silva looks inside the folder again and says, "The bullet passed between the heart and the lungs." He says it did so without touching either one. And without hitting the spleen or liver or any major blood vessels. And without striking and ricocheting off any ribs or vertebrae. "It's quite remarkable," he says, shaking his head, face still stuck inside the folder. "I have never seen such a clean through-and-through gunshot wound to the torso."

Neda gasps. And then come the tears.

She, too, starts crying.

Dr. Silva says to my folder, "God must really like you."

Me drunk texting my drug dealer [*click*] while driving [*click*].

Me ignoring my tenth-grade girlfriend's pleas to stop just before we had sex for the first time [*click*].

That last slide, it isn't mine. It couldn't be.

Neda says something I don't catch. Says something else, then taps me on the cheek. "Zero, everything okay?"

I just stare at her. She asks, "Where'd you just go? You were kind of catatonic there for a minute."

I shrug, as much as my exit wound allows, and Neda turns to Dr. Silva. He assures her it's quite normal.

As I'm pretending to sleep, Dr. Silva tells me I need to rest. But first, he says, he has just a couple more questions.

"How is your pain level?"

"Hard to tell," I say, and Dr. Silva follows my eyes to the bag of morphine hanging next to my bed.

"Ah," he says, nodding. He glances at Neda, then back. "Your wife told me. Actually, the surgeons and I already knew."

Dr. Silva says when I was brought in, the Suboxone in my system tipped them off to my addiction. However, he tells me, an opioid analgesic was their only option. "Without it," he says. "you'd go into shock due to the severe pain caused by your injury, as well as from the surgery." He glances at Neda and back again. "As I told your wife, it's a clear case of the benefits outweighing the drawbacks."

I gaze up at the ceiling and shake my head in disbelief—not at what Dr. Silva just told me, rather at what my post-coma brain claims I did to Lauren after the junior prom.

Dr. Silva apologizes and says, "We never *like* to give someone with substance abuse issues such medication, but sometimes it's necessary."

"Impossible," I say to myself, eyes fixed on the ceiling.

And Dr. Silva goes, "What was that?"

"Huh? Oh … nothing."

Neda moves in real close, like she's checking for pupil dilation, then looks at Dr. Silva. He mouths, "Completely normal" as he waves off her concern with his hand.

"Now," Dr. Silva says, looking at me, "your wife said you are getting help and have been clean for a couple of weeks."

I point to the IV line that delivers my morphine, and he says, "Aside from that."

He tells me he, along with the hospital in LA I'm moved to in a couple of days, will do everything they can to keep me from relapsing. "This includes keeping you on the lowest dose possible for your level of pain, weaning you off the morphine—and the diazepam—gradually, and getting you back on the Suboxone."

A nurse stops in the doorway and Dr. Silva waves her in. She smiles at Neda and me, then hands Dr. Silva a pair of exam gloves.

"Before I check your dressing and let you rest," Dr. Silva says to me, "do you have any questions. Any concerns?"

Lauren in my Mustang saying maybe we should wait [*click*] telling me it hurts [*click*] whimpering in the backseat [*click*].

"Nope," I say, missing the peace and quiet of my coma. "I'm good."

"Okay then," says Dr. Silva as he snaps on the latex gloves and trades positions with Neda beside my bed. "Let's just have a quick look at you." The nurse adjusts a couple of my tubes to keep them from tugging or getting tangled while Dr. Silva carefully removes the tape holding the gauze holding me together. Neda turns around to face the doorway. Dr. Silva starts to undo the gauze just above my abdomen and I shut my eyes but catch the stench. Blue cheese with a hint of iodine.

"Oof," says Neda. Through my squint she's halfway toward the door, her back still to me. "Smells infected," she says.

Dr. Silva goes, "Nah. Totally normal." He tells her it just needs a fresh dressing. Says the sutures look good. "No new bleeding or seepage."

Hard to tell what's making my stomach churn more right now—the word "seepage," the odor coming off me, or the morphine mixed with muscle relaxants mixed with antibiotics mixed with laxatives.

Of course, a three-decade-old date rape that didn't occur might also be to blame.

The nurse helps Dr. Silva turn me onto my side so he can check where the bullet left the middle of my back. In this position, no amount of morphine can help. "Excellent," says Dr. Silva as the nurse dabs the pain streaming down my cheek with a tissue.

After helping the nurse change my entry and exit dressing, Dr. Silva picks up my folder from the side table and says he'll pop in again in a couple of hours to check on me. Neda takes his hand and thanks him, then comes back to my bedside. And I say, "Before you go, doctor, there is something I wanted to mention."

"Of course," says Dr. Silva, sticking his folder-free hand into the pocket of his lab coat. "What is it?"

I say, "It's my memory," and he tells me not to worry. He says it's totally normal to suffer some temporary memory loss following even a light coma.

"Yeah, memory loss isn't really the issue," I say as I pick at the new gauze over my entry wound. "What I'm experiencing is more like … memory *gain*?"

Neda leans in and checks my pupils again. Dr. Silva tilts his head and asks me to elaborate.

Talking to the ceiling, I tell Dr. Silva my past seems clearer than I remember. That a barrage of personal moments will suddenly flash through my mind in intricate detail.

I look at Neda, then at Dr. Silva and say, "I'm even

remembering things I don't think ever happened."

Neda eyes me head to toe, as if to make sure I haven't been replaced by an exact replica. I tell her it's okay, that I feel fine. "I'm sure it's completely normal," I say, then turn to Dr. Silva and go, "Isn't that right?"

Dr. Silva, his face back inside my folder, shakes his head and says, "That's actually kind of weird."

CHAPTER SIXTEEN

Sometimes to get the vacation you deserve, you need only get shot point-blank by a pimp.

This is the first time Neda and I have been outside the country together since Santo Domingo for our tenth anniversary. That was three years ago. She joined me there after one of my missions. I was exhausted, so not the best trip. But at least I could feed myself.

"Nothing wrong with your appetite," says Neda as she spoons a lump of brown goop into my mouth. It tastes like chocolate and how a dirty sponge smells. I force the goop down my gullet and open wide for more.

"Slow down," Neda says. She peers into the small plastic container. "You're almost through your second one this morning."

I tell her this protein pudding is my only hope for not needing a new wardrobe. "Nurse Fernanda says it's loaded with good calories. Keeps patients from wasting away."

A chocolate sponge burp bubbles up my esophagus. I close my mouth but it escapes through my nostrils. Neda curls her lip and says, "Gross." Like she hasn't seen and smelled so much worse in the two days since my awakening. I'm wearing a diaper, for chrissake—another big difference between this vacation and the Santo Domingo one.

Neda digs the spoon into the goop container, scraping the sides, and here comes the choo-choo train. I open wide again and—

"It's okay, it's okay," says Neda as she caresses my hand, the one clutching the gauze covering my entry wound. "Just breathe," she says. "Try to relax." My writhing tests every suture in front and back. Neda takes a hand towel from the side table and wipes the sweat pouring from my scalp. What she misses leaks through my gritted teeth. My tongue catches the salt of it.

"Breathe, baby, breathe," she says and I do my best. The room sounds like childbirth.

I miss Santo Domingo.

"Silva lowered the dosage too much," I say through a spasm. "On the morphine *and* the muscle relaxants."

"You're doing great, baby," says Neda, one hand holding mine, the other toweling me dry. "He told us flare-ups like this are—"

"Normal. I know, I know."

Neda reminds me it's going to get easier and easier. That this is the worst part.

I tell her I know that, too. With Dr. Silva starting to wean me off the morphine, I know a lot of things. I'm getting sharper every day. So smart, it hurts.

A text message lights up Neda's phone and nearly buzzes it off the small table by my bed. She grabs the phone, skims the screen, then laughs and says, "You're a very popular guy these days."

"Who's this one from?" I ask, the spasms starting to subside.

Neda says it's Barrett again and holds the phone in front of my face.

"Just read it to me," I say, turning my head away. "All these messages are making me dizzy."

Neda tells me to say please, and I do, and in her best baritone Barrett voice she says, "I'm still glad you're not dead. Keep hanging tough. Hugs and shit, B."

"He's the sweetest," says Neda. "All of them are. Checking up on you four, five times a day like they've been doing."

I tell her they just feel guilty for abandoning me here mid-coma and flying off to the next party.

"Stop it," says Neda. "I know you're joking, but I don't like it."

I start to apologize and through her tears she reminds me how Barrett, Malik and Caleb kept me from bleeding out until the ambulance arrived. How they sat in the ICU waiting room through ten hours of surgery and by my bedside until she arrived from LA. How they comforted her through her panic attack. And how pained they were when they had to leave for a jump in Buenos Aires before I regained consciousness.

She taps her phone screen a few times, then turns it toward me. "Don't forget this," she says, pointing emphatically at the photo she already showed me two days ago—the one she took of Barrett, Malik and Caleb huddled in a circle over my coma, all three with their head down, one arm around each other, one hand touching my face my shoulder my hand.

"Damn it," I say with a wince while wiping my nose with my forearm. "You know crying activates my core muscles."

Neda stifles a laugh and says, "I wouldn't have to resort to torture if you'd just show a little more gratitude."

Her phone buzzes again and again and it's Barrett again and again telling us Buenos Aires went well. Twelve girls rescued. Three pimps arrested. No shots fired. Another text comes in and it's him adding, "Helluva lot better than the jump there two years ago."

A pimp getting shot in the throat running from the cops [*click*] a stray bullet clipping a twelve-year-old's shoulder [*click*] and striking a ten-year-old square in the temple [*click*].

"Zero? Zeeeero? … Zero!"

My earlobe gets a flick. "What?" I snap, and Neda shoots me the "don't give me that tone" glare, then asks, "What should I text back?"

"Tell him 'glad to hear it' and 'hope to see you soon.' Or just send a thumbs-up emoji."

As she's typing, I ask if there's been any progress on the search for my phone. She says the ambulance guys and hospital staff are still looking. "Anyway," she says, "focus on getting better and stop worrying about your phone. We have mine, and everyone knows they can reach you through it."

They sure do. Neda's phone hasn't shut up since I stopped being dead. All this caring and attention from concerned friends and family makes it hard to enjoy my self-pity. Also, it would be nice to have a few uninterrupted moments with my wife. The bullet that tore a hole straight through me has really helped mend our relationship.

Neda's phone buzzes and it's Fynn for the fifth time apologizing for not making it down here, asking when I'll be back stateside, telling me to take all the time I need.

I ask Neda to tell her "no apology necessary" and "air ambulance to Cedars-Sinai tomorrow" and "thanks."

Neda's yellow and white floral print sundress. It's the same one she wore on our outing to Vista Hermosa Park last summer. I point at one of the dress straps. "Nice to see you got the blueberry stain out." She looks at her shoulder, then smiles like a picnic.

The phone buzzes and it's Malik seeing how Neda's holding

up and saying they're in Tijuana for a jump and will see me in LA when they land in two days. I show Neda a thumbs-up and she types in something seemingly more substantial. After hitting send, she closes her eyes and lets out a yawn bigger than her face.

"You sure you don't want to get a hotel room?" I ask. "You haven't really slept in three days." Neda shakes her head, yawns again and glances at the fold-up cot—the one Nurse Fernanda brought her the first night—leaning against the wall. "I'm perfectly comfortable right here with you," she says.

The phone again. Neda's mother for the tenth time making sure Neda's safe and asking if she's been fasting for Ramadan. Another buzz and, "I almost forgot, how's your husband?" I tell Neda she doesn't have to share every text with me. Neda takes a bite of the Snickers bar she got from the vending machine earlier this morning and lies to mama. "Sorry I ruined the holy month," I say.

A stunning woman stumbling on the steps of a Chicago mosque [*click*] me breathless, introducing myself as I help her to her feet [*click*] she wasting more than a decade hoping I'll get back on mine [*click*].

An "I love you" bubbles up my esophagus. I open my mouth to let it out and—

Buzz. Principal Bert tells Neda the whole school is thinking of us and that the substitute teacher has everything covered.

Buzz. Drew sends a selfie of him and his wife Carla holding up a sign that says, "Come home soon!"

Buzz. Lauren tells me thanks for destroying her trust in men.

Buzz. And for sending her into a spiraling depression that lasted until her suicide in 2003.

Neda snaps her fingers in my face. "Finally, I got your attention," she says, shaking her head. "Now for the third time, is it okay if I take a photo of you and send it to Drew and Carla?"

***

Post-Traumatic Stress Disorder. False memories. Schizophrenia.

Some guys look at porn when their wives are asleep. Me, I'm researching what the fuck's wrong with my past in the present. Doing it in private browsing mode on Neda's phone so she'll never see the pages I'm visiting. Some things are worse than bukkake and golden showers.

Like hypermnesia. Found it while googling "weird memory shit." A dictionary I trust even on the Internet says, "hypermnesia: specific instances of heightened memory experienced by people whose memory abilities are unremarkable under ordinary circumstances." Says it's typically brought on by hypnosis.

Or by trauma.

The audible "no way" that escapes from me causes Neda to stir in the chair she's napping in. After a couple of moans, she's out cold again. Good thing, as there's plenty more private browsing to do, and these IV lines taped to the back of my hands aren't helping me work any faster. Nor is the ever-increasing amount of morphine Dr. Silva has me off. Or all the muted interruptions from loving friends and colleagues.

The Internet's being a bit presumptuous, making it sound like hypermnesia is a good thing. Yeah, I get it, most people would be thrilled to have a heightened memory, but then most people haven't spent years planning pedophile parties with slave owners. Most people didn't take things too far with their dead prom date in the back of a Ford. Possibly.

Not having gone to med school means there's still a chance. A chance I've misdiagnosed myself. It's still possible the Lauren incident is an inauthentic or exaggerated recollection. Unfortunately, WebMD pretty much just ruled out schizophrenia for me. For one, it says the disease is typically diagnosed in the teen years, and rarely after thirty. Secondly, one of the main symptoms after delusions and hallucinations is lack of emotion, yet one look at Neda in her sundress, one thought of Sung suffering, and much of the saline being pumped into me right now comes out of my eyes.

It's not looking good for Post-Traumatic Stress Disorder, either. If being shot had caused me to suffer PTSD, the memory haunting me the most would be of me being shot, or at least the moments leading right up to it. *Not* Lauren having her virginity stolen. Perhaps.

A box of text from Bert slides across the top of the phone. I ignore it and go back to hypermnesia. There's so little authoritative information and no real case studies on the topic. Not even a Wikipedia entry. No wonder Dr. Silva looked like I was crazy.

Neda starts whistling through her nose. A ray of early afternoon sunlight has fooled the window blinds and illuminates her bare shoulder. Why can't *that* be the memory haunting me.

A box of text from Barrett slides in and says, "Wish you were joining me for poolside margaritas in Tijuana, coma-boy." Suppressing my laughter angers my bullet holes. The spasms cause me to fumble the phone, and the reflex response to grab it angers my holes even more, and fuck Dr. Silva for following protocol. My bedrails rattle. That and the sound of my sweat merely nudge Sleeping Beauty into a new position in her chair.

This is a good place to stop with the research. Besides, Neda's phone battery is at three percent.

I know how it feels.

A box of text from Caleb says, "Rise above your pain through forgiveness and compassion." Another one slides in and says, "To conquer oneself is the greatest task of all." I'm in too much pain to roll my eyes. A tear drops from one.

Hopefully someone's been keeping Barrett and Caleb separated in my absence.

As my spasms relent, another box from the little Buddha arrives. This one's not for me.

"Sending you strength, Neda. I've spent far too much time ..." I click the text box to see the rest. "... sitting beside loved ones in hospitals, asking the universe to make it stop. So I sort of know."

Nurse Fernanda walks in with her poufy silver-blue perm. I press my index finger to my lips and look her toward Neda, who's mimicking my coma. Nurse Fernanda mouths "ahh" and nods, then tiptoes over to the bed and checks my fluids.

"Saline almost out," she whispers, I think. Difficult to know for sure with fifty or sixty years of Portuguese and cigarettes driving her accent.

The phone lights up on the bed. I tap the home button to disappear my mother-in-law while Nurse Fernanda changes my bag of sweat and tears.

"*Ay, tão bonita,*" she whispers, looking over at Neda. I grin and say, "She sure is."

Nurse Fernanda checks my vitals on the monitor. She then asks me either how I got or how I met such a beautiful woman. To cover both bases, I say, "Just lucky."

"You treat her good," Nurse Fernanda says, pointing at Neda and frowning at me. Like she knows.

The phone lights up and a Brazilian telecom company tries to upsell my wife in Portuguese. Before I can delete the message, the screen goes black. Nurse Fernanda asks if I need a charger. I tell her no thanks. She looks at my dressing, then at me, then over at my mostly dormant morphine drip. "Your pain, okay?" she asks.

"Meh," I say.

Nurse Fernanda sighs and looks at my dressing again. She shakes her head and says, "I no like guns." I say that makes two of us.

She tells me Dr. Silva told her about the work I do. "It must be very difficult, no?"

This always seems like a trick question.

I just shrug.

Neda whistles through her nose and we both look over at her and smile. Then Nurse Fernanda looks at me and asks if I plan to continue doing my job once back on my feet.

I pick at my gauze and nod.

"Really?" says Nurse Fernanda. "Why?"

The dead phone lights up and it's Lauren telling me she hopes the next bullet paralyzes me—from the waist down, at least.

"I'm not sure why," I say to Nurse Fernanda. "Repentance, maybe."

CHAPTER SEVENTEEN

Home at last. Well, not home exactly—Cedars-Sinai Medical Center. Still, it feels good to be back in LA. Even if it hurts like hell.

Since arriving here from Rio yesterday, I've been busy getting to know my new caregivers, bitching to them about my morphine shortage, and continuing to silently thank the Brazilian paramedic who found my phone mere hours before Neda and I boarded the air ambulance. Were it not for him, I wouldn't be able to do the thing that's been keeping me the busiest. Looking at a photo Alice texted me over a week ago. The photo I'm looking at right now.

Sung's wearing a princess tiara cut from yellow construction paper. Her teeth are showing, but she's not smiling. She's growling or roaring along with a toy tiger she's holding, and swiping at the camera with the claws of her free hand. I turn my phone sideways so the photo fills the screen.

Every time I look at her, I laugh in a way that should make me cry in pain but doesn't.

I reread the message Alice texted along with the photo. "She's a feisty one. Think she's got some tiger in her. Getting stronger and more confident every day."

I texted Alice back this morning to apologize for the late reply and to thank her for the update. Told her to keep them coming.

I click out of the message, ignore the seventy-three unread ones from well-wishers, and go to a web page to continue the one other thing that's been keeping me busy. It's supposed to make me more present and to connect with others. It's supposed to make me less judgmental and enable me to open my heart. It's supposed to eliminate my desire for immediate gratification and pleasure. It's supposed to help me accept and even embrace reality.

Nevertheless, I'm willing to give it a try. As soon as Nurse Eric, who just entered, leaves.

"You buzzed, Mr. Slade?" he asks.

I nod and ask him to help me out of bed and into the three-position clinical recliner next to it.

"Kind of soon for you to be doing your sitting exercises on your own," says Eric.

I shake my head and say, "That's not what I'm going to be doing. Those exercises hurt like hell."

"Ah," says Eric. "You just wanted to get out of that bed and take in some sunshine."

"Something like that," I say.

He endures my curses and groans while helping me and my phone out of the bed and into the special recliner. My legs, they look like I donated most of their muscle to the hospital.

"You mind turning me toward the window?" I ask Eric after getting situated. He obliges and the sky taunts me with its endless blue. He says, "Just press the chair remote whenever you're done," then heads out of the room.

I take a deep, painful breath and click the home button on my phone to bring me back to the earlier web page.

The page says to set aside some time.

Check.

The page says to find a quiet space.

Check.

The page says to sit comfortably.

The page can fuck off.

The page says to keep my eyes open and just observe the present moment as it is. The vagueness of this makes me anxious, but then I read on to see that the goal of this step is not to quiet the mind or achieve a state of total calm, just to pay attention and feel my breath. So another check, I guess.

The page says to let all judgments roll by. I try but am having a hard time letting go of how "judgments" is spelled incorrectly with an "e" after the "g." I take a few more deep, painful breaths and move past this. Checkaroo.

The page says to return to observing the present moment as it is. I do and find the present moment hasn't changed much since my last visit a few seconds ago. And now I'm back to judging—namely the author of this article. I read the final basic step, which is to be kind to my wandering mind, to not judge myself for any thoughts that crop up, to just practice recognizing when my mind has wandered off and to gently bring it back. After muttering a few more curse words, I'm right where the page wants me to be.

Except my chest and back are on fire.

The page says that, while mindfulness meditation is easy, it's not necessarily simple. I say the expert who wrote that is just covering his ass. The page assures me if I keep practicing, changes will take root. Changes that alter the structure of my brain and its response to physical pain. The page says, in time, results will accrue.

I tell the page that's why meditation has a tough time competing with morphine. Waiting for results to accrue isn't nearly as appealing as instantly appeasing the brain's opioid receptors. It's why you rarely hear of anyone breaking into a Zen center or a yoga studio in search of a mindfulness fix. It's why nobody ever sells family heirlooms or their wedding ring or their body for the latest instructional CD by Thich Nhat Hanh.

Still, mindfulness meditation is my best chance of managing my pain without falling into a crater-sized relapse and dying before my next birthday. It's my best chance of keeping my marriage intact and getting back to work.

My new doctor, Dr. Mugheri, has picked up right where Dr. Silva left off with the weaning process. She told me she plans to have me off the morphine completely within the next two days. Then it will be back to Suboxone for help with the opioid withdrawal, and on to some tri-cyclic antidepressant for help with the pain. After hearing about the side-effects of the latter meds—blurred vision, drowsiness, dry mouth, nausea, lightheadedness, weight gain, difficulty thinking clearly, constipation, difficulty urinating, and heart rhythm problems—I told Dr. Mugheri that all sounds fun, but then asked about more holistic alternatives. I've never been a big proponent of prescription drugs that don't require you to lie through your teeth to obtain.

And that's when Dr. Mugheri mentioned mindfulness meditation. Based on what I've read about it, the only negative side effect is being overly positive. Based on my brief experience with it, the only negative side effect is remaining in a lot of pain.

And having your buddy bust your balls.

"Looks like you've caught whatever Caleb has," says Barrett as he enters the room and catches me facing the window focusing on my breath. I'd ignore him, but my practice calls for me to embrace the present moment as it is. If only the present moment didn't involve half my ass hanging out of a hospital gown.

"It's about goddamn time," I say, keeping my eyes fixed on the window in front of me, following Dr. Mugheri's orders regarding no twisting or over-rotation of any kind.

Barrett enters my peripheral vision and stops. It's great to almost see him.

"Sorry, man," he says, still standing off to the side. "Would have come sooner if I could have."

I shift my weight in my special chair and tell Barrett to stop apologizing. "Now, come stand in front of me. What, am I *that* tough to look at?"

Barrett does as I say, but doesn't respond to my question, not even with a joke. So I know the answer. Knew it before asking. Haven't looked at my reflection much since the shooting, but I know what an emergency blood transfusion, hours of surgery and a coma does to my visage. Add in the bandages, the bed sores, the IV bruising, the chapped lips, the atrophied muscle and the flappy gown, and I'm not at all ready for my close up, Mr. DeMille.

This room's florescent lighting isn't helping.

"I'd give you a hug," says Barrett, eyeballing the IV line running from my forearm up to the pouch on the pole beside my chair, "but I, uh, don't want to, you know, cause any more damage."

I extend my non-IV arm toward Barrett, who gives me a delicate handshake, then asks where Neda is.

"Back at work," I say. "Her students ate the substitute teacher while she was down in Rio with me."

Barrett goes, "You make it sound like a vacation." I tell him it was close.

"Malik and Caleb should be here soon," he says as he picks up the little plastic doo-hicky the nurses make me blow into so I don't get pneumonia. "Drew wanted to come, but had to fly back out today."

I nod and tell him Drew's been in touch via text, then cry out as knives pierce my shoulder blades.

"Shit, you all right?" asks Barrett, crouching like a catcher in front of my chair.

"Yeah, yeah, it's okay," I say while pressing the "rescue me" button on the remote in my lap. "Just my sutures pulling. The nurse will be here in a sec."

I close my eyes and take several deep breaths. A thousand milligrams of mindfulness would be helpful right about now.

Barrett asks if there's anything he can do and I tell him I'm fine. He watches me struggle to find a bearable position in the chair. Judging from his face, he's in as much pain as I am. He needs something to take his mind off my agony.

"So," I say, gritting my teeth, "Sounds like things went well in Buenos Aires and Tijuana."

Barrett nods. "Still, it wasn't the same without you there getting arrested with us."

I press the button on the remote again, so hard my thumb knuckle pops.

"You want me to run out and grab someone?" asks Barrett, his face again mimicking mine. He can grimace all he wants, I'm not sharing what little morphine they're letting me have.

The sound of nurse sneakers in high gear. Then Eric nudging Barrett out of the way and helping me out of the chair. "Sorry," says Eric, "I got caught up assisting one of the other nurses with a PICC line. We're a bit understaffed today. And tomorrow and forever."

Eric takes my phone and sets it on the table by my bed. He then has me hold on to his left arm and uses his right one to grab the rolling IV pole as we inch toward the bed, with him facing me and moving backward. He's strong as hell, especially for a guy weighing under a buck fifty and dressed in violet pajamas.

"What were you doing in the chair that would make you sweat this much?" he asks as we move an inch an hour. I say, "Meditation." He tells me I'm probably doing it wrong.

We reach the bed and Eric says, "Okay, this is always the hard part."

The perfect title for my autobiography.

He turns me around so I'm facing away from the bed and helps me sit down near the head of it. Barrett's face tells me how much pain I'm in.

"The most important thing to remember," Eric says, "is don't hold your breath."

Still sitting up on the bed, dreading what for most people is a quick and simple set of physical maneuvers, I say, "Funny, I was just going to tell you the same thing."

"C'mon, Zero," says Eric. "You got this."

Judging from Barrett's face, Eric's wrong.

"Hug your pillow, lie on your side, bring up your legs, roll onto the bed" sounds like a line from a children's bedtime song. But it's actually a verse Satan wrote for post-surgical patients.

I take a deep breath, let it out, and repeat. Just as I'm about to try to defy Barrett's expression and make Eric proud, in walk Malik and Caleb.

If I could smile at them right now, I would.

Eric holds up a hand and says to them, "Sorry guys, you—"

"It's okay," I say, bracing myself on the edge of the bed. "They can stay."

Eric says only two visitors at a time are allowed. "Hospital rules, not mine."

Hate to do this, but it's time to play the hero card.

"These three guys," I say to Eric, "they work with me in rescuing victims of child sex trafficking. They were there when I got shot."

Eric looks at Barrett, then over at Malik and Caleb, and then back at me. "Fine," he says. "But I want you back in that bed now."

I nod, close my eyes and start slowly counting to three in my head. On three I clutch the pillow and proceed to follow the rest of Satan's instructions, with Eric spotting me through each stage of hell. Yelling at me to breathe.

Once in the proper horizontal position, I open my eyes. The faces of Barrett, Malik and Caleb say I'm in three times more pain than before. It's killing me to make my friends suffer so.

"Good work," Eric says to me.

"Fuck you," I say to Eric without speaking a word.

He checks my cardiac monitor leads as I try to catch my breath and ignore the incessant signals certain neurons are sending to my brain. My three visitors are standing next to each other far enough from my bed for Eric to finish up.

"Sorry you guys had to see that," I say.

"Yeah, that looked painful," says Malik.

"I meant my ass."

Malik and Barrett laugh. Caleb says, "It's just good to see you, brother." He presses his palms together and gives me a Namaste bow.

Caleb's a lot less annoying when he's a pedophile.

Eric tells me Dr. Mugheri should be in to check on me within the hour. He turns to the guys and says, "If you tell anyone I gave the okay for all three of you to be in here, I'll deny it."

The guys nod as they make room for Eric and watch him leave. The look on their faces, it's like they'd rather he'd stay. Like they'd be more comfortable with a stranger in the room. Seeing me like this was probably much easier for them when I was in my coma.

The three of them step closer to my bed, pretending not to be put off by the sight of me. It's a struggle, and this from guys highly trained to keep their game face on in a room full of children who've suffered unimaginable abuse.

Caleb says, "You seem to be in good hands."

Malik says, "Way to hang tough, my man."

Barrett says, "It smells like piss and vitamins in here."

In fairness to Caleb and Malik, Barrett has had a little more time to adjust.

What none of these guys may realize is it's just as difficult for me to look at them as it is for them to look at me. The last time we were all together, *I* was all together. Physically at least. This visit is a stinging reminder of the last time I was able to piss into a toilet rather than through a tube. What I wouldn't give to be back in that Rio mansion right now unwittingly destroying brain cells with gasoline and glue.

Then I remember I need to learn how to embrace the present. To let all judgment of myself and others roll by. To just breathe.

Caleb would be so proud. So I can't let him find out.

"I really appreciate you guys popping in," I say.

Malik gives a dismissive wave. "You kidding me?" he says, "We couldn't wait to see you."

Caleb nods and says, "It was hard to focus during the jumps

knowing what you were going through."

"Couldn't have been that hard," I say. "Heard you guys crushed it at both parties."

And they launch into a play-by-play account of what Barrett merely glossed over earlier. How one of the Argentine pimps pissed himself during the bust. How, in Tijuana, Caleb shouted, "No cell can hold me!" and laughed maniacally while getting cuffed. How three of the girls nearly took down a cop who got a little rough while trying to get them out the door.

It's nice being brought along on the mission I missed. It's good seeing the guys light up as they take their victory lap. It's great just sitting here listening and smiling and not being pummeled with pity.

This is the best I've felt since falling in love with my wife a few days ago.

This is the type of present moment I can get behind.

"Excellent work, gentleman," I say.

Malik says thanks and tells me it felt good to get a couple of wins after what happened in Rio. We all nod.

"And after hearing about what happened in Cambodia," adds Malik.

"Why, what happened in Cambodia?" I ask, and the guys— distracted by the loud, rapid beeping sounds—all turn their attention to the machine monitoring my heart rate.

"Hey, hey, relax," says Barrett. "Nothing to get too worked up about." He says a couple of the girls we rescued in Phnom Penh got abducted from their safe house several days ago. He says, "It sucks, but, you know, it happens."

I swallow without the aid of any saliva and ask, "Do you happen to know which safe house?"

The cardiac monitor again draws everyone's attention. Caleb

looks at me and says, "Deep breaths." To Malik and Barrett he says, "That's enough talk about work for now, fellas."

Putting my new mindfulness skills to practice I manage to get the monitor to pipe down. I look at the guys and again ask which safe house.

All three shake their heads. "Not sure," says Malik. "All we know is one of the girls taken was that tiny one who wouldn't let go of you."

BEEPBEEPBEEPBEEPBEEPBEEPBEEPBEEPBEEP …

CHAPTER EIGHTEEN

Sweat pours off my forehead and nose and chin and pools on the black foam mat beneath me. Tanya is standing over me telling me that's enough for now. But I keep going. Tanya shouts for me to stop. She can shout all she wants. I'll stop when I'm done, and I'm not even close.

The pain is exquisite.

"What the heck, Zero!" yells Tanya as she tugs at the back of my soaking wet gray T-shirt.

I grunt and continue to hold my plank position.

Tanya lets go of my shirt. "Darn it," she says, "I don't know what you're trying to prove. You're just going to cause more frigging damage and set yourself back."

Tanya never swears. If she plans on sticking with me, she might want to start.

I tell myself just three more seconds, and I go five. And then five more. Perspire, scream, repeat. Some would say this is self-abuse. Others might call it self-control. They'd all be right.

It's my cruelest punishment and my greatest achievement.

After just a week of physical therapy, I'm three weeks ahead of schedule. That's what Dr. Mugheri told me. She said she's never seen anything like it. She said at this rate, I'll be out of here in no time. The trouble is I have no time for no time. My three weeks ahead of schedule is nearly two weeks too late. And counting.

I tell myself two more seconds, and I go ten.

And then I collapse. Flat on the foam mat with my head turned, the whole right side of my face bathes in the liter of liquid I've lost. I can't tell where the pain from the lactic acid buildup and the pain from my wound and sutures begin and end. It'll be even more fun when the Suboxone wears off.

I have a whole new appreciation for pain meds now that I actually need but can't have them. I hate my new appreciation.

Still, this session with Tanya doesn't hurt as much my first several with her. So either I'm gaining strength or causing nerve damage.

"The goal is to get stronger slowly but surely, not to kill yourself," Tanya says, shaking her head at me sprawled out on the mat. "This isn't a race."

"You wanna bet?" is what I'd say if I could catch my breath.

Tanya says, "I think we'll hold off on the resistance strap exercises until your afternoon session."

"No," I mutter into a puddle. "I'm ready."

"You don't *look* ready," says Tanya. "You look like you just got run over."

The sadistic personal trainers I always see torturing their clients at my gym, I wish Tanya were more like them. They get off on pushing people beyond their limits. Tanya is intent on pulling me within mine. Though, in her defense, I'm probably a little too motivated. Certainly more than the saggy soccer moms and dads who join my gym mainly for the free daycare. All they really want is a break from their kid. All I really want is something like the opposite.

I push myself up to a kneeling position, closing my eyes and breathing deeply to douse the flames between my shoulder blades. After getting to my feet I smile and say to Tanya, "C'mon, let's do this," but I make the mistake of clapping hard on "this." Looking at Tanya's expressionless face, I can't tell exactly how much pain I'm in.

But she can.

"Sorry, Hercules," she says. "We're done until three o'clock."

I plead for twenty more minutes, and Tanya shakes her head. "Why are you so intent on destroying yourself?" she asks.

I tell her it's the only way for me to save someone else.

"If this is about your job," says Tanya, "you're going to have to accept you'll be out of commission for a while."

She must have been chatting with Dr. Mugheri, or with Eric or one of the other nurses. I've yet to share with her what I do for work.

"I don't need to be able to deadlift five hundred pounds," I say. "Just need to be able to place a valise in an overhead compartment."

Tanya shakes her head again. "Listen, I admire your dedication, but not your stupidity. You *do* realize a blazing hot chunk of metal went into one side of you and came out the other, right?"

I tell her I don't expect her to admire my stupidity, just understand it.

"Okay," says Tanya, pointing to the wheelchair beside her, "how 'bout you explain your stupidity to me while I wheel you back to your room."

"I'm not getting in that thing," I say, then drop back down to my knees.

See also: Begging.

Tanya places her hands on her hips and tilts her head back. "Zero, I have no time for this."

I tell her I have even less.

Tanya grips the back of the wheelchair and rattles it. "Damn it," she mutters.

It's her first curse word. I've finally broken her. Maybe now she'll do what I ask and break *me*.

"So," I say looking around the room, "where are those resistance straps?"

"Shit," says Tanya.

She's really coming around now.

I say, "I think I'm good for several sets."

And Tanya says, "I guess I don't really have a choice."

Looks like I've got her right where I—

"I'm going to page Bruce and have him *put* you in that wheelchair."

Bruce is the head of Physical Therapy at the hospital. And bigger than Barrett.

Tanya starts toward the door of the therapy room. I stand back up and tell her to wait. She stops and says, "So you're ready to cooperate?" And I go, "Did you know there are more than five thousand child prostitutes in Cambodia?"

Tanya just taps her foot on the floor and points at the wheelchair.

I say, "They're taken from their families, or sold by them, and forced into sexual slavery."

Tanya scowls. "That is very sad," she says, "but it doesn't change the fact that—"

"The children who resist sex or who try to run away, they are beaten. Cut. Burned. Some receive electric shocks. Others are shot dead and disposed of. They are the lucky ones."

"Zero," says Tanya, "I get what you do is very—"

I say the average age of these girls is twelve.

"Zero, please——"

I say some are as young as six.

And Tanya goes, "Six? Fuck."

The mouth on this one.

I reach into the right pocket of my damp gray sweatpants and pull out a plastic zip-lock sandwich baggie. From the baggie I retrieve the picture of Sung and the toy tiger that Eric was kind enough to print out on photo paper for me a few days ago. "This girl here," I say, holding the photo up for Tanya to see, "she's five."

Tanya lets go of the wheelchair and moves in for a closer look. She covers her mouth, then asks, "Who is she?"

"She's the reason I need to get the hell out of here."

Tanya lifts my hand and looks at the photo again. "Five years old," she says shaking her head. "Tell me, how is such a thing even possible?"

I wish I had a better answer than "high demand," but I don't. So I say nothing and just stand there looking at Tanya looking at the photo, her eyes filled with fury and disgust and disbelief. All the things I used to feel before getting too used to this sort of thing. And the meds.

"So," says Tanya, "is this one of the girls your team's going to rescue?"

I wish I had a better answer than "we already did but it didn't work." A better answer than "shit happens." A better answer than "now it's all up to me." But I don't.

Only this time I make sure Tanya knows this. Sometimes the best thing you can say is the worst thing you can say. Sometimes the truth works in your favor.

Tanya stands there stunned after hearing what I've just told her. That the precious child in the photo's only real chance for liberation lies in the hands of a man who a week ago couldn't make a fist.

Tanya looks like she's about to cry or punch a wall or both. At least now she knows I'm not crazy. Or at the very least understands why I might be.

And I go, "I'm assuming we can get started on the resistance strap exercises now?"

And Tanya says, "Absolutely not." Then, ignoring my look of disbelief, she walks over to the wheelchair and releases the brake. I stay put and wave the photo in the air.

"I'd love to help you save that little girl," says Tanya, "but I'd hate to lose my job."

"You're a physical therapist," I say, "administering physical therapy *is* your job."

Tanya says what I'm asking her to do isn't physical therapy, it's physical destruction. "I build bodies up," she says, "I don't break them down."

I remind her what Dr. Mugheri said about my amazing progress. "How can you say I'm breaking down?"

Tanya points to the wheelchair and says, "I know a body on the brink when I see one." I tell her there's nothing she can do to stop me. And she says, "You're right."

I just stand there with my head cocked. To fill the silence, Tanya says, "If you decided to just up and walk out of this place today or tomorrow, nobody in this hospital can legally stand in your way."

I cock my head to the other side. Tanya points to the wheelchair again, and I limp over and have a seat. Then, defying doctor's orders, I rotate my torso and turn my neck to look back at her. She gives me a wink and starts wheeling me out of the room.

***

Freedom is just another word for ignoring common sense.

I'd probably enjoy mine more if I were dressed better. But time is of the essence, and there isn't enough for me to call Neda to bring me a nice change of clothes. Also, I'd be an idiot to call Neda to bring me a nice change of clothes.

It's easier to ask for forgiveness than for permission.

Cambodia is ringing in my ears. Sung is screaming in my sleep. There is a hole in me that isn't from a bullet.

I won't be able to live with myself if I don't go. Neda won't be able to live with me if I do. But considering the level of danger involved, there's a good chance she won't *have* to.

Abandoning reason appears to be the most logical choice.

The clock on the wall in my room says it's 5:35 p.m. I peek outside the doorway to see if the coast is clear, which is stupid because I'm free to go. And because the coast is never clear. Still, I hate saying goodbyes, especially to people to whom I owe my life and who still aren't convinced they've saved it.

After one more visual sweep of the room to make sure I didn't leave any important items behind, I start on my hundred-foot journey to the elevators. I'm wearing a dirty hoodie, T-shirt and sweatpants and carrying a garbage bag filled with more dirty hoodies, T-shirts and sweatpants. In the pocket of the hoodie I have on is a vial of Suboxone.

You've heard of going out in style. This isn't that.

Every step is accompanied by a grimace and a grunt and the sound of pills rattling around. But this is a hospital, so nobody pays me any mind.

Ten feet from the elevators, a man calls out, "Zero!" Could be he's addressing someone else with that name, so I continue walking.

"Mr. Slade! Stop!"

Without turning around, I press the down button. The doors of the middle elevator slide open immediately.

"Wait!" the voice shouts as I step in. My finger presses the L button for lobby, then the inward-facing arrows button for catch you later. Keeping my hooded head down, I close my eyes to: 1) use mindfulness in an attempt to stay calm and relieve pain; 2) telepathically get the fucking elevator doors to close like I commanded; and 3) avoid eye contact with the man who's sprinting toward me shouting, "You can't leave yet!"

Not sure who I'm more pissed at right now: Tanya for telling me nobody could stop me; the man who's trying to do just that; or the moron in charge of elevator maintenance.

The doors tell me they're finally sliding shut, and I open my eyes. A short, heavy man in a suit is just a few feet away and gaining. It's the patient support advisor who's spoken to me a couple of times since I was admitted. I lower my head again, this time in shame, and in rapid succession press the button with the inward-facing arrows three times, as if this might provide the turbo boost the doors need. Seconds later, they bounce off Mr. PSA's forearm and slowly slide back open.

"Going down?" I ask, averting my eyes.

"You haven't … been cleared for … release," says Mr. PSA, panting. He raises his index finger up as he hunches over to catch his breath, all the while keeping his foot pressed against the edge of the elevator door. Behind him the corridor is filled with doctors and nurses and aides and volunteers, who have each decided my unauthorized discharge deserves more attention than the sick and the dying.

"I'm not going back," I say to Mr. PSA, who's still doubled over, wheezing.

"I need you to … come with me," he says.

Even in my impaired condition, I could probably take this guy. Don't care how many witnesses there are right now. Don't care how many security guards will be waiting for me. I'm going down to the lobby. A quick jab to the throat and then a shove, and I'll be free to make my descent.

Mr. PSA says, "We can't … let you leave …"

My right arm rears back, my right hand balls into a fist.

"… until you sign … a waiver."

He could have just opened with that.

"Sorry," I mumble while stepping out of the elevator with my garbage bag. "Thought it was okay to just split."

Mr. PSA says it will be once I relinquish the hospital and all its staff of any liability henceforth.

This guy is fluent in waiver.

He says, "Follow me," and, watching me struggle, offers to carry my garbage bag down the corridor. We arrive at a large beige cubicle, where I sign and initial a document after pretending to speed-read it. Judging from Mr. PSA's grin, either I've just saved his job in the event of my death, or I've handed him the deed to my house. I, too, am grinning a little, just happy not to have to wear a suit to a cubicle every day.

Mr. PSA tells me I can leave now. But since I've already signed the waiver, he doesn't offer to help me with my garbage bag again.

On the elevator ride from the sixth floor down to the lobby, a wave of optimism rolls over me. A sense of power and purpose. A feeling that nothing can stop me. Such positivity is very unlike me. It's very unlike *anyone* wearing pajamas in an elevator.

The elevator stops. I step out of it and drag my garbage bag through the lobby, filled with more natural resolve and confidence than I've ever experienced.

And then I see Caleb walking through the hospital entrance.

Sometimes all it takes is a Buddhist to knock you out of your Zen zone.

I'm in no condition to dart down a hallway or crouch behind any lobby furniture. And besides, it's too late. Caleb has just spotted me. He looks as confused as I do ridiculous.

He approaches, bows his usual bow, and says, "So ... they're releasing you?"

"Yup," I say to an abstract painting on the lobby wall. "I'm all clear."

Caleb eyes my ensemble and my garbage bag and the sweat beading on my forehead. He turns to look behind him, then back at me. "Is Neda waiting for you outside?"

I tell him she's got a parent-teacher night at the school.

"Ah," says Caleb, scanning the lobby. "Is someone *else* here to take you home?"

I tell him I was just going to grab a taxi.

Still looking around, not really listening, Caleb says, "Don't they usually have an orderly or someone bring you out in a wheelchair? Or at least help you with your things?"

I tell him they offered but that I said no thanks.

Caleb nods. Then he shakes his head. "What's going on, Zero?"

"Nothing," I say to the painting. "What do you mean?"

Caleb says when he and Malik and Barrett came to see me last week, they spoke to my doctor. "She said if all went well, you'd be back home in three to four weeks."

I tell him things have gone *better* than well.

"I'm glad to hear that," says Caleb, "but—and don't take this the wrong way—you don't look like a guy who should be walking out of a hospital on his own right now. Or at all."

I tell him he doesn't know what he's talking about. "Feeling great," I say, my eyes closed to ease the throbbing. "And you'll be happy to know a lot of it has to do with the mindfulness meditation I've started doing."

"Interesting," says Caleb. "Now what do you say you let me help you back up to your room before you hurt yourself more."

Looks like I may get to throw that throat punch after all. I'll just have to be sure to aim about a foot lower than usual.

"I'm telling you, I've been released."

Caleb folds his arms across his chest and says he's not buying it. I reach into the pocket of my sweatpants, retrieve my copy of the signed waiver, and snap it in front of his face. He takes the wrinkled piece of paper and looks it over.

"Oh, Zero," he says, shaking his head. "Why would you do this?"

I say don't worry about it, then snatch the paper from him and stuff it back into my pocket. "Now if you'll excuse me, I gotta run."

"Run? You can barely walk."

I tell Caleb walking's not a problem, then grunt as I start to drag my garbage bag around him. He shifts over to block my path.

Scratching my cheek, I say, "You'd be wise to move."

"You'd be even wiser not to," says Caleb. "And that's not a threat. Pretty sure it's doctor's orders."

I tell him I'm a lot stronger than the doctor anticipated. "Anyway, it's not your concern."

And Caleb says, "The heck it's not."

All these people averse to cursing. It's really getting on my fucking nerves.

"Not sure why you're so adamant about keeping me here," I say. "You're the one who told Neda you understand how hard it is spending time in hospitals. Well, me leaving means you won't have to come visit this place anymore."

Caleb glares at me like I'm a cop and he's in character.

"What was that text all about, anyway?" I ask. "Who—"

Caleb shakes his head. "This isn't the time."

He's right. There's not a minute to spare. I go to drag my garbage bag past him again, and he again steps in front of me. I stop, close my eyes, and take two deep breaths. Caleb says, "You're not ready. You need help."

"Then help me," I say.

"I am," says Caleb. "By stopping you."

I tell him that doesn't help anyone. "Now kindly move."

Caleb says, "Sorry, Zero, but there's no way I'm going to just let you go out and start using again."

I laugh and he goes, "I saw how you were on that flight to Mumbai. You need to heal up and face your demons."

I shake my head and tell him he's got it all wrong. "You don't have to worry about that," I say. "I'm clean."

Caleb points at my midsection and says, "Then what's that I heard rattling in your pocket?"

"Pills," I say. "The ones I've been *prescribed* to keep me *off* the others." I reach into my hoodie pocket and pull out the vial of Suboxone. The photo of Sung tags along and falls to the floor. I squat to pick it up, but Caleb beats me to it.

"Who's this?" he asks as we both return to a full standing position.

I grab the photo from him and slip it back into my pocket. "Nobody you know."

"She's adorable," says Caleb.

I shake the vial I'm holding and say, "So anyway, here are the pills I was—"

"Wait a minute." Caleb points at my hoodie pocket again. "Is that the little girl Malik and Barrett were talking about?"

I stare at Caleb and say nothing.

"It *is*, isn't it?" says Caleb, almost gleeful. He looks down at the floor, then back up at me with a solemn grin, and says, "She must have really gotten to you."

I tell Caleb to mind his fucking business.

Caleb turns around and looks at the giant rotating doors leading outside. He shakes his head, then turns back to me and says, "This is crazy."

He looks at my hoodie pocket and tells me I must be out of my mind.

Then he snatches the garbage bag from me.

And he says, "I'm in."

CHAPTER NINETEEN

I hate the New York Yankees and everything they stand for. But I always knew Derek Jeter would come through for me one day.

"Well, the card's authentic," says Billy, the owner of Billy Z's Sports Memorabilia, as he lays his magnifying glass on the desk in his cluttered, windowless office in the back of the shop. "And you took good care of him."

"Not me," I say. "My brother."

"Does your brother know you're selling his card?" asks Billy, looking at me with his one good eye while his lazy one wanders the periphery. I just hope he used the correct one to examine Jeter.

"Nope," I say. "My brother's dead."

"Ah shit," says Billy. "Sorry, man."

I say it's okay, he's been gone for years. I say Jeter's just been sitting in a safety deposit box ever since.

"Well, then you *did* take care of him," says Billy. "You'd be surprised how many numbskulls keep their valuable cards in a shoebox and take 'em out all the time to drool on 'em."

"Yeah, well, I don't really care about baseball or baseball cards," I say. "No offense."

Billy laughs. "The best collectors never do."

I say my brother wasn't what you'd call a collector. I say he won Jeter in a high-stakes poker game from a guy who was cash-poor. "Pretty sure it's the only baseball card my brother ever owned."

"Well, he picked a damn good one," says Billy, gazing at the card and the wall simultaneously. "A Derek Jeter 1993 Upper Deck SP rookie card in mint condition, that's a rare find."

So are two plane tickets to Phnom Penh for just seven hundred dollars each. But I'll need to hurry.

"So," I say, "how much we talking here?"

Billy looks over the card again, then closes his eyes and starts rubbing his hands together. "I can give you fifteen hundred," he says.

I did a bit of online research before coming here and I know for a fact the card is worth no less than twenty-two hundred. So I look at Billy, slap my hand down on the desk, and say, "Deal."

Billy gets up and asks me to wait in his office while he fetches the cash. He closes the door behind him, leaving me alone with Jeter.

And Hank.

Hank asks why the hell I'm selling his card—and for seven hundred dollars under market value. I tell him I don't really have time to go into it all. I say just know I need fast money and can't have Neda finding out. I say she keeps close tabs on all of our accounts. I tell him I'm sorry.

The office door swings open and in comes Billy holding a white business-sized envelope, which he hands to me. "Count it to make sure it's all there," he says.

I want to say "no need" to show trust and further cement our solid rapport, but I can't take any chances with that eye of his.

For all he and I know, a few one-hundred peso bills got lumped in with the legit C-notes.

"Fine, if it'll make you happy," I say as I lift the flap of the envelope and flit through the bills with my thumb, counting fifteen Benjamins. I nod at Billy. "We're good," I say, but he can tell that's a lie by how long it takes me to stand up and extend my hand. He looks at my hand, takes a moment to adjust his focus, and gives it a shake.

"If you find yourself feeling guilty tomorrow," says Billy, "I'd be happy to give you the card back. All it will cost you is twenty-five hundred." He chuckles and gives me a wink with his good eye while his other one looks at the ceiling.

I tell him don't count on me returning. I say my brother and I just talked it over, and he seemed okay with this.

"Wait," says Billy, "so your brother is alive?"

"God, I hope not," I say. "He'd kill me."

And with Billy looking straight at me and the water cooler perplexed, I hold up the envelope and go, "Then again, so might this."

***

I'm so torn and distracted by what I have to do tomorrow, I almost order a salad. Neda's so baffled by how enamored and attentive I'm being, she almost orders pork.

I hate that I have to act like I feel what I actually feel for Neda.

I love that she's buying it, even though I'm not selling anything.

I say, "Baby, it's wonderful to be here with you right now." I say, "No way that hospital could keep me from you any longer." And what I'm saying is true, but I'm focused more on where Neda might have put my passport.

"I still can't believe you were released so soon," says Neda, glowing as she takes a sip of her Sauvignon blanc. "Or that you didn't have me come get you."

"I told you, love, I wanted to surprise you," I say, gazing at Neda adoringly and wondering if Alice has responded to my latest email regarding Sung's whereabouts.

Neda says she was certainly surprised, and takes another sip of wine. "It was very nice of Caleb to pick you up from the hospital and drive you home."

I nod and say that guy would do anything for a friend.

"Well," says Neda, "you did … you know … kinda save his life and all."

I say I'm pretty sure he'd do the same for me. Then I go, "Enough about Caleb. Tonight is about just you and me." I raise my glass of Italian sparkling water and clink Neda's second glass of wine as I breathe in her beauty and try to remember if I still own a Kevlar vest.

The waiter brings our starters—a salad for Neda and beef carpaccio for me. I watch as Neda creates the perfect forkful of kale, arugula, roasted beets, golden raisins and goat cheese, then holds the fork up and presents it to me across the table.

"No thanks," I say. "That's all you."

Neda continues to hold the fork in front of me. "This one bite contains more nutrients than ten plates of carpaccio, and you could use some nutrients."

The old me would have pushed her fork away. The old me would have then stuffed his mouth full of cured meat, chewing it slowly and grinning while staring defiantly at his wife. The new me, he smiles gratefully and leans forward to accept the offering from the goddess he should have lost long ago. The new me nods and hums "mmmm" and takes her hand, caressing it with both of his. The new me winks at the love of his life and prays his Jagdkommando Integral Tri-Dagger Fixed Blade Knife makes it through Customs.

Neda says, "I love you, Zero." She says, "I'm so grateful to have you back." She says, "I'm proud of you."

I don't know why she has to make everything so difficult.

She's wearing a black dress against which I have little defense. And the way she looks at me after each bite of food and each sip of wine, it's enough for me to call the whole thing off. Enough for me to send a text to Caleb simply stating "abort, abort" before crushing my phone with the heel of my shoe.

But then Sung leaps into my arms [*click*] and ruins my neck, my ribs, my shirt [*click*] and asks me if I'll come visit her again [*click*].

The waiter brings our entrees. Grilled branzino for Neda and veal saltimbocca for me.

"Don't get mad," says Neda as she grabs my plate and slowly drags it across the table next to hers, "but we're going family style with these." She takes half of her fish and most of her sautéed vegetables and puts them on my plate. Then she takes half of my veal and most of my potatoes and puts them on her plate. Then she pushes my plate back to me, grins and says, "Get used to it, big guy. Going forward, there are going to be some changes around here."

I just smile and nod and start eating. And hope to hell she's right.

After a minute or so of comfortable silence while we each enjoy our dinner, I say, "I'm sorry."

"For what?" asks Neda, dabbing her lips with a napkin.

"Everything," I say.

Neda shakes her head and tells me I've already apologized

enough. What she doesn't realize is, with this apology, I'm being proactive.

I tell her she means the world to me. That I'd never do anything to hurt her. That I hope to make up for all I've put her through.

I tell her everything I'm feeling deep down, and nothing from the back of my mind.

The waiter comes with the dessert menu. Neda tells him she'll just have coffee. I tell him nothing for me.

Neda smiles at me and says, "I see you drooling. Go on, get something."

"Yeah?"

"Sure, baby," she says. "You deserve it."

This woman so gets me. And is dead wrong.

I pick the dessert menu back up from the table and resume salivating. Should I get the tiramisu? Should I get the amaretto cheesecake? Should I get the chocolate mousse? Should I check in early tomorrow afternoon to see if I can get upgraded to business class?

Neda taps the last drop of wine onto her tongue and looks around for the waiter. The way she's eyeing that empty glass, it's not the check she's after.

"Sorry you have to drive us," I say to her. "Someone as gorgeous as you shouldn't have to operate heavy machinery." Yes it's a tad chauvinistic, but also strategic. Another Sauvignon blanc and she might have to call in sick tomorrow. That will make it very difficult for me to sneak out of the country.

"Just one more small glass while you have dessert," Neda says, holding her thumb and forefinger an inch apart. "I'm fine to drive."

She's given me no other choice and deserves much better. But here goes.

"Aaghh!"

Neda scrunches up her face and tells me to breathe as I clutch at my exit wound. The couple at the next table are riveted by the performance.

"Just a little twinge," I say through my teeth to Neda, "I'll be fine. Don't let this ruin our—"

"Check please," Neda calls out to the waiter as he approaches with her coffee. He nods before turning around and heading toward the computer register by the bar.

"We need to get you home," Neda says, looking at me with such tenderness and pity I want to punch myself. She sighs and goes, "Or maybe back to the hospital?"

I shake my head and say it's nothing, just a little spasm. I tell her I'd die if I had to spend another night away from her.

Not proud about the lying. Not thrilled the lying's painfully close to prophecy.

The waiter arrives with the check. I go to fish my wallet out of my pants pocket, wincing all the while and not faking this time. Neda halts me with a hand and gives the waiter a credit card from her purse.

"You're going to have to learn to let me help you," she says, reaching across the table to caress the back of my hand. "You can't do this on your own."

She's absolutely right. And has no idea.

I lift her cinnamon-vanilla hand and kiss it. She smiles at me like she may never again. We are perfect right now. So perfect, the waiter had better hurry his ass up with that card.

CHAPTER TWENTY

The stout guard watches us with his M16. The skinny one pats us down and turns our bags inside out. This is after Alice's okay has already come through the big guy's walkie-talkie loud and clear. After she's identified us through the surveillance camera staring at us from atop the concrete wall encircling the grounds.

It's been years since I visited five weeks ago. Good to see they've stepped up security. Crippling to remember why.

There's no Pich. No golf cart. No smiling. Just heavily armed men giving us the eye and digging through our underwear. No complaints here. Other than easy with the fake Versace jacket, and you guys are a few weeks late.

After getting the nod from Slim, Big grabs the muzzle of his M16 and slides the strapped rifle around until it rests on his back breasts. He then undoes the latch on the gray steel gate in front of us and kicks it open while Slim, sporting an open-holstered nine millimeter, escorts us onto the grounds.

There are no girls in sight, but I smile just in case. To get Caleb to do the same, I look at him and point at the corner of my mouth. As for Slim, he can do whatever he wants with his face. The girls know him well enough by now.

Alice is standing on the front porch of what I recall being her office. As we get closer, I can see she, too, is doing her best to smile. She steps off the porch and shouts, "Thank you, Prak!" in Khmer as she waves off Slim, who turns around and marches back to his post.

We are ten feet from the porch, and through her clenched grin Alice says to me, "What in the world? I thought you were in the hospital." The look on her face. Like she just received a bad gift.

"Rumors of my condition have been greatly exaggerated," I say.

Alice moves in for a hug, which is what I was afraid of. Stepping back I say, "Okay, so maybe I'm exaggerating the exaggeration," and then extend my hand for her to shake.

The look on her face now. Like she received a broken gift.

And another, much smaller one.

"This is my colleague, Caleb," I say. "Caleb, Alice."

"A pleasure to meet you," says Caleb.

Alice smiles and nods at him, then turns back to me and goes, "I had no idea you were coming ... or were even *able* to come."

Normally I'd call before dropping in on an acquaintance who lives eight thousand miles away. It's just, I didn't want Alice to worry about straightening up. Laying out clean towels. Preparing a welcome drink. She's got enough to deal with.

Also, she would have told me ...

"There's really nothing you can do."

I tell her nothing's what I've been doing for the past few weeks. I say now I'm ready to try anything. "But first, I really need to lie down."

The searing pain shooting down my lower back and radiating to both legs, it's all Caleb's fault. I was doing just fine until he insisted on using a wheelchair to rush me to our connection at Hong Kong International. We hit more turbulence than the flight did.

Caleb needs to be more careful when risking his life to help me.

"Please, please, come in and rest," says Alice, holding the door open for us. "Feel free to sprawl out on the sofa, Zero. Do you need us to help you lie down?"

"Nah, I got it, thanks."

And with both of them watching me size up the sofa, I realize "Hug your pillow, lie on your side, bring up your legs, roll onto the bed" isn't going to work here. There's no pillow and not much room to roll. So I improvise a little. And sound more like a man easing into a scalding cauldron than onto a couch.

After assuring Alice and Caleb I'm okay and convincing neither, I say to Alice, "Don't worry about me. How are *you* doing?"

"Well," says Alice as she and Caleb each take a seat near the sofa, "like I've mentioned in my messages, it's been pretty rough."

I tell her I can only imagine how awful it must have been. I tell her I'm just glad they didn't hurt her like they did Pich.

"How's he doing?" I ask.

She says he's still on the mend from the broken ribs. "For such a sweet and gentle boy, he really put up quite a fight."

"Brave kid," says Caleb. "Please give him our regards."

"I shall," says Alice with a sad smile. She tells us Pich's sister Mau has been keeping her updated every couple of days. "Mau says even though it still hurts him to breathe, he never complains. Says all he cares about is getting back to his job here."

If anyone understands that, it's me. Sometimes excruciating

work is the only thing that helps with the agony. Sometimes to keep going, all you can do is everything you can't.

I search for a more comfortable position on the sofa and say to Alice, "I know you said in an email you didn't get a very good look at the two men, but anything you can share would be very helpful."

Alice looks at me like a mother preparing to tell her child the truth about Santa. "Anything I can share, I've already shared with the police," she says. "And no offense, but they are probably a little better equipped than you to handle this."

That hurt, but nowhere near as much as trying to sit up on the couch to prove her wrong.

Alice goes, "I respect your intentions, but you have to let the police do their job."

"It's been two weeks," I say, eyes closed, still horizontal. "Either they don't want to do their job or they don't know how."

"Oh, Zero," says Alice. "I know you just want to help, but you have to be realistic." She reminds us how we haven't a clue regarding who took Sung or where they're keeping her. How we have no idea how many men we'll be up against or what weapons they might have. How I haven't the ability to sit up on the sofa.

The nerve of her to throw solid facts in my face out of concern for Caleb's and my safety.

"Granted," I say to Alice, "the odds are stacked against us, but if you could just tell us whatever you saw, anything you suspect."

"It will be like finding a needle in a haystack," says Alice. "A haystack the size of Cambodia."

I tell her that's where she's wrong. She says she hopes I'm right.

"We're not searching for a needle," I say. "We're searching for men who know where the needle is."

Alice looks at me like I just gave her a koan to solve.

"What's more," I say, "when these men find out we're looking for them to show us the needle, they're going to be eager to do so."

"I'm afraid you've lost me," says Alice.

I push myself up to a seated position on the sofa.

"What I'm saying is we aren't here to rescue Sung. We're here to become her new pimps."

***

I never expected to get such a high from reaching a new low.

Or for Caleb to know so much about the Dark Net.

It pays to have an FBI guy around when you're ready to buy a child on the black market.

"Wow, look at you go," I say as Caleb opens up five different sex slave sites in ten seconds. I tell him to hold on while I walk over to lower the blinds in Alice's office. Looking at what we're looking at, where we're looking at it, it's like building a bonfire in a burn unit.

Alice is with the girls over in the art center. Said she won't be back for an hour. Told us she didn't want to see what we're doing. Pointed out for the record she doesn't approve. Still, she was kind enough to provide her Wi-Fi password. And a few helpful clues.

"Wow, you're good," I say to Caleb while we browse scores of Cambodian children for sale.

"You guys didn't get trained on the deep web at the CIA?" Caleb asks.

"Sure, we dabbled in it in a little," I say, "but you, you're like a hacker up in here."

"I had a few friends in the IT department," says Caleb.

I'll be forever grateful to him for granting me access to the worst place you can imagine. Can't thank him enough for the rage and the nausea I'm currently experiencing. You could say this makes us even for me saving his life in Rio, but it doesn't. I owe him big time.

None of the girls featured on any of the sites are Sung. That's a good thing. Once a girl like her goes privately public, all the worms come out of the woodwork and the bidding war begins. You don't want a war.

What you want is to be proactive. To get to the owner before he even knows he wants to sell. To make him an offer he can't refuse before refusal is even a factor.

At least that's what all the experts say in the online forums I've been hanging out in of late. Over the past few days, I've learned a ton of invaluable tips and tactics from some of the world's leading miscreants. Thanks to them and their willingness to share their insight, I stand a real chance at becoming the monster I aim to be.

It's a big jump from pedophile to pimp. Just because I have years of experience pretending to rent young girls doesn't mean I know how to pretend to purchase them. The key to success at the higher levels of sex trafficking is to understand your limitations.

And then act invincible.

Caleb knows all this because it's all I talked about on the plane yesterday. Quietly. In-flight whispering is one of the first things they teach you at OE. The whole "If you don't have anything nice to say, don't say anything at all" thing doesn't cut it in our line of work. We never have anything nice to say, but we have to say it. And usually in mid-air. With a half dozen strangers practically sitting in our laps or us in theirs. Go up a few decibels when talking shop or strategizing with a colleague in this biz, and you'll be placed on a supersonic jet to the no-fly list.

Based on the expertise I shared with Caleb for hours in a crowded pressurized cabin, he's right now putting a call out online for a five-year-old prostitute. Not Sung, per se. Just someone like her. Using her name and describing her to a T mere weeks after a successful sting and a subsequent abduction is how you lose her forever. We'll never find her if we try to find her. We're not looking for her. We're just looking.

Privately. Whatever happens on the dark web may stay on the dark web, but still, there are a ton of people in the room. If you ask for the youngest girl possible openly in a forum, soon everybody will want her. Or one just like her. It's herd mentality. The whole "I'll have what he's having" thing. Keeping up with the creepy Joneses.

So Caleb, he's reaching out on various sites to individual traffickers via direct message. Only he's not Caleb; he's MnyTalks.

MnyTalks types, "Seeking young Cambodian girls. If you got the goods, I'll pay more than market price. Highly motivated." Then he hits submit, sending the message to a Mr. P!tV!per.

Seconds later, my phone rings and buzzes. I look at Caleb and shrug while reaching for it in my pocket. Caleb looks at me like he just encountered a koan he can't solve.

The caller, it's not Mr. P!tV!per.

It's someone even more dangerous.

"You can't keep ignoring your wife," Caleb says to me after I hit "Decline" on my phone screen.

"I'm not," I say. "I'm just trying to avoid a huge cell bill."

"I see," says Caleb. "So then I assume you've at least been

answering the text messages she's been sending ever since we landed."

"Our cell plan doesn't include unlimited texting," I say, struggling to my feet from the sofa. Caleb asks me where I'm going and I say, "Be right back. Need to use the bathroom."

I'm not going to just sit here and get preached to by someone with a name like MnyTalks. Besides, I think I have to throw up. Fishing for five-year-olds is making me nauseous. As is the Suboxone combined with the thoracic pain combined with the guilt.

I head toward the bathroom in Alice's office and try to remove from my mind what must be going through Neda's.

Thirteen and twenty-two. That's how many voicemails and text messages from Neda were waiting for me when I turned my phone on upon arrival in Phnom Penh. And that's how many I've yet to respond to. Add to that the five calls and eight texts I've since received and evaded. In my defense, I did ask Neda—in the rather cryptic letter I left on our bed—not to contact me. In her defense, that's like asking a lioness to stop hunting gazelles.

I turn the knob of the bathroom door and enter. Not sure if I need to vomit into the toilet or do something that requires sitting atop it. To cover all bases, I sit and then grab the small wastebasket beside the toilet. It could be worse—Alice could have opted for a squat toilet so prevalent in these parts. I'm just trying to look on the bright side. Doing so, however, seems to have exacerbated my gastric distress.

I sweat and wait and sweat some more. Few things are worse than throwing up and shitting simultaneously. Abandoning your wife, for instance.

"Everything okay in there?" Caleb shouts.

"Comparatively," I shout back.

And Caleb goes, "Huh?"

"Just give me a few minutes."

You know how when you're nauseous and crampy so you focus on something serene and soothing to settle your stomach? I don't have that option.

Where most people would be picturing ice-cold popsicles and babbling brooks and fields of flowers right now, I'm picturing Neda reading my letter then calling me then texting me then calling again then shouting a stream of obscenities then texting again then running crying into the master bathroom and shattering the vanity mirror with her fist or forehead.

And still I can't crap or puke.

I consider sticking my finger down my throat to get the show started, but I haven't washed my hands in hours and can't reach the sink. So instead I think about whether I'm going to die at the hands of sex traffickers or my wife. The woman I'd never hurt but do. The woman I'd never abandon but have.

The letter told Neda I love her. The letter told her more than ever. It said she has every right to never speak to or see me again. It said I hope she has a choice in that matter.

What the letter didn't say is where I went. Or why. Or with whom.

It didn't ask her for forgiveness. It didn't ask her for patience. It asked her only to not alert Fynn or Barrett or anyone else from OE about my disappearance. And to please not change the locks.

I could stuff my shirt in the toilet and it would come out dryer than it is right now. The bathroom refuses to sit still. The butterflies I had for breakfast have been obliterated by the solar flares. Inside I'm lava. Outside I'm raining.

What I wouldn't give right now to be murdered by sex traffickers or my wife.

Caleb knocks on the bathroom door. "You sure you're okay?" he asks.

And I don't say a word but it's okay because it must have been a rhetorical question.

Besides, it's time.

If only I had some hand sanitizer.

I open my mouth, press my index finger down on the back of my tongue, and, cradling the wastebasket with my arm, ruin the babbling brook and every fucking flower in the field.

Dr. Mugheri told me there are over two hundred muscles involved in human regurgitation. Most of them are found in and around where I have an entry and an exit I'm not supposed to have. In and around where thousands of my nerve endings haven't slept in weeks. So Caleb isn't pounding on the door right now because of the gagging and hacking and gurgling he just heard. He's pounding on the door because he assumes a wounded jaguar is in here with me.

"Zero!" he shouts, sounding as un-Zen as I've ever heard him. "Zero, open up!"

I tell him I just did, and that everything came out.

Caleb gives the knob another try and goes, "Do you need any help?"

And even though I know it must have been a rhetorical question, I lie and say, "No."

I say, "I'm fine."

I say, "I'll be out in a second."

"Good," says Caleb. "Because MnyTalks just got a response."

Hearing there's a stranger on the Internet eager to deal us a child makes my gastrointestinal tract and abdomen and back feel a lot better.

While washing my face and hands at the sink, the mirror

recommends I sit back down. If I always did what my reflection tells me, I'd never get anything done. So I continue cleaning up. The jasmine and lavender scent of the hand soap is nice, but it's no match for the alpha smell in the room. We'll just have to tell Alice a truck hauling butyric acid collided with a truck hauling raw sewage.

"What should I do with this?" I ask Caleb while holding up the clear plastic bag that was lining the wastebasket.

"Oof, I don't know," says Caleb, his face like that of a civilian stumbling upon a crime scene. "Anywhere but here, please. And hurry. A second seller just took our bait."

He looks up from the laptop and sees me hobbling toward the front door toting the contents of my stomach. "Oh jeez, I'm sorry, Zero," he says, setting the laptop aside and standing up from the couch. "Let me take care of that for you."

Caleb walks over to me and reaches for the plastic bag, his face more contorted than before. He pinches one of the loops of the bag's tied end between his thumb and forefinger and holds the bag as far away from his nose as possible. Then, just like the mirror, Caleb says to me, "You should go sit down." He heads out the door to dispose of my guts and I head to the couch to check out the sex merchants.

A Mr. Style4M!les and a Mr. F*ckF@ce. These are the two gentlemen MnyTalks has heard back from. Each seems eager to do business, but Mr. F*ckF@ce's reply is much more courteous, so I doubt we'll be working with him. "Dear sir" and "if you'd be so kind" and "it would be my pleasure." There's no place for that kind of language here. Anyone with his level of diction and etiquette doesn't have it in him to pedal the preschooler I'm looking for.

Then again, his name is F*ckF@ce.

In the chat box I type, "Thanks for the prompt response. Is

there a way to see what you have on offer? The younger, the better." Before sending, I copy the message, paste it into the chat box for Mr. Style4M!les and fire it off to both parties at once.

It's a good thing my stomach is empty.

Mr. Style4M!les types back, "2 hot girls, 7 and 8. Youngest bitches I got. No pics, but can get."

Mr. F*ckF@ce types back, "I have a fine selection of girls that fit your requirements. Please click on the link below and kindly let me know if any are of interest so we can make subsequent arrangements."

Who knows what deadly viruses are attached to the link, but this is Caleb's laptop so I click on it and it brings me to a page featuring nothing I haven't seen before. Girls in micro-skirts and makeup clutching Barbie dolls. Garter belts on kindergartners. Toddlers twerking.

You get the picture. But you try your best not to.

I may have misjudged Mr. F*ckF@ce. He's definitely got the goods.

But he doesn't have Sung. At least I don't see a photo of her anywhere.

I type to him, "Lovely assortment. Before I decide, are there any new arrivals who aren't pictured?"

Mr. F*ckF@ce types back, "I'm pleased you are impressed. I did just acquire another beauty, but she's almost twelve and thus, I'm afraid, too old for your purposes."

The front door swings open and in comes Caleb without my innards.

"Thanks, man," I say. "I owe you one."

Between the blood I spilled all over him in Rio and the bag he just discarded for me, Caleb has really gotten to know what I'm made of.

"Any progress?" he asks as he heads back to the couch to join me.

"The opposite," I say, pointing at the two chat boxes open on the screen. "Both leads are dead ends."

Caleb skims my exchanges with Mr. F*ckF@ce and Mr. Style4M!les and goes, "That's okay. We're just getting started."

If only the same were true for Sung.

I scoot over on the couch, allowing Caleb to retake the reins while I stare up at the ceiling and gnaw on the inside of my lower lip until it bleeds. This is the closest I ever come to praying.

To keep from spiraling, I think of my dead brother.

Hank's telling me, "Minus ten for being a pussy." He's telling me, "Minus twenty for being a pussy." He's telling me to stop sulking. He's telling me to stop being so negative. He's saying if you want something, go get it. I'm telling him I'm trying, but it isn't easy. I'm telling him this is uncharted territory. And he's telling me, "Minus fifty for being a pussy. Minus sixty for being a pussy."

Alice walks in and Caleb and I startle even though we've been expecting her. Caleb lowers the laptop lid like we're hiding porn even though it's far worse and we have nothing to hide.

Hank tells me, "Minus ninety for being a pussy."

Alice shuts the door behind her, and when she turns back toward us I can see what little makeup she wears is trickling blue-gray down both cheeks.

"Everything okay?" I ask.

Alice sits down on the end of the couch without saying word, but it's okay because the three of us know it was a stupid question.

She puts her hand on my shoulder and looks me not in the eyes. My blood sugar's too low for me to panic.

"We just got word that Akara, the girl who was abducted along with Sung, has managed to escape," says Alice. "She was found just outside downtown Siem Reap in rough shape, but is going to be okay."

My core's too weak to brace myself.

"That's great," says Caleb, and he's right, but shut the fuck up, Caleb, and don't interrupt her again.

My eyes plead with Alice to finish me off.

"Akara told the police she and Sung were separated the night they were taken. She said they were both blindfolded and that Sung was screaming and crying, begging the men to let them stay together. Then Sung grabbed onto Akara's leg and—" Alice chokes on the lump in her throat. My fingernails slice through denim and into the flesh of my thigh. Through snot and tears Alice says, "One of the men whacked Sung with a cane several times until she let go and got into one of the cars."

And breathing like an asthma attack I wait for the rest. But Alice, she's just sniffling with her hand still on my shoulder, rubbing it. Consoling me. Not saying a word. Unaware what she just told us might be the best news I've ever heard.

CHAPTER TWENTY-ONE

By the sound of Anders' voice, his eyes aren't open. He asks me if I have any idea what time it is and I do but don't care.

I tell him to think back to the last mission in Phnom Penh. To think real hard and tell me if he remembers the name of the pimp he arranged the party with the day before the rest of us arrived.

Anders yawns then curses. A faint voice asks him who is it, and he tells the faint voice nobody and to go back to sleep. Then to me he mumbles what the fuck and how's he supposed to remember and why in the hell do I need to know that now.

I say I don't have time to go into it. To jog his memory, I remind him how he was making fun of the pimp that one day. Telling us the guy was nuts, had a bandaged eye, was playing with a yo-yo.

Anders snorts and says, "Oh yeah, *that* clown."

"Think, man. Gotta have that name."

"Ah, dude, I don't remember." Anders yawns again and goes, "Where are you?"

I tell him not to worry about that. "You said he chucked the yo-yo against a wall and started cracking up, then he—"

A snore like narcolepsy. I pull the phone away from my ear,

hold it in front of my mouth and shout, "Anders, Wake up!"

"Jesus, dude," he grumbles. "I'm as awake as I'm going to be this time of night."

And I say, "A cane."

And Anders goes, "Huh?"

"After he chucked the yo-yo," I say, "you told us he grabbed a cane that was hanging from the handlebars of his scooter and started twirling it around."

The faint voice asks if everything's okay and Anders tells the faint voice yes and shhh. Then all groggy to me he says yo-yos and canes and shit like that are easy to remember but names are not. He says he doubts if the pimp even provided it. He goes, "You might want to check with Fynn, or a member of the Advanced Team who did all the initial legwork for the mission to see if—"

"Can't," I say. "And neither can you."

"What ... why not?" asks Anders.

I tell him he's just going to have to trust me on this one.

And Anders goes, "Yo, man, you in some kind of trouble?"

"No," I say. "Someone more important than me is." Then I talk over his next couple of questions by telling him sorry for waking him and to keep thinking and to let me know immediately if a name pops into his head. And I click off the call.

Anders is one of the best fixers at OE. And useless.

I shout "fuck" loud enough to make the motel room's lights flicker. Loud enough to knock Caleb out of his meditation on the lumpy twin bed next to mine.

"It's okay," he says, unwinding his legs from the lotus position and sitting up on the edge of his bed. "We already have plenty to go on."

I shake my head. "We need a name."

Caleb stretches his arms above his head and says, "You really don't think we could find him by asking around town for a guy with—"

"No," I say. And slapping the back of my right hand against my left palm as each word is uttered, I go, "We. Need. A. Name."

I already explained this to Caleb during our jarring twenty-minute tuk-tuk ride from the safe house to this eighteen-dollar-a-night motel in downtown Siem Reap. I already explained how we can't just hit the streets with "We're looking for a man with a cane and maybe a yo-yo and a scar on or near his eye" and expect to be trusted or taken seriously. How we have to go in like we own the place and know what we want. How we need to convince any potential connections we're ready to talk business with the one they call X, where X equals Anders better fucking call us back.

Also, it's not that simple.

We have to remember X had three of his colleagues busted and is smart and stupid enough to still be running free. And we have to remember anyone who knows X knows how smart and stupid he is, knows smart and stupid equals crazy, and knows crazy will kill anyone who leads the wrong people down the right path.

"I get it," says Caleb, back in the lotus position in the middle of his bed, eyes closed, breathing controlled. "But what if we can't get a name?"

What I should say is we'd be fucked. What I should say is there'd be nothing left to do but pack up and go home. What I actually say is, "Then we'll just go with your plan and hope for the best."

This knocks Caleb out of his meditation even faster than before, when I shouted. His eyes are wide open, mouth agape.

It's a normal reaction to me being open to compromise.

My phone buzzes and it has to be Anders and of course it's not. It's a text from Alice asking if everything's okay and why we left her office in such a hurry. I type everything's fine and it's just I wasn't feeling so hot and didn't want to distract her from her duties.

Awaiting her reply, I look and Caleb's meditating with one eye closed and the other on me.

Another buzz. Alice says we were no distraction and that's she's sorry she couldn't be of more help. Sorry I had to hear about Sung like that. Sorry I came all this way for nothing. Says she could have saved me a long trip and a lot of discomfort if I'd let her know I was coming.

The Suboxone is taking effect and I'm almost smiling, almost relaxed, so Caleb's back to meditating with both eyes. My fingertips tell Alice sorry for showing up unannounced. I tell her I knew she'd try to convince me not to come and was worried she'd alert Fynn, who'd have insisted I stay put and maybe would have contacted Neda to ensure it.

The guest in the room above ours just started pogo-sticking or having sex or both. Hopefully not asbestos is now drizzling onto the carpet between Caleb's and my bed. My phone buzzes and Alice reminds me there's nothing stopping her from alerting Fynn now. I wait to see if she follows this with a winky-face or a smiley-face or a little devil emoji, but she doesn't so I can't tell if she's playing with me or not.

I type yes there is something stopping her from reporting me. I type what's stopping her is she wants Sung back just as badly as I do.

The pogo-stick asbestos sex show and Caleb's quiet acceptance of detachment and impermanence continue as I await a response from Alice. The Suboxone and the jet lag have teamed up to tug on my eyelids. I fight back with a sip of pineapple and kerosene flavored energy drink I bought from the kiosk next to our motel before we checked in.

Still no response. Not even a blinking ellipsis showing one is in the chamber. Maybe I should have taken a kinder, gentler approach to make sure Alice says nothing to Fynn. Asked her nicely rather than hinted she wouldn't dare. It's not too late to add an emoji to ease the tension, but my fingertips and every fiber of my being won't allow it.

I type I didn't mean to be rude, then delete it. I type please don't tell Fynn about all this, then delete it. I type it's in nobody's best interest if … and I delete it and replace it with a colon followed by a closing parenthesis, and hit send.

Smile, I just sacrificed all I hold sacred.

And still no response.

The energy drink has synchronized my heartbeat with the pogo-stick. I watch some flakes of malignant mesothelioma float down from the ceiling and land in Caleb's hair. But I need even more entertainment, so I grab the TV remote despite what I've heard about motel TV remotes and point it at where the TV is supposed to be. Then just to feel like I've accomplished something, I point the remote at the ceiling and press the volume up arrow before pointing it at Caleb and pressing the off button.

The Suboxone working means my pain is somewhere between a fender-bender and a mid-speed motorcycle crash while wearing a helmet. Not enough to panic about, but enough to keep me from getting out of bed to scrub my remote control hands with soap and scalding water.

My phone buzzes and the pain increases to a shark attack because it isn't Alice succumbing to my smile. It's Neda saying she can't sleep and she still loves me wherever I am.

Another buzz and the pain increases to Prometheus getting his insides eaten by an eagle for all eternity because it's Neda saying still loving me wherever I am is killing her.

Another buzz and the pain disappears.

Because it's Anders saying he's pretty sure the nut-job's name is Trans Am.

CHAPTER TWENTY-TWO

We're on Khmer Pub Street, the heart of Siem Reap's lesser-known party zone, and I really should have had Sung laminated. The photo doesn't even look like her anymore. Marks all over her face. A hole in her cheek. And one of her eyes, it's scratched out.

"Put that away," Caleb whispers to me as we walk, with zero intention of singing, toward the first karaoke bar of the afternoon. I slide the decaying photo into the back pocket of my pseudo-linen pseudo-Zanella trousers. Caleb says, "You need to be more careful."

"I need to have her face, what's left of it, fresh in my mind," I say.

Caleb catches me wincing as I flatten a wrinkle out of the front of my short-sleeve button-down Bugatchi knock-off, and he goes, "You sure you're okay to walk?" I tell him I'm fine as long as we keep taking it slow. This can actually work to our advantage, I say. "Sauntering and ambling establishes a look of power and ease. An air of dominance."

Now if I could just get whoever's hair I'm wearing to stop itching my scalp. This goddamn wig. The talcum powder was supposed to help.

"If you don't stop scratching," says Caleb, "the pimps will think you have lice. Also, you smell like a newborn baby."

Ever since I went blonde an hour ago, Caleb hasn't shown me the same respect.

He points out some talcum in my eyebrow and on my shirt collar. I stop and brush both with my hand, but he shakes his head and points again. I tell him it's fine, that the pimps will take any white residue on me as coke and assume I'm the real deal. I say he might want to shake a little on himself next time just to be safe.

And we amble and saunter. Amble and saunter. Caleb decked out in almost Armani, almost Brioni, almost Ferragamos, with a copy of a copy of a Rolex on his wrist. Dressed how he is, we're on the same level. He still comes up only to around my entry wound, but we both look like two guys who really know how to lure minors onto yachts.

From the outside, the karaoke bar looks like a karaoke bar. Just like all the other karaoke bars we'll probably have to visit. Cheap, modern construction. Superficial stucco pillars. No windows. And a small sign on the facade that blinks "KTV," which is what they call karaoke bars in these parts. Even legitimate karaoke bars.

We enter and Caleb says something, but I can't hear him over all the red light and the darkness. The perfume and the Lysol.

Electronic instrumental Gloria Gaynor mixes with electronic instrumental Katy Perry mixes with electronic instrumental Neil Diamond in the background as rows of pre-teens in micro-skirts twist their hair and undress us with vacant eyes. Some of the girls even stand up from their chairs. None of them are Sung, but we pretty much knew that coming in. *That* young isn't advertised.

It's still light outside so the place is devoid of tourists. They are waiting until the sun goes down before crawling out from under their rocks and coming to choose a twelve-year-old or a ten-year-old or an eight-year-old they traveled two thousand miles or five thousand miles or ten thousand miles to rape. Tourists who know about Khmer Pub Street, they're not the same sunburns in cargo shorts you'll see lined up for miles outside the entrance to Angkor Wat. For one, nobody here carries a camera.

A short but not Caleb-short man in a dark blazer, white T-shirt and skinny jeans approaches us, and all smiles he goes, "Gentlemen! Welcome!"

We nod at him.

The manager says, "You come nice and early so you get best girls!"

Doubtful he's this enthusiastic with all customers. He's just turned on by our outfits. They mean he can charge us quadruple what he charges sunburns in cargo shorts. We just have to hope he doesn't look closely at our labels.

"Very nice selection," I say as I gaze at the girls flirting with us from afar and begging us to leave. "But we aren't here for usual business."

The manager steps back and frowns. "So, just drinks?"

I shake my head and say, "My associate and I were told we could find a gentleman around here who might be interested in selling to us."

The manager steps forward and whispers, "Drugs?"

I shake my head and go, "Girls. Young ones." I pat my back pocket to gain resolve. And to apologize.

The manager takes another step forward and smiles. "Yeah, yeah, I help you!" Without looking, he thumb-points behind him, and says, "You can have any girl. Many only twelve, thirteen. I give you good price."

Caleb clears his throat, then reaches out to brush some lint off the lapel of the manager's blazer. "I'm afraid we're not being very clear," he says. "We don't want to *rent* girls. We want to *purchase* girls. You know, *acquire* them." Then he points to what's on offer in front of us and goes, "But not *these* girls. Much younger."

The manager takes two steps back and says, "I, I don't sell. Can't."

Caleb says, "We know that. We're hoping you can point us toward the man who can. We hear he goes by the name of Trans Am. Know him?"

"I know many Tran," says the manager. "Very common Vietnamese name. Many Vietnamese in Siem Reap."

I step in and ask, "Do you know any with young girls?"

The manager looks down and scratches his head, then shakes it.

I go, "Any with a cane or a yo-yo?"

The manager looks at me like I've snorted too much talcum, and shakes his head again.

Caleb says, "Is there someone else here we can speak with? Someone who might know who we're talking about?"

The manager says maybe his boss or his boss's boss, and Caleb says bingo. The manager says, "Wait here," and disappears into the red lights and the darkness as instrumental Elton John mixes with instrumental Queen mixes with instrumental Madonna. That he would leave us alone this close to the girls and this close to the exit means he's either an idiot or sees us as rich and evil enough to trust. Probably both.

A few of the girls are still looking over at us. Most of the girls, though, have gone back to staring at their fingernails, the floor, the walls.

What I wouldn't give for the cops to roll in right now and handcuff Caleb and me. But not getting arrested is the price you pay for going rogue.

The girls don't know what they're missing.

I reach for my back pocket and Caleb slaps my hand away. "Don't," he says.

I tell him to never do that again, and he says, "Get it together." He says he's concerned about me.

I point to my back pocket and go, "Be more concerned about her."

"I am," says Caleb. "Even more so because I'm concerned about you." Or something like that. Caleb never makes sense when I don't listen.

He continues with something about how I'm too emotionally involved and too physically impaired to do what needs to be done. Some nonsense about me jeopardizing Sung's safety by trying too hard to save her. Talking out his ass about how I need to stay in character and show better judgment.

I dismiss him with my hand, and walk through the perfume and the Lysol toward the girls as Caleb whisper-shouts for me to stop. Two of the girls meet me with false enthusiasm halfway and I show them the photo I've pulled from my pocket. "You know her?" I ask. "You see her?" The girls look at the picture, then at each other, and shake their heads. I say, "You sure?" and they just giggle and shrug. One of them tries to run her fingers through my hair, but I dodge her reach to avoid going bald.

Caleb over there is pssst-ing at me repeatedly. He sounds like a sprinkler.

Two more girls come to look at the photo. They each go "aww" and smile. I point at them and then at the photo and then at them again and go, "Yes? Yes?" Their awws and smiles melt away and all four hurry back to their spots.

Caleb's now snapping his fingers and flailing his arms like a mother whose kid refuses to get out of the pool. I put Sung away and start back toward him. He mouths "What. The. Hell?" This is no time for him to unravel.

I walk back over to him, shielding my eyes from his glare. Caleb opens his mouth to tear me a new exit wound, and the biggest Cambodian I've ever seen comes out of the shadows to save me. He's wearing a black suit with a red satin shirt unbuttoned down to a gold dragon pendant pinched between his pectorals. His presence wipes anything resembling a smile off the faces of the girls. And lands my hand on my back pocket.

With the manager standing behind him, Boss says to us in a thick Khmer accent, "You want talk to me?" It sounds more like a command than a question.

"No," I say as I step closer to him, my eyes even with his throat. "*You* want to talk to *me*."

Boss and I squint at one another like boxers at a pre-fight weigh-in. He glances down at Caleb and scoffs, then peers at me again. "I busy man," he says to the top of my head. "Talk or leave."

I turn to Caleb while pointing at Boss with my thumb. "This fucking guy," I say as I try to hold back my fake laughter. Caleb nods and smirks, then cracks his knuckles.

"What you just say?" Boss asks, the creases in his suite smoothing out as he puffs up.

I shuffle forward till the toes of our shoes touch. "There's a way to speak to men like me," I say. "I suggest you figure out fast what that way is."

Boss's eyes can't believe what he's heard. His jaw muscles ripple as I lean in closer and whisper, "I'm going to give you three seconds to try again."

Heat from his flaring nostrils hits my forehead, and I go, "One."

"I'd take his offer," Caleb says to Boss, sounding almost bored. "He doesn't make it very often."

Boss doesn't blink or budge. The manager, still hiding behind him, takes a couple of steps backward. Then a couple more. Then he orders the girls to a back room.

Behind me Caleb hums along to "Like a Virgin."

I just stare into Boss like I'm in love, and go, "Two."

His eyes dart back and forth between Caleb and me. A bead of sweat drips from his earlobe onto the shoulder of his suit jacket. I glance at the drop then back at Boss and grin. He swallows hard. Drip goes another drop.

"Last chance," I whisper. And I reach for my back pocket.

"Whoa, whoa," says Boss as he steps back and holds his palms up. "Relax."

I keep my hand on my pocket. Like I'm holding a grenade pin in place.

The manager turns and runs toward where he told the girls to go. I yell to him, "If you call anyone, I'll kill everybody."

Boss, looking a foot shorter than before, says to me, "No need for gun. We talk, okay?"

I nod at him just as a local comes out of one of the second-floor rooms, his face flushed. He fiddles with his unbuckled belt and burps. Following him out is a girl a quarter his age looking as pallid as a brown girl can. Boss and I relax our stances and smile at the awful couple while they descend the stairs single file, the man four or five steps in front of the girl. Caleb laughs like Boss or I just told a joke.

The customer scans the space and in Khmer asks Boss what I'm pretty certain is, "Where are all the whores?" Boss says something like, "We had an early rush," and the customer just looks at his watch and goes, "Huh." Then he tucks his shirt in and heads for the exit. The girl, she staggers over to the greeting room and has a seat, seemingly oblivious to that fact that none of the other girls are there.

With my hand off my secret weapon, I lock eyes with Boss again. "Let's go somewhere and chat," I say. Boss nods, then reaches into his suit jacket. I jerk my hand back to my pocket and, wincing from the jolt, say, "Don't even think about it." Boss holds up one hand, smiles and says, "Phone" while the other hand continues deeper into his jacket. I'm not buying it. I feign a more menacing grip and try to hide how adrenaline and Suboxone are no match for Boss calling my bluff.

Then behind me Caleb goes, "Stop or you're dead."

And every overgrown muscle in Boss's body seizes. His face, it's frozen like a Vesuvius victim's.

I turn around, and there's the little Buddha—his shirt un-tucked—using both hands to steady a chrome-plated Desert Eagle forty-four. He's pointing it over my shoulder at Boss's head while Michael Jackson mixes with ABBA mixes with the B-52s.

"A phone, just a phone," says Boss, holding his position, looking like Napoleon getting sworn in.

Caleb takes closer aim and says, "Bring the hand out slowly." I step to the side to give him a clearer shot, just in case.

Boss draws his meat hook from the jacket and holds up a smartphone the size of a tablet. He points to the back room where his workforce has retreated to and says, "I text manager. I tell him everything cool now. Okay?"

Caleb looks at me and I nod, then he nods at Boss, who starts thumbing a message on his phone. I say to Boss, "Tell him we're going somewhere outside to talk," and he lifts a meat hook to give me a thumbs-up.

After several more taps on his phone, Boss looks up and says, "Gentlemen" as he motions toward the front door. Caleb tucks his Eagle into what has to be a custom-made holster inside his waistband, on the hip. He keeps the top strap of the holster open and says to Boss, "You first." Boss carefully slides his phone back into his jacket, then even more carefully slides his hand back out and wipes the sweat from his face. He steps past me and Caleb, and we follow him. Keeping him in front of me is a priority. I need him to continue thinking Caleb isn't the only one armed. Also, how in the hell is Caleb armed? Guess he knows how to use the dark web for more than just pedophilia. And guess I took a nap earlier.

The late afternoon sun blinds us the second Boss cracks the exit. We each hold up a hand to save our retinas as The Village People and Whitney Houston and Sister Sledge disappear with the air conditioning.

"Over there," I say, pointing across the street to a restaurant with some outside tables covered by an awning.

Boss says, "Okay, but food no good."

I say we'll make do, then motion for him to lead the way. He starts walking and I move Sung from my back pants pocket to the breast pocket of my shirt.

The locals we encounter while crossing the street and on the sidewalk by the restaurant, some of them wave and smile at Boss. But most just cower. One, the tiny hostess who offers to seat us, does both.

Before sitting down at one of the green plastic Heineken tables under the awning, Caleb adjusts his trousers in a way that makes the hostess even more uncomfortable than Boss does. I wait for Caleb to get situated before easing into a chair on the opposite side of his gun, in case he adjusted wrong and has the safety off. Boss, he removes his suit jacket and folds it over the spare chair, pulls at the places his satin shirt sticks to his sinew, then plants himself across from us. The hostess turns into a waitress and her voice quivers as she asks us what we'd like. Boss and Caleb each order a beer, but I'm on Suboxone and in Narcotics Anonymous. So I order a whiskey.

"Don't know how much your manager told you earlier," I say to Boss while touching my shirt pocket, "but we're looking to buy fresh young meat, and—"

Boss is looking at me like I've given him a trig equation to solve. "Too fast," he says. "Slower."

I scan the patio to make sure no other customers are within earshot and, speaking a little louder and slower than before, I say, "Girls. Very young. We want to buy."

Boss looks at me and nods like he finally gets trig.

I say, "Looking for a man named Trans Am." I say, "We hear he has what we want." I ask, "Do you know him?"

Boss shakes his head and shrugs.

Caleb lifts his hand above the table for Boss to see, then places it on his hip. He leans in toward him and goes, "Are you sure?"

Boss looks around at all the people passing by and dismisses Caleb's attempt at intimidation with a laugh. Caleb lifts up the side of his shirt and scrapes one of his gold rings across the Eagle's steel grip. "What, you think I haven't shot a liar in public before?"

Boss's smile slides away and, more angry than scared, he says, "Not a liar. Don't know a Trans Am."

Caleb stares him down for a few seconds, then looks at me.

My tilted head tells him easy tiger, and he removes his hand from his hip and leans back in the chair.

Boss says to me, "I have young girls."

I ask how young and he says ten and I say not young enough.

He smiles and goes, "Ahhh, I see … you want Chicken Farm girls. Down in Sihanoukville."

Looking puzzled, Caleb opens his mouth to speak but I shut him up with a raised finger and say to Boss, "The girls at Chicken Farm *are* very young, it's true. But no way the owners will sell to a white man. Only by the hour."

Boss just nods. And the reason he just nods is I just earned the kind of street cred not even a forty-four tucked down your trousers can earn you around here.

"But now you have the right idea," I say. "Little girls like the ones in Sihanoukville, those are the kinds of girls we hear Trans Am can supply. The kinds of girls we pay big money for."

Boss hoists his elbows onto the table and clasps his meat hooks together, then leans forward to rest his chin on them. "Maybe I ask around for you," he says. "And maybe if I find your Trans Am, you give me commission."

Caleb looks at me wide-eyed, like Boss's offer is a blessing. Me, I play it cooler, turning my head toward the windows lining the wall by our table, pondering the proposal while I watch the patrons dining inside.

And Caleb goes, "That sounds—" I grab his shoulder to again shut him up. I'm not even looking at him but can tell he's pissed and he should be.

But there's been a new development.

"Actually," I say to Boss as I continue to peer through one of the windows, "I don't think that will be necessary."

I stand up and nearly take out the waitress and the tray of

drinks she just brought us. I apologize to her smile, then grab my whiskey off the tray and shoot it. Going down it burns less than my back.

To a perplexed Boss I go, "Sorry for the trouble," and then head as straight as I can for the restaurant's entrance, with Caleb calling after me.

Inside it's all curry spice and cigarette smoke and stares. Everybody's looking at the only blonde in the place. Everybody but one guy. Over by the bar. He's too busy dancing to a Billy Idol song on the jukebox to notice me.

And for someone nursing recently broken ribs, he's moving around pretty good.

CHAPTER TWENTY-THREE

Hard to tell who's queasier right now. Me from the Suboxone and the bumpy tuk-tuk ride back to our motel, or Pich from all the blood he's swallowing.

Caleb, he's looking at me like the elbow to the mouth was unnecessary. Shaming me for resorting to violence. When this is all over, he'll no doubt ask me why I didn't just let the massive gun he's got shoved in Pich's face do the talking. But what Caleb's not getting is Pich would much rather take a quick bullet to the brain than endure whatever Trans Am might do to him for ratting him out. Me cracking Pich in the kisser, that was just to show him I'm every bit as vengeful and sadistic as a crazed pimp king.

That said, I probably should have started by breaking one of his fingers rather than knocking out a couple of his teeth. For one, I wouldn't be in need of an elbow bandage and tetanus shot right now. But more importantly, it would be a lot easier to understand what the hell Pich is saying. His English was bad enough before I created a gap between his incisors. Now he sounds like Mike Tyson awakening from a twelfth-round KO. The crying doesn't help.

"Pleeth sthtop! I thorry!" he cries, a mist of blood and spit spraying from his mouth and speckling my pants.

I warn him to keep it down, then hand him a roll of toilet paper for his eyes and nose and a damp hand towel for his upper lip and gums.

"Sorry doesn't help us," I say, standing over the toilet Pich is slumped on in our bathroom. "Doesn't help Sung, either. Now tell us where she is, or we're going to need a lot more towels."

"I don'th know!" Pich lisp-shouts.

"Yes. You. DO," I say, backhanding him across the jaw. He yelps on contact, then bows his head and sobs as he rubs his cheek.

Caleb, standing in front of the closed bathroom door, shakes his head at me and points at the Desert Eagle he's gripping. He's either trying to tell me the gun's more than enough for our purposes, or warning me he's going to pop a cap in my entry wound if I don't ease up with the hitting.

As if I'm enjoying this. Caleb's gotta know breaking this boy's face is breaking my heart. Watching the kid bleed and blubber and beg for mercy. Ruining his spotless white shirt and pants. Forcing him to spend a large chunk of his recent earnings on reconstructive dentistry.

I go, "Talk!" and then thwack the top of Pich's head with my ringed hand. As he cries out, more red spittle speckles him and me and the toilet seat and the floor. Caleb clears his throat or growls, and I glance over to make sure the gun's still pointed at the right guy.

Truth is, I can't say I wouldn't have done exactly what Pich did to deserve this had I been in his shoes. It's not every day you're offered the chance to make in a few minutes what you'd be lucky to make the rest of your life, while avoiding a cane beating to boot. By pretending he got pummeled within an inch of his life the night

Sung and Akara were abducted, Pich essentially saved his, got rich, and became a hero in the eyes of Alice.

Almost. He picked the wrong time and place to groove to "Dancing with Myself."

Pich peeks at me through his blood-wet fingers. He's crying so hard I hate him. The least he could do is curse at me, spit in my face, take a swing, do something—anything—that would help me forget he's not all the monster I'm treating him like. The genuine terror and shame in his eyes right now, it makes things difficult. It reminds me of his only can of cola. It reminds me of years with a key to the safe house. It reminds me that deep down and not even that deep this little bastard has a heart.

I just hope he doesn't force me to rip it out.

"Tell you what," I say as I take a knee in front of the toilet, "you get us to Sung, and I won't say anything to Alice or the police about what you've done."

I motion for Caleb to lower the cannon still aimed at the kid. Pich watches as the weapon comes to rest on Caleb's thigh, then exhales relief and some more red into the hand towel he's holding. Out of the corner of my eye, Caleb nods his approval of the new tack I'm taking.

"Also," I say to Pich while pointing to Caleb, "if he and I get caught by Trans Am or anyone else when we go for Sung, we promise to leave your name out of it."

I tell him this way we get what we came for and he gets to keep his money and his freedom. And his face. I tell him time is running out. I tell him this is his chance to make up for his mistake. His chance to undo all his awful. His only chance.

Pich removes his non-towel hand from his face. A string of crimson snot arcs between a nostril and his pinky finger, then stretches too thin and snaps as he moves his hand to his lap. I run a fresh towel under the sink, squeeze out the excess water, and offer it to him. He drops the blood-soaked one onto the no longer all-white tile, then takes the new one from me and uses it to dab the wreckage where his smile used to reside. The bathroom, it smells like bleach mixed with sweat and pennies.

"So, you ready to help us?" I ask.

A ray of contemplation breaks through the fear and confusion in Pich's eyes. He looks at Caleb and then back at me, but there's still too much blood where the words need to come out.

And then he nods.

If only I'd given the softer approach a go before I took his teeth.

He mutter-lisps something into the towel he's clutching as pink water drips down his chin and onto his shirt and pants.

I go, "Huh?" and he says something as incomprehensible as his previous attempt.

"Maybe he can write it down," says Caleb.

I ask Caleb if he has a pen and paper anywhere and he says no. I say damn it me either and we both look at Pich, who pats his pockets and shakes his head. I say I'll go search the room for writing implements, and Caleb moves away from the door. With my hand on the knob, I turn back to Pich and go, "Don't try anything stupid, understand?" then point to Caleb's Eagle. Pich nods and I exit the torture chamber, shutting the door behind me.

There's no motel stationery in sight, but for paper we could always use one of my T-shirts or one of Caleb's or the hairless side of one of our forearms. The pen is the bigger issue. I look under the bed and behind the console and in every drawer, and nothing. I could ask for one at the front desk, but I can't expect the clerk to just ignore the light blood spatter I'm sporting. And changing clothes hurts like hell.

From the bathroom I hear Caleb say what sounds like, "Keep that on your mouth."

"Everything all right in there?" I call out as I feel around where the mattress meets the headboard of my bed.

"Yeah, fine," Caleb calls back.

I check the other bed, then walk over to the upholstered chair by the window and lift up the seat cushion but find only a paperclip, a candy wrapper and some fossilized crumbs.

There's a faint grunt and groan followed by "Sit back down." I call out, "Problems?" as I hobble toward the bathroom. No immediate response from Caleb, so I pick up the pace and the volume. "Hey! What's going on in—"

"It's okay," Caleb says through the door. Behind it there's sliding or shuffling.

"You sure?" I ask, and Caleb says yeah. Then he says, "But come on in anyway."

I say I haven't found anything to write with yet and Caleb tells me it doesn't matter just come in. Then he opens the door. And there's Pich off the toilet and down on his knees, letting blood drip from his mouth into a cupped hand, using the index finger of his other hand to scrawl red letters and numbers on the white tile floor.

What looks like a suicide note is an address. The street's about twenty letters long, probably named after some ancient Cambodian king. Even if Pich had all his teeth earlier when trying to tell us what he just bled, we wouldn't have understood a thing.

I point at the death scribble and say to him, "You're sure this is where Sung is?"

Pich dips his pointer into his palm, then paints a capital Y and then a capital E and—

"You can just nod or say yes," I say, but Pich finishes up the capital S and adds an exclamation point for good measure and more of a mess.

I squat down to look him in the carnage. "Okay," I say. "But know this—if you're leading us down the wrong path, I'll kill you so slowly you'll be begging me to hand you over to Trans Am. Got it?"

"Yeth," says Pich, wincing as the word slips through his raw gap.

I ask him if the address is in Siem Reap. He nods and, for emphasis, points to the bloody affirmative painted on the floor.

I ask if it's a karaoke bar. He starts to finger a capital N but I shout, "Just shake your head!" Pich startles, then gives me a wobbly, drunken shake as his eyes roll around in their sockets. He's clearly lost too much ink. I need to hurry.

"So it's a regular brothel then?" I ask, and Pich's head wobbles east then west.

I go, "Then what? Just a house?" and Pich points yes.

I go, "And it's open for business, right?" And I'm bloody correct.

Then I go, "Are barangs like us welcome there?"

Pich, eyes now closed, drops from his knees to all fours and sways back and forth like an escaped zoo animal hit with a tranquilizer dart.

I go, "Hey!" and his eyes open. I go, "Will we get in?"

Pich just blinks slowly, struggling to stay upright. Caleb sighs, then bends over and holds the Eagle in front of Pich's face. I push the gun away and scold Caleb with a stare. Then I turn back to Pich and go, "C'mon, just a yes or a no. Can. We. Get. To. Sung?"

Pich collapses flat on his belly, one arm straight against his side and the other bent in an L with his hand palm-down by his head, which is turned away from me. His eyes are closed. I poke his shoulder and order him not to pass out yet. The eye I can see opens and blinks, then shuts again. I go, "Just show me one finger for yes, two fingers for no."

On the hand up by his head, Pich folds in every digit but his index. I sigh in relief, then turn to Caleb and give him a thumbs-up, but Caleb points me back to Pich, who's finger-painting again. We watch as he bleeds what looks like a number two, only with its tail missing. He then lifts his finger, moves it down an inch, and presses it to the floor again, leaving behind a single swirled dot.

What we're looking at, it pretty much encapsulates the last month or so of my life.

A big, bloody question mark.

CHAPTER TWENTY-FOUR

D o not disturb.

The three words hang from our door handle like a prayer. Like please God, let the maid understand English. Please God, let whatever music she's listening to not distract her to from the sign. Please God, let no bored, bratty kids snatch the sign while scampering past our room.

Declining fresh sheets and new bars of hand soap is a small price to pay for freedom. I'll take a room that looks like assault and battery over a police interrogation any day.

Just as important as the sign hanging on the outside of our door is the one taped to the inside of it. The one we wrote after we changed out of our spattered clothes and got what we needed from the front desk. The one telling Pich that, when he wakes up, he is to stay put and keep quiet until we get back, and that if he doesn't he's going to wish he were dead long before we kill him.

The two Suboxone and four ibuprofen I chewed back in the room allow me to walk almost as well as an outpatient. Caleb and I stride by the front desk and wave to the clerk who earlier gave us the pen, paper and tape. He smiles and waves back. Hopefully he isn't wondering what happened to the nervous-looking local he saw us come in with an hour ago.

Though spotless, what we're wearing now is even worse than what we changed out of. This is so we can blend with the crowd. Caleb's got on knee-length khaki cargo shorts and an aquamarine tank-top, the front of which sports a white outline of the Angkor Wat temple with the words "Angkor Wat" printed in red block letters inside. On his feet are dark-brown, leather-like sandal-sneakers with chunky soles that give Caleb an inch up on himself. Me, I'm still blonde and have gone with gray cargo shorts and a black "I heart Siem Reap" tee where the "heart" is a valentine. I, too, am wearing sandal-sneakers, only mine are light brown and twice the size of Caleb's. Also, I'm sporting an accessory. A large blue fanny pack that hangs heavy like our lives might depend on it.

It's night out front of our motel. The tuk-tuk we rode in on at sunset is still right where we made Pich park it. Caleb raises his hand to hail us one with a conscious driver, and I push his hand back down. Over the drunk tourists and traffic I go, "We want a taxi not a tuk-tuk tonight."

We turn right, down a side street where it's easier to find a vacant ride with four wheels and a real engine. Before either of us even signals, a yellow Toyota Camry rolls by and beeps twice. I give a thumbs-up and the driver pulls over to the sidewalk just ahead of us. When Caleb and I catch up, the driver asks, "Where to?" through the rolled-down passenger-side window. I tell him the bloody address from memory but botch the pronunciation and he laughs. Then Caleb steps in and gets the address right. The driver laughs even harder.

"No, really," I say to the guy as we climb into the back. "And please hurry."

The driver stops laughing and shifts into first. The green

cardboard pine tree dangling from the rearview mirror doesn't quite cut Caleb's cheap cologne or my talcum powder. I ask the driver how much for the ride and he says about three or four dollars, then he asks if I'm sure I have the right address and I say yes. Through the rearview mirror, he looks like I'm confused.

Caleb whispers to me, "Assuming Pich is still there when we get back, what are we going to do with him?"

I say we'll worry about that later, but Caleb looks intent on worrying about that now. I need him focused, so I say, "We'll get him to a dentist," and then turn away to look out my window.

The crowds and the shops and the eateries and inns fall further behind us, giving way to nothing you see in Siem Reap brochures. Abandoned apartment buildings full of families. Tattered rags hung with care from moonlit barbed wire. The locals on the street who peer into the taxi look at us like we're going the wrong way. This is how we know we're on the right track.

"About how much longer?" I ask the driver.

"Five minutes," he says.

I say thanks and tell him we'll pay him double the normal fare if he waits for us after we arrive. He asks how long we'll be and I say I don't know, anywhere from five to twenty minutes. What I don't tell him is it's okay to leave if we never come back out. Or that he's going to need to ignore the speed limits and stop signs if we do.

The driver nods, then glances at the meter, which reads $1.70. The rearview mirror shows him still looking like we're confused, but he's also smiling. This could be a big night for him.

Outside my window we're nowhere.

I interrupt Caleb's meditation or nap with a tap on the shoulder. "Let me see your phone," I say. Caleb unzips and reaches into one of the ten or so pockets of his cargo shorts, then another, then another and pulls out his Android and hands it to me. It's charged only twenty-seven percent, but that's more than enough. I hand Caleb his phone back and tell him he'll need to be faster on the draw, then shift my fanny pack to retrieve my phone from the first pocket I try and say, "Like that." Checking my charge, I'm at nineteen percent. Not checking my messages, I'm at twenty-six unread. And maybe divorced.

The meter reads $2.45.

Outside my window we're farther away and getting closer.

I put my phone away and pull out Sung. She's never looked better. I show Caleb the photo and remind him she's not this folded and torn in person.

"Don't worry," says Caleb as he glances at Sung. "I'll recognize her from the first thirty or forty times I saw her." Then he points at the picture's creases and scratches and adds, "Before all this happened."

I remind him it's likely to be dark inside the house. "And she'll be wearing makeup. You have to be certain."

A tinge of nausea creeps in. I can't tell if it's from the Suboxone and ibuprofen, or from how I just instructed Caleb to make sure he doesn't rescue another tortured little girl by accident. Judging from the shaming look he's giving me, it's both.

"If it'll make you feel better," Caleb says, "I can bring the photo with me." He reaches for Sung, but I close my hand around her and shake my head before sliding her remains back into a pocket.

The meter reads $3.95.

Outside my window there's no turning back.

The driver turns onto an unpaved road lined with houses

made out of plywood and rust. Every bump we hit stabs me in the back. My grunts and grimaces ask the driver to slow down. He turns onto another unpaved road. Pebbles crack and pop beneath the tires as we roll by several vacant lots. The driver kills his headlights, then pulls over by a sea of weeds with a two-story house set back in it. Several motor scooters are parked in the weeds. The house is twice the size of those on the previous street but with half the windows. Curtains are drawn across the window on the ground floor, and iron bars ensure no one steals them. The window on the second floor, it's boarded. Nobody lives here and lights are on.

The driver points at the house and says the address we gave him earlier. In the rearview mirror, he looks like Caleb and I are lost.

The meter reads $4.10.

Outside my window has finally arrived.

"This is for you," I say to the driver as I reach between the front seats and hand him a ten. "Keep the change, and keep the meter running." The driver nods into the mirror.

I open the passenger door to faint laughter leaking out of the cracks in the house. Then maybe shouting. A faraway dog barks somewhere over by the nearest neighbor as I work too hard to exit the taxi. The soles of my sandal-sneakers touch the ground. The rest of me is still in the vehicle catching my breath and cursing Suboxone and bullets and doctors. And Caleb. He already got out on his side and is standing in front of me offering a hand. I say I'm good. I say just give me a sec. Caleb says, "Whenever you're ready." Then he steps back, does a quarter turn to look at the house and says, "She's right inside."

And I'm up. And the hot breeze. It almost puts my wig crooked as I guide Caleb along a worn path through the weeds to the way in.

**

"Happy birthday, Doug!" I say to Caleb as I remove the red and white handkerchief from his eyes. He looks as surprised as the Samoan guy blocking the doorway is wide.

Caleb rubs his eyes and goes, "No way!" while trying to peek around the Samoan into the house. "Is this … this isn't … is it?"

I tell him it is, and he reaches toward the sky with two fists and shouts, "Fuck yeah!" Then he turns to me for a high-five.

The Samoan just stands at the door in his black shorts and black T-shirt, watching the celebration with folded arms. His wild kinks are pulled into a ponytail. He smells like nicotine. I look at him and go, "Sorry. My friend here, he gets a little excited."

Caleb squats down to catch a glimpse of what's behind the Samoan, then springs into the air like a Jack Russell terrier in an attempt to see over him.

"So," I say to the blockade, "how does this work? Do we pay you, or do we come inside first, or … you tell me."

Caleb says, "Oh man I can't wait," and I say, "Doug, settle down."

The Samoan unfolds his arms and scratches his scruff with a bandaged hand. "How you know about here?" he asks me.

I tell him a tuk-tuk driver gave me the address the other day. The Samoan looks out at the road and sees the taxi. He asks if it's our ride and I say, "Yeah, but that's not the guy who told us about this place." I say, "In fact, he seemed very surprised when we told him the address."

There's some shouting upstairs followed by some whimpering followed by more shouting followed by silence. I squeeze my pocket of Sung and swallow hard to keep my hand off my fanny pack.

"Look," I say to the Samoan, "It's Doug here's birthday, and I really want him to have a special time. We hear you have some special girls." I pull a wad of dollars from one of my pockets, point to Caleb and say to the Samoan, "Little Dougie here, he likes 'em young."

Caleb says, "Damn right," and I go, "Chill, Doug."

The Samoan eyes the money, then glances behind him as footsteps approach. He turns back to me with different eyes. Eyes like he's no longer in charge. He steps aside, but not to let us in. Rather to make room for a short, wiry man wearing a silver satin kimono and dark shades. Doing rock the baby with a purple yo-yo.

I almost say his name out loud.

"Looking for directions?" Trans Am asks us, then laughs and with his elbow nudges the Samoan to do the same.

Caleb and I both chuckle. "Nope, pretty sure this is where we want to be," I say as my fingers fan out the fives and tens.

Trans Am smiles and moves from rock the baby to hop the fence, then splits Caleb and me with a quick around the world. He snatches the yo-yo with a palm smack and says, "All the KTVs in town for barangs, and you barangs come all the way out here?" He sounds like Pich might have ignored our note.

"They don't have what we want in town," I say, my wrists crossed over my fanny pack, fingers primed for the zipper. "The girls in town, they're pretty, but too old for my friend's birthday present."

Trans Am lowers his shades. His one good eye moves from me to Caleb and back to me. His other eye isn't one. Just a slit of skin like a cat fight. Just as he's about to speak, someone in the house stumbles behind him and the Samoan, lightly bumping them. The Samoan grabs the man, shoves him to the floor and shouts in Khmer what I think is "Stupid drunk!" The man cowers, then laughs an apology as he struggles to sit up.

Still facing Caleb and me, Trans Am rolls his only eye and says to us, "One moment."

With yo-yo in hand, he turns toward the drunk on the floor and walks the dog. Caleb and I both turn away and cringe just as the yo-yo cracks against the shrieking man's head. Out of the corner of my eye, Trans Am continues, going around the world several times—each trip damaging a different piece of his victim.

The tricks stop right after the screaming does. Trans Am steps aside to allow the Samoan to pick the bleeding mess up off the floor and hoist it onto his shoulder.

"Use back door," Trans Am says to his bouncer.

Caleb looks at me and I give him a quick nod before turning to look back at the road. Our driver missed the yo-yo performance. He must have—he's still here.

We watch Trans Am watch the Samoan haul off the drunk. The kimono in sunglasses then turns to us. He points to the handkerchief Caleb is still holding and says, "May I?"

Caleb hesitates, then says sure and hands the handkerchief to Trans Am, who uses it to wipe the sweat from his brow and the blood from his yo-yo. He offers it back and Caleb says, "Please, I'd like you to have it."

Trans Am thanks him and tosses the handkerchief on the floor. "Where you guys from?" he asks as he does a double or nothing with the now-shiny yo-yo.

"Canada," I say. "We're both from Vancouver."

He nods, then turns to Caleb and shows him a slack trapeze. "How young you like?" he asks.

"As young as you got," says Caleb, his eyes following the yo-yo's pendulum.

I'm thinking either Trans Am is very inquisitive or a hypnotist. He looks my way, the fanny pack reflecting in his shades. "And you?" he asks.

I point to Caleb and say, "I'm just here for Doug."

Trans Am does a sidewinder and says I can't come in unless I get a girl too. He does a loop the loop and says no spectators.

"Completely understand," I say. "I don't mind waiting in the taxi."

Trans Am splits the atom. Then he executes a pinwheel. Then he turns to show us the black dragon embroidered on the back of his kimono and starts walking away.

"Happy birthday, Doug" he says without looking back. "Follow me."

CHAPTER TWENTY-FIVE

Snap a kitten's neck. Eat a bag of feces. Go to a mall. That's about it.

The list of things I wouldn't do for a single oxy right now is short.

Caleb has been inside the house for roughly eleven minutes and seventeen seconds and counting. This according to the stopwatch on the phone I'm clutching hard enough to need a new phone. The phone is also reminding me a wife and a boss and several friends I'd take another bullet for would love to hear back from me. What the phone isn't telling me is all I'm waiting for.

I lean against the passenger door on the driver's side of the taxi. Sitting inside the taxi would draw less attention, but right now less attention is less important than response time and mobility. I'd rather stick out like a sore thumb than get stuck in a back seat.

Adding up as fast as the seconds on my stopwatch is what I owe the driver. He keeps glancing at the meter and singing a Khmer tune out his rolled-down window. Through the side view mirror he's as happy as he is tone deaf.

"Why you not go in?" he asks me, pointing at the house. "No boom-boom for you?"

I keep my eyes on my phone screen and just shake my head to say go back to singing.

I pat Sung in my pocket and pray Caleb's with her in the house. Thirteen minutes and thirty-eight seconds and what if he's in a room with no cell coverage?

I type, "Everything okay?" even though I promised I wouldn't, and hit send. Under my wig is all itch and sweat. How anyone has hair in this heat is beyond me. And Caleb isn't answering.

A scooter comes buzzing down the road and, just a few feet from me and the taxi, turns into the weeds and parks by the other scooters near the side of the house. A silhouette hops off and heads toward the front door as I rest my hand on my fanny pack, fantasizing about a silencer and good aim. The silhouette knocks on the door and moments later is let in by a silhouette triple the size.

Sixteen minutes and seven seconds and what if Caleb's battery is old and twenty-seven percent is now dead?

Out the window the driver sings even louder to the tune of me matching his monthly salary. While I'm happy to help, I don't need him singing every cent. Every second of nothing happening fast. Every minute of Sung slipping away.

I close my eyes and take deep breaths to lower the volume. Then even deeper ones to slow the speed in my chest. But breathing isn't working. All it's doing is shortening the list of what I wouldn't do for an oxy. An oxy and—

A text. "I'm done." But it's not from Caleb.

It's from Neda.

I click on it to see everything I've been missing with my phone off most of this trip. And what I've been missing is the letter I left wasn't nearly enough.

What I've been missing is the new me after the coma is worse than the old me.

What I've been missing is I'll be the only one receiving mail in our mailbox if I ever come home.

And now what I'm missing is enough phone charge to make an international call. Instead I key in, "It's impossible to explain, but I hope to," and don't hit send. I key in, "Soon this might make sense," and don't hit send. Then I key in, "LOVE," and off it all goes.

Standing here outside the taxi, the end is just getting started.

The meter reads half of what I have left.

My phone buzzes Neda's reply. "You lost me at impossible."

I go to key in more love and that I'll call ASAP, and in comes another text.

"Now."

From Caleb.

It's about time. And couldn't have come at a worse one.

I text back, "coming," then give the roof of the taxi a knock to stop the singing. The driver looks out his open window at me, and I go, "Whatever you do, don't leave." I'm a few steps into the weeds when he calls out, "Boom-boom!"

Eighteen minutes and twenty-two seconds and I wish it were that simple.

The path I'm taking through the weeds is not a path. Just weeds. A different way than Caleb and I went before. This way is darker and deeper and greatly increases the risk of contracting Lyme's disease. This way also keeps trying to trip me, enough to make me consider murdering a kitten. This is by far the safest way.

I glance back at the taxi. The driver is too busy getting rich to notice how safe I'm being. He doesn't see me hacking and stumbling through the tangle as I loop around toward the side of the house opposite where all the scooters are. The last thing I need is the driver honking to redirect me. Yelling through the window something like, "Boom-boom *that* way!" while pointing at the front door of the house. Who knows, maybe he has noticed me and just doesn't care. Could be he's stupid enough to assume I know what I'm doing.

I'm now close enough to the house to hear if anything has gone horribly wrong. But all I'm catching is the muted laughter of men I hope die slowly, so we're probably good. I stop and lean against the side of the house, out of the possible view of anyone, then slip my phone out of its pocket and text "ready" to Caleb.

Along the splintered wood siding I inch toward the back of the house and will need tweezers if we make it out of here. I peek around the corner at a backyard lit even worse than I'd wished for. One step into the abyss I hear a moan and I hop back into hiding so fast I'm willing to kill a whole litter. Tears join the sweat streaking down my face. There's another moan and it's not mine but it should be.

Who knows how many minutes and how many seconds and I don't have the luxury of time.

With my finger on the zipper of the fanny pack, I start walking toward where there'd goddamn better be a door. There's another moan and some rustling in the tall weeds. Then the stench of piss and whiskey and I know. The drunk who got yo-yoed within an inch of his life. If he wants to keep that inch he'd better shut up and stay down.

A light turns on upstairs and some of it shoots through a hole in the board covering the room's window, enough to show me the door down here. I lean up against the house where when the door opens I'll be behind it. Just in case.

The only thing I need more than oxy right now is the sound of inside footsteps heading my way and then that goddamned door to slowly open. But instead I get more moaning and more weeds rustling and what comes to mind is the Holocaust. That movie where a mother hiding from the Nazis smothers her own crying baby to avoid being captured. I hope this doesn't come to that.

The light in the room upstairs goes off and everything outside goes even darker than before. Louder, too. And what comes to mind is a chokehold that hopefully won't kill him but put him to sleep.

I take out my phone and type "?" then hit send. The response I get is like a window opening. Coming from where the light was and then wasn't. Now the board covering the window, is it being pried off? All I can see is sound. Plywood cracking just overhead. Men laughing far off inside. Weeds moaning right in front of me.

Then, from above, Caleb's voice.

"What's the landing like?"

I step away from the house to get a better look at what can't be happening up in the window. To a shadow I whisper-shout, "No fucking way," and the shadow goes, "No other choice." The shadow then straddles the sill and, cradling a smaller shadow, asks, "Rocks or anything below?" and I say, "Just weeds, but wait!"

Then I shut my eyes and turn away as the two shadows drop as one.

A thud and a grunt like a stomach punch. I whip around to weeds being steamrolled but no shrieking or crying and I need shrieking or crying, even if it gets us killed. I step toward the groaning black mass on the ground and whisper, "Is everyone okay?" and a tiny whimper joins in and I'll take it.

"Caleb, can you stand?" I ask. Then all I do is blink and his outline is up and on the move, limping as it carries the smaller outline through weeds waist deep. I set off behind them and ask, "Is she conscious?" but whatever Caleb just murmured got drowned out by the drunk's loudest and longest moan yet. Caleb's outline turns around and I whisper, "It's just the yo-yo victim. Keep going."

We're almost to the side of the house and there's an earthquake inside. The back door flies open just as we turn the corner and I don't have to see the Samoan to know. I reach out for whatever piece of Caleb I can grab and pull him to a stop. The drunk's moaning camouflages our huffs and puffs against the side of the house. No thunder on the ground tells me the Samoan isn't in pursuit. But his voice. A booming "Hey!" out the back door cuts through and quiets the night and everything in the house. A wheeze then a whimper comes from the outline Caleb's holding and he quickly moves to cover her mouth. I feel for his arm and follow it to the end to make sure it's not covering her nose too. This isn't the Holocaust. I have the fanny pack.

"You still here?" shouts the Samoan. Still no thunder on the ground but the weeds say he's stepped outside. The outline of Caleb's head turns to me and I whisper, "Wait" as I clutch his shoulder. There's another moan out back. Then more steps through the weeds followed by the Samoan saying something in broken Khmer. Something like "Shut up, you make too much noise all night." Something like he doesn't suspect a thing.

With it quiet now but the Samoan still outside, Caleb and I have to hold the breath we're trying to catch. Finally the back door slams. I wait for aftershocks inside the house to confirm that the Samoan is on the correct side of the door.

"Go," I whisper as I give Caleb a light push with the hand

that's been holding him in place. "Slow and quiet."

The slow is a given considering our condition. The quiet, not so much. Whatever Caleb did to his leg during his two-story drop and roll, it's not conducive to straight lines or silence. In his throat I can hear a sprained ankle or knee or hip as he carries the outline clinging to him. We're moving about a mile a week toward the front area of the house, doing our best to keep our suffering and desperation from disturbing the occupants. It's a good thing there's no oxy around or we might kill one another for it before reaching the taxi.

"Maybe I should try to carry her," I whisper but Caleb just grunts and continues plowing crooked yet forward. I go, "Let me take her," and he snorts to remind me of the pain and dehydration and withdrawal clouding my judgment.

Draw a horizontal line from the front corner of the house to the perimeter of the weeds and that's where we are right now. Maybe half a football field away from the quiet inside. About to cross the threshold of nowhere to hide. The taxi, it's still waiting on the road so close and forever far. Caleb is three limps ahead of me. Now two. Now one, and I reach out to touch the tiny outline of one of the hands draped over his back. The fingers I get are warm but don't grip mine back. I let go and to Caleb whisper, "Did she hit her head?" Caleb shushes me and murmurs, "Valium," then grunts to say let's just get to the car. Moving in unison I whisper, "How much?" and Caleb holds up two fingers. I whisper, "Two? Milligrams?" and he shakes his head.

The Valium was good thinking and too much and thank God she isn't screaming and I hope to hell she can.

After a few more staggered steps in roughly the right direction, the front of the house casts just enough light for me to see. I overtake Caleb by a length then turn around and walk backward to look without stopping. It's only her profile and a closed eye but it's her. Even with the sweat-smeared makeup and dirt all over her she looks better than she does in my pocket. She bounces almost lifeless in Caleb's arms as he moves. Each of her whimpers keeps me going.

Caleb hisses me back into position behind him and I can't argue. It's where I need to be. Again, I have the fanny pack. And this is what "cover me" means.

We are now closer to the taxi than to the house. Close enough to hear the far-off songs of the driver's net worth increasing.

And then there's a shout from the house. Not like the shout out back before. Louder, and out the front. I turn to see a solar eclipse in the doorway. Another shout and now a silhouette like God with a shotgun is gaining on us.

I go, "Run!" but Caleb's way ahead of me, and not. We're both sprinting like when you try to in a dream. Getting nowhere as quick as we can.

Not that it matters.

Even in peak condition we wouldn't catch a speeding taxi.

"no No NO!" I scream as the driver leaves us and everything I owe him behind. Over the road a cloud of dust and exhaust billows, lit red for a second by taillights.

I whip around and see God getting bigger every second. He slows to a trot with his sawed-off propped against a shoulder, the barrel pointing up. He's laughing. Running behind him to catch up is another silhouette, much smaller and flapping in the breeze, holding a glow-in-the-dark purple dot. Several panicked scooters peel out and vanish from the premises.

Smooth like I'm not moving I feel for the pull tab of the fanny pack zipper. I glance back at Caleb holding Sung and say,

"Get down," then take a few steps toward what's coming. The Samoan is close enough for me to see him shaking his head. Trans Am is far enough behind him to not be blocked. But they're both still just contours and hopefully I am too. If not, I'll never know what happens next. I give the pull tab a yank to access our only hope and I can't believe it has come to this.

A broken fucking zipper.

Me dying with a fanny pack on.

I try pinching the nub where the pull tab snapped off, and behind me Caleb goes, "Zero?"

I try sliding the nub using just the edge of a fingernail, and Caleb goes, "Zero!"

I try tearing the whole fucking pack apart using everything I've got.

And in front of me the Samoan goes, "Don't move!"

I look up and he's so close he has a face. The shotgun he just pumped is no longer pointing up. My hands are. I backpedal until there's breathing behind me.

"DON'T MOVE!" shouts the Samoan as the yo-yo and then its master come into full view beside him.

Trans Am yawns and says, "Give me the girl."

A couple more scooters rev up and peel out. I take another step backward and squat down in front of Caleb and Sung, then lower my hands.

Trans Am drops the yo-yo into the pocket of his kimono, grabs the shottie from the Samoan and, gripping it in one hand, he growls, "Give her or I shoot."

Now he's got the right idea.

Then he nudges the Samoan and says, "Get the girl." The Samoan starts toward us, and forgive me.

"Stop or I'll snap her neck!" I shout as I turn sideways and place a hand on each of Sung's warm cheeks, keeping my body in front of her and Caleb. She moans. The Samoan pauses and looks back at his boss.

"Let go or you're dead," says Trans Am, raising the weapon to the ready position.

"Another step and *she* is," I say.

Then Caleb clears his throat and goes, "Let us buy her from you."

Trans Am laughs and the shottie doesn't budge. "Not for sale," he says.

"We can give you a lot of money," says Caleb.

Trans Am laughs harder and says, "No you can't."

I admire Caleb's effort, but we're not dressed for it. And the little cash still on us, it's already Trans Am's.

Caleb opens his mouth to continue dead negotiations and I shake my head and whisper, "Don't." He looks at me like it's just hitting him, and I whisper, "I'm sorry."

"Shut up, you two!" Trans Am screams, startling the Samoan still frozen between us.

I let go of Sung's head, turn and scream, "Fuck you!" to Trans Am as I give the nub of the zipper another tug, and nothing. Just bleeding fingertips.

Trans Am takes aim and I'm staring at both barrels and begging him to pull the trigger. Hoping it's a strong enough gauge. Praying Sung doesn't feel a thing. I close my eyes, say a quiet goodbye to Neda and again go for my gun because who knows and either way I win.

The hum of a motor coming the wrong way and we're all still alive. I open my eyes and Trans Am isn't even aiming at us anymore. He's got the shottie on a single headlight bouncing and zagging on the road toward us. Maybe a drunken scooter but the sound's too smooth and strong, so a motorcycle? The Samoan crouches down. Trans Am drops to a knee, keeping the barrels pointed at the light and the speed. Bright and loud. Sung stirs and moans in Caleb's arms. He lets go with one and reaches for my fanny pack and the tugging and pulling is killing me and he has as much luck as I've had. Just this thin fucking layer of nylon is keeping us dead and I scrape the ground for a stick or a rock or broken glass. Anything. And all this movement catches the eye of the crouching giant. He's half-watching us and half-watching what Trans Am's aiming at.

Over the approaching torque and internal combustion, Caleb goes, "Try to grip the trigger." I try but the gun's so big there's not enough give to the nylon around it. I undo the strap to free the pack, and the Samoan's out of his crouch. Headed this way. I feel for the trigger again and get closer. The headlight is almost here and illuminates everything. Trans Am shouts something and whatever the light's attached to honks, stopping the Samoan as I continue to claw. Caleb goes, "Got it?" and I just touched what I need to pull but can't. Caleb screams, "Hurry!" like I'm blind, then the tip of my finger catches the curl but slips off as I point the pack at the wall closing in on us.

And a blast stops everything.

The Samoan's on the ground inches away. Looking at what we're looking at.

Trans Am pumps the shottie for another go. Not at us. At the motorcycle. But it isn't a motorcycle. It's a tuk-tuk.

"Thstop!" cries the driver, holding his hands up for Trans Am to see. "Ith me! Pich!"

My finger's got a better hold this time and I—

***

Weeds. Up my nostrils. The house sideways through an eye and that's Sung crying. Caleb's too quiet to still have her.

My hand throbs and is empty like the other one. Voices like victory all around nearby. Next to me is my hair. One of my eyes is swollen shut and I can barely turn my head to expand my view. I taste blood.

All I can really move is one leg. I reach with it till my foot touches what must be Caleb and give a soft kick. Then another one. One more and I get a groan. He's still alive. He deserves better.

Whatever they're waiting for is torture. Everything is killing me and nothing hurts. Not as much as Sung's sobbing and the Samoan shouting for her to shut up. I'd roll over, but then I'd see. Plus I can't roll over.

Caleb groans again and I tell him he's going to be okay. I say this will all be over soon.

Weeds crack and crinkle an approach. The distant voices off to the side I can't see are getting loud enough to become words.

"Dey attack me. You see what dey do to my mouf, my teef."

I almost forgot Pich is here. Son-of-a-bitch didn't listen to what we wrote.

"Good." It's Trans Am, laughing. "You are too pretty before."

Pich tells him it's not funny and Trans Am says relax. Sung's crying has stayed behind, back where the Samoan's still scolding her. Hopefully far enough away to one day forget what she's about to see. I should have snapped her neck when I had the chance to save her. And I'd kill for one more crack at the fanny pack, wherever it is.

"Let me do it," says Pich sounding almost close enough to spit on if I had any saliva. He says, "I need to."

Trans Am laughs again and says, "You don't even know how."

"Yes, I do," says Pich.

Every word the weeds get louder. Something metal clacks with each step forward.

I tap Caleb with my foot again. To thank him and to apologize. To say goodbye and to not be alone. He isn't moaning anymore. Just deep, controlled breaths.

The green all around my face smells like my first summer job.

"Fine," says Trans Am, his voice as close as point-blank. "But don't fuck up."

The metal clacks like a transfer of power.

"Both of you go to hell," I say.

And the double-scratch of a pumped gun and here comes the final painkiller and Neda I love you and Sung I tried.

My ears explode and I scream, too long to be dead so Caleb must be. "Fuck you!" I shout into the ground where nearby something splattered. The Samoan's shouting too and pump goes the gun but softer than before. Sung is shrieking so I defy physics, every torn fiber working me onto my side. Still blind to everything I hear.

"Drop her!" yells Pich like he's moving away from me. Sung screams like she is too. Caleb? Is that him behind me catching his breath?

Another explosion cracks the earth and sky as I make it onto my back.

Caleb is off to my side sitting up, as broken and bloody as I, looking at me like we're immortal. Trans Am lies at my feet and appears to have lost his head. Over by the tuk-tuk with the motor still running is a pile of Samoan with his motor shot out.

And far behind the headlights, a tiny silhouette runs toward the house, not realizing the murderer chasing her with a shotgun and getting closer is here to make amends.

CHAPTER TWENTY-SIX

Take a concussion, a fractured eye socket, a herniated disc, a torn hip flexor, a sprained wrist and two broken fingers. Add some minor contusions and lacerations. Then take that sum and add it to an unhealed hole near my heart. It equals me never feeling any better than this.

I don't even have to start over. The two pills the nurse just gave me are prescription-strength ibuprofen. They may ruin my liver and cause me to bleed out, but I get to keep the orange key tab I never picked up from NA.

"No stronger pills for you?" asks the nurse with a smile I'd like to import to the States.

I go to nod but my cervical collar makes that painfully impossible. "Yes, I'm sure," I say, grimacing. "No narcotics." And Nurse Smiley looks at me like my concussion is keeping me from understanding my options.

"When can I see the girl?" I ask.

Nurse Smiley checks the bandage covering my eye and says, "She still recovering."

What Nurse Smiley doesn't get is Sung has her whole life for that.

"But she's going to be okay, right?" I ask for the third or fourth or tenth time tonight.

Nurse Smiley tightens my wrist wrap and says, "Yes, don't worry. Just a little shock and dehydrated. Getting fluids and rest."

I tell Nurse Smiley to make sure they test Sung for HIV. For gonorrhea and syphilis. For hepatitis and tuberculosis. For urinary tract infections.

Nurse Smiley reminds me I already told two doctors all of that and assures me they know what to do. Then she moves in for a look at the stitches on my chin and cheek.

I tell her to check Sung for vaginal tearing and rectal trauma. For pelvic bruising. For an existing concussion or signs of past ones. For burns and scars and broken teeth.

Nurse Smiley takes a tissue from the box by my bed and dabs the tear running from my good eye. She tells me she didn't find any of those things during the initial examination.

I say don't forget to screen her for food deprivation and vitamin deficiencies and any other form of malnutrition.

Nurse Smiley presses the button to lower the head of my bed, then puts her finger to her lips and starts for the door.

I go, "Wait, wait," and she stops and turns around with a smile too wide to hide her contempt. "What about the other girls?" I ask.

She takes a few steps toward my bed. "Other girls?"

I ask her if four or five girls in similar condition as Sung have been brought in, maybe dropped off by a young woman, and Nurse Smiley says not that she's aware of.

"Never mind," I say, and she turns back around, hits the lights, and leaves.

And I'm thinking when I get out of here, I may have to elbow Pich in the mouth again. Since I can't hit his sister.

The whole room smells like gauze and iodine. Even with the

lights off it looks a lot like where I was living and dying in LA and Rio and LA again. The only notable difference is the privacy partition a few feet from my bed. A little voice tells me the privacy partition isn't working.

"I knowiz hard," the slurred voice murmurs, "but tryta gessom sleep."

Easy for the voice to say—it's coming from a body with half my injuries and ten times the pain medication. Twenty times, if you take weight into consideration.

"Yeah, no," I say through the partition. "I won't be getting any shut-eye tonight."

The digital clock on the wall says I don't care.

The voice on the other side of the screen says, "We diddit."

I say yeah sort of. I say, "Sorry it almost got you killed."

Silence on the other side.

I go, "Hey, Caleb, you still with me?"

A pause and then, "Yezz, good. Evvything realllly good."

I know exactly how he feels. I'm trying my best not to ever again. The ibuprofen is doing its part to help me by doing almost nothing.

The hospital doesn't have Suboxone and the rest of mine is back at the motel room and it doesn't matter. Withdrawal isn't the problem right now. My perfectly functioning central nervous system is.

Sure it feels great knowing Sung is out of harm's way, but tell that to my eye socket.

I close the eye that isn't already slammed shut and bandaged, then try focusing on my breath. Observing the present moment. Trouble is, the present moment is in the bed next to mine high on everything I need. With each attempt at positive visualization, all I see is Caleb dancing in a field of poppies. With each slow inhale and exhale, all I hear is him stealing my drugs. It isn't fair that Caleb gets to enjoy my bad habit while I fail miserably at his. It's hard to locate your third eye when you're starting with only one.

My anger toward Caleb only exacerbates the pain in the upper and lower and middle and outer sections of my body. But I just remembered something that can help alleviate all that.

Everything he's done for me.

Including letting me use his phone to make an international call to Neda right now. I'm sure he won't mind.

Thanks to an earlier mix-up by one of the orderlies, Caleb's phone is on the small table next to my bed. Thanks to an earlier stomp by an enraged Samoan, my phone is smashed to pieces in the pocket of some weed-stained shorts that are who knows where. I reach for Caleb's phone and let out a cry, then let out another cry as I bring the phone in. Through the partition, Caleb responds to my agony with incoherent utter joy.

The clock on Caleb's phone says Neda's wide awake. I rest the phone in the palm of my splint-fingered hand, then go to punch in her number but forget the 001 in front. I go to punch in her number again, but forget her number. After three attempts and three apologies to perfect strangers in Los Angeles, I mutter, "Fuck." Through the partition, a gleeful Caleb goes, "Gesundheit."

To kill the time while trying to remember how to speak to my wife, I have a look at Caleb's text messages and find a list of people I don't know with opening lines that don't interest me. The LA Zen Center wants Caleb to know about an upcoming retreat. Below that a guy named Elias asks if Caleb's up for lunch at Veggie Heaven when he gets back into town.

I call Neda again and apologize to a man in Spanish.

Someone named Sky tells Caleb she can't, she's busy next Friday.

Someone named Erica tells him she can't, she's busy next Saturday.

Across the partition, Caleb starts humming the theme song to *Sesame Street*. I'd yell at him to stop, but he's had enough rejection for one night even if he doesn't know it.

I try Neda again and hang up on a funeral home.

Someone named Jessica tells Caleb to please just sign the divorce papers.

I rub my eye to make sure my lack of depth perception isn't playing tricks on me, and all the same words are still there. After clicking on the message to open the full exchange, I'm greeted by a series of gray and blue bubbles revealing Jessica and Caleb's history in reverse. The last part of it, anyway. I scroll up to see more.

Across the partition, Caleb sings about a sunny day sweeping the clouds away.

Jessica's been asking Caleb to sign the papers for weeks. Caleb's been stalling with short messages like "Traveling for work" and "I'll get to it soon" and "Why the sudden rush?" I scroll up to go months back.

Across the partition, Caleb sings to come and play. He sings how everything's A-okay.

A message to Jessica from Caleb says it's been almost two years. He says he misses Lizzie so much he can't stand it.

A message to Caleb from Jessica says she knows. She reminds him he isn't the only one who lost a daughter.

Across the partition, Caleb is still singing. Hoping someone can tell him how to get to Sesame Street.

I hit the call button, and after less than a minute Nurse Smiley enters. "Need something?" she asks.

I point at the partition and say, "Please make sure my friend over there is comfortable. Maybe an extra blanket."

Then I remind her to come tell me the second I can see the girl.

***

The clock on the wall says Alice doesn't give a damn about visiting hours. It also says I lied a little about not getting any shuteye.

"You must be out of your damned mind," Alice whispers, illuminated by all the monitors as she stands over my bed. "Thank God for that."

I blink like a cyclops to get my bearings. "How'd you even—"

"Shhh," says Alice, glancing at the door. "Please, keep it down."

Across the partition, Caleb's meds are wearing off.

"Is that, what's his name?" asks Alice

I say Caleb and yes. She asks if he's going to be okay. I say he'll be fine. I tell her this is nothing compared to what he's been through.

Alice walks around the foot of my bed and peeks around the partition. "Hard to really tell, but he looks better off than you," she says. And I go, "Don't be so sure." As she heads back to the side of my bed, I notice a small backpack hanging from her hand.

"Is that for Sung?" I ask. "Is she all right?"

"Yes, this is hers," says Alice, looking at what my only eye is fixed on. "And I *hope* she's all right. I haven't been able to sneak into her room yet. Security is tighter over in the children's wing, thank goodness."

I tell her last I checked with the nurse, Sung was doing fine— considering. Alice says glad to hear it. She says she doesn't understand how I'm not dead.

I tell her there's still time.

"Sounds like you've heard what happened," I say.

"Yes," says Alice, "but I'm still trying to believe it." She tells me how one minute she's sound asleep, then the next a guard is pounding on her door saying Pich's sister Mau is out front with a car full of little girls, and that Mau is rambling about how Pich is trying to make things right.

"Oh good," I interrupt, "so Mau *did* rescue the girls from the house. She was supposed to bring them here to the hospital, though, not out to you."

Alice says Mau had seen some policemen outside the hospital and panicked. Says Mau panicked because she had a shotgun and a handgun Pich had given her to hide in her car trunk.

I make a mental note to kiss Pich if I ever see him again, then apologize to Alice again for having been drawn into this mess.

"It's fine," she says, "I'm just glad the girls weren't left behind. A double-murder scene is no place to be abandoned."

And yet it would have been an improvement over what they'd gotten accustomed to.

I tell Alice I'm sorry for not bringing all the girls to the hospital ourselves, pointing out they were too traumatized, the tuk-tuk too small, and me and Caleb too battered. "It was good of Pich to call Mau," I say.

Through her teeth Alice goes, "Both of them can go to hell."

I get why she can't forgive Pich, but I ask what she's got against Mau.

"Who do you think covered for Pich after the kidnapping?" spits Alice. "Lying to me and the police about how he'd been beaten, making us think that miserable coward was a hero."

I go, "Ah."

The clock on the wall says it's time I start paying more attention.

Across the partition, Caleb reminds us why morphine was invented. So loud, we didn't hear the footsteps. Nurse Smiley is standing in the doorway.

"This no visitor time," she says, glaring at Alice.

"It's okay," I say, "she's my mother."

Nurse Smiley apologizes and says how nice it is my mom could come. She smiles at Alice. Alice doesn't smile back. I don't think she likes passing for my mom.

"How's the girl?" I ask Nurse Smiley, and she says the girl is still fine. I ask, "Can we see her?" and she says maybe when morning visits begin.

The clock on the wall says not for another two hours.

Across the partition, Caleb is haunting the place. I ask Nurse Smiley if she can bring him more pain medication. This is like an obese man who hasn't eaten in days ordering pie for someone else. This is like a breakthrough. Except I could kill for some pie.

As Nurse Smiley heads out the door, I shout at the partition, "Hang in there, man. Relief is on the way." My raised voice rattles all my broken pieces and I let out a groan to match Caleb's.

"Why didn't you request any pain meds for yourself," Alice asks, eyeing me from bandaged head to stubbed toe.

"I'm fine," I say. "I've had plenty."

Alice looks me over again and says as wrecked as I am, it's still better than prison.

I again say there's still time.

And Alice goes, "Actually, you're probably in the clear. You were never there tonight."

My neck collar keeps me from cocking my head to the side.

Alice says, "Pich turned himself in a couple of hours ago and, according to Mau, he's telling the police the same thing he told the hospital when he brought you in."

"Care to refresh my memory?" I ask. "The ride here and the whole admissions process, it's all a bit fuzzy."

Alice says sure and she explains. And apparently I have the night all wrong. Apparently what happened was Pich accidentally ran over two innocent tourists with his tuk-tuk while rushing Sung to the hospital after rescuing her from the two men who had kidnapped her last month. Apparently he couldn't in good conscience just leave us there bleeding on some side street.

"That's the version he gave to the emergency room," says Alice. "In the version for the police, 'after rescuing her from' was to be followed by 'and killing.'" She points out that, in both versions, me and Caleb were merely just stupid Americans not watching where we were going. In neither version were we stupid Americans trying to kidnap a kidnapped girl.

I tell Alice for a guy whose teeth we knocked out, Pich keeping his mouth shut is an awfully nice thing to do. Even nicer than saving our lives.

I'm wondering if he had time to clean the blood in our motel bathroom, to boot.

"He can still go to hell," says Alice. "I hope he rots in jail forever for what he has put Sung and Akara through."

That's understandable. Me, I'm a bit torn. Between wanting to rip his head off, and thanking him for me still having mine.

I say, "I wonder how the cops reacted when Pich, you know, told them he took money from a pimp to let the pimp kidnap some girls he was protecting, and then killed that pimp to get one of the girls back."

Alice says, "He only confessed to the murder, not to the kidnapping."

My neck collar is really getting in the way of my natural reactions.

Across the partition, Caleb expresses my pain. I go to buzz the nurse for him, but need a little more information first.

"Not following," I say to Alice.

She says Pich doesn't want to implicate Mau. Says if he confesses to collaborating with the kidnappers, the police will arrest Mau for aiding and abetting, seeing as how she got a cut of the money and covered for Pich.

First he saves me and Caleb while rescuing Sung and the others, and now he's come almost clean to pay his dues and protect his sister. The most shameful act of Pich's life seems to have brought out the best in him.

"Also," says Alice, "if Pich confessed to the kidnapping, he'd get killed."

My eyebrow pulls the cuts on my face, and I go, "But the guys who'd kill him are already dead."

And Alice says, "The pimps, yes. The police, no."

She explains how a couple of cops are in on this, and I say surprise, surprise. She says that, according to Mau, they took a sizable bribe from Pich to help tone down the investigation.

I curse the cops and say it sounds like quite the co-dependent relationship. Then I ask Alice if she plans on telling the police the whole truth.

"No," says Alice. "While I hope Pich rots in hell, I don't think he should have to die."

She says she doesn't want to cause a rift among the police force either, as that could result in less protection for the safe house and her girls. "Not only that," she adds, "if I expose Pich, I'm afraid he might expose you and Caleb out of spite."

I tell her thanks, but point out that even if Pich doesn't implicate us, there's a taxi driver who might. I say, "There's also Sung. She probably got a pretty good look at Caleb in the house, and at both of us on the ride here."

Alice says hopefully the police won't question Sung since Pich already confessed. She says maybe they'll leave her be after everything she's been through. "As for the taxi driver, I wouldn't worry about him. Locals tend to not get involved in police matters that don't involve them."

I tell her worst comes to worst, if Caleb and I are placed at the scene, I'll just play our OE card and apologize to the cops for not following protocol.

"Fynn will fire our asses," I say, "but that's probably happening anyway."

Across the partition, things can only get better.

Nurse Smiley emerges and knocks twice on the doorjamb as she enters, holding a paper cup. "Lights on?" she asks and flicks the switch regardless, then heads over to the louder side of the room.

Sung's backpack, it's light blue with black and yellow bumblebees on it. It's stained with travel.

Through the partition I ask Nurse Smiley, "What are you giving him?" and she says tramadol.

"Make sure he gets some hyrdromorphone or hydrocodone or oxycodone," I say. "And make sure you don't give him any to take with him when he's released."

Alice looks at me like I know what I'm talking about. I point at the partition and whisper to her, "Don't want him continuing with that junk after the pain has stopped." Even though his pain never will.

With the lights now on, Alice's face looks different. Like I don't look so good.

"Maybe Pich really did run you over," she whispers, then smiles as if to cry.

I say that would have been a lot easier.

Alice folds her arms and shakes her head. She sighs and says, "I just don't understand."

I ask her what she means as if I have no idea.

She waves her hand at everything bandaged and wrapped and splinted and stitched, then smiles and says, "All this. All this for a little girl you hardly know."

If I could nod and shake my head, I would.

Alice says, "Don't get me wrong, I'm grateful. And I'm sure when she's old enough Sung will be grateful, too. But I, I don't know, I guess I'm just wondering—"

"Why her," I say.

Alice points at the words as they leave my mouth and says, "Exactly."

Before I can answer, she recites my bio to me, saying I've been with OE for years and have helped rescue hundreds of girls. Saying many of the girls I've helped rescue have ended up right back at what I've helped rescue them from. Saying that is the hardest part of the job but one I've learned to live with.

"So, yeah," she says after pausing to catch her breath, "I can't help but be curious. Why her?"

The clock on the wall says you'd think I would have figured that out by now.

"Honestly," I say to Alice. "I don't really know."

I tell her there was just some strange connection that day we did the jump in Phnom Penh. I tell her I can't explain it because I don't think it's explainable.

What I don't tell her is maybe that strange connection turned into a strange addiction to replace my existing one. That maybe I felt a dangerous cause could be my new drug. That maybe I saw saving a child as a more acceptable way to destroy myself.

Nurse Smiley comes around the partition and apologizes for interrupting my chat with my mother. She says it's time for my medication, then places two ibuprofen tablets and one amoxicillin capsule on a small metal tray and I'm thinking what a tease. I don't ask her about Sung. I don't ask her because apparently I just met Sung on a tuk-tuk that ran me over, and asking would be weird. As would barking out medical orders to all the doctors and nurses caring for her.

After I down my Tic Tacs and Nurse Smiley leaves the room, Alice says, "I have to ask, were you serious when you sent me that email about the possibility of adoption?"

I tell her sorry about that and laugh. I tell her I was kind of drunk when I sent that. I tell her I tend to get overly sentimental when I drink.

Alice asks what about the text message I sent about adoption.

I say same. I say I drink to forget about work but that it sometimes has the opposite effect.

"Okay, good," says Alice, "because adoption would be next to impossible."

I say of course it would be, then laugh again.

The ibuprofen is starting to take effect. I can tell because everything hurts the same.

Alice pats her stomach and says, "I'm starving. If I don't get some food in me, I'll pass out and miss visiting hours." She says she's going to grab some breakfast in the cafeteria downstairs and asks if she can leave the backpack in my room so she doesn't have to tote it through the food line. "I'll come back up for it before I go to see Sung," she says. I say of course, and that maybe she can wheel me over there when she goes.

"Are you sure you're allowed out of bed?" she asks.

I say yeah and give her a thumbs-up, inadvertently using my

hand with the splinted fingers, so it looks like I'm pointing a gun at her. "I've been worse off than this and just walked out of hospitals."

Alice plops the backpack on a chair over by the wall.

"Actually," I say, pointing at the backpack with my gun, "do you mind if I hold on to it for you?"

Alice wrinkles her brow. "You hardly have any room on that bed as it is," she says, then catches herself and smiles and nods. She picks the backpack up off the chair, walks it to my bedside and sets it between the bedrail and my good hip.

"This thing managed to stay with Sung from the time she was trafficked in Thailand to the time she was delivered to the safe house," says Alice. "Pretty sure she has had it since she was three or four."

I ask why she assumes that, and she says the backpack contained several pieces of adorable clothing that were way too small for Sung when she arrived at The LifeLong Center. She says the clothing had Thai labels and weren't anything a trafficker would ever buy.

I say, "Strange that a mother or father would care enough to pack nice clothes for the preschooler they're selling into sex slavery."

Alice says from what Sung has told her during play therapy, Sung's father died before she was born and her mother died a year or so ago. Sung then went to live with her uncle—her mother's brother. "The uncle's the one who sold her," says Alice.

I grit my teeth until I feel it in my eye socket. For Sung, and for all the girls with all-too-similar a story.

"I'm sorry, but I really need to eat," Alice says, grabbing her stomach with both hands and starting for the door. "Want me to get the lights on the way out?"

"No, no, thanks," I say, my hand resting on the backpack. "You can leave them on."

Alice leaves. I raise the head of my bed up as far as my ache allows, then pull the backpack in a little closer so it's leaning on my hip. It's more like a toy than it is a piece of luggage. I slip two fingers through the loop where the top strap's attached and gently pull up. Everything Sung owns weighs next to nothing.

The bumblebees on the front are embroidered. Some of their stitching is coming loose. Their yellow isn't what it used to be. I find the zipper tab for the main compartment and give it a light tug, half-expecting the tab to snap off but it doesn't. Another tug and the short sleeve of a tiny purple T-shirt peeks out. The fabric is coarse like commercial laundry. This doesn't feel like an invasion of privacy. Not even when I reach in and gently burrow down past more cotton and some denim and then the laces of a canvas sneaker.

Across the partition, Caleb laughs at nothing in particular. In a voice like ether he goes, "Whadeverdanurse gave me … magic."

He doesn't know the half of it. The other half.

As I ease my hand out of the backpack, my pinky knuckle catches on a seam on the padded interior wall. My pinky tip tells me the seam's a zipper. My thumb and pointer find the tab and slide it to open a compartment just big enough for my hand to fit inside. I touch what feels like a thick piece of paper. What I pull out is a small, square red envelope. The kind fourth-graders are forced to stick Valentine's cards inside and give to one another. The envelope is creased and worn, but still sealed. Nothing's written on it. I set it on my thigh and hold it in place with the thumb of my gun hand. The pointer of my other hand traces the thin edges of whatever's inside.

I know better than to open someone else's Valentine.

It doesn't stop me from slitting the throat of the seal flap.

With two fingers I fish out a photo, but it flicks out of my grasp and flutters to the floor before I get a look. Can't see where it landed, and not for a lack of trying despite my body screaming don't. I press the nurse call button.

Across the partition, Caleb is useless and I couldn't be happier for him.

The clock on the wall says I hope Alice chews slowly.

Nurse Smiley arrives with eyes that sparkle in a way that says now what. I point to the floor and say, "I dropped something." She looks down as she approaches my bed, then looks up, sees the baby backpack by my lap and rolls her eyes. I say, "Don't worry about that," and point down again. "Look for a small picture."

Nurse Smiley quickly scans the floor around the bed and shakes her head. I say please keep looking, it has to be there. She sighs. A few seconds later she goes, "Aha," and bends down beside the bed before partially disappearing under it.

"Found it?" I ask.

She grunts, "Uh huh," then backs out from beneath the bed and stands up, eyeing the photo pinched between her fingers. All I see are indecipherable symbols scribbled on the back.

"This you?" Nurse Smiley asks.

I hold my palm out and she places the photo in it. And I look.

"You okay?" asks Nurse Smiley as she glances at the monitor and all my vitals rising.

I bring my palm closer to my face, wink twice and look again.

Nurse Smiley says something, I have no idea what.

Even with just one eye. Even with the creases and the scratches and the fading. There's no doubt. It's him.

The clock on the wall says I just became an uncle. Five years ago.

Behind me, the monitor sounds like a pinball machine. Nurse Smiley calls for a doctor. I tell her all I really need is the phone that's down by my feet. She hands me the phone, shakes her head as she looks at the monitor, and calls for a doctor again.

While I still can't remember Neda's phone number, I do know her email address.

I lost her at impossible. But impossible just started to make a lot more sense.

NOTE FROM THE AUTHOR

Thank you madly for taking the time to read *In Wolves' Clothing*.

I hope you'll consider posting a review of the book on **Amazon**, **Goodreads** and/or any other site where people look for truth in fiction.

Sincerely,

Greg Levin

ACKNOWLEDGMENTS

While it's my name on the cover of this book, there wouldn't even *be* a book were it not for the following people:

My wife, Miranda. Miranda's humanitarian trip to Cambodia in 2016 is what sparked the idea for this novel. And her innate ability to earn actual money is what enabled me to sit around in my pajamas for a year writing what she sparked. Also, she kept me alive while I was killing myself to meet my editor's deadline.

My daughter, Leah. Had Leah not made friends with people old enough to drive her around this year, I wouldn't have completed this book until 2019 or 2020. That said, I regret not having been there more for my daughter. In my defense, she's embarrassed to be seen with me.

Radd Berrett. Radd spent over two years risking his life and sanity while traveling the world to help rescue victims of child sex trafficking. My interviews with him were invaluable in helping me create and develop the characters and plot for this book. Radd is both a badass and a sweetheart, and considering he has the strength to bench-press my entire family, he is the last person I'd want to forget to thank.

Suzy Vitello. "If you knew Suzy like I know Suzy …" Actually, I don't know Suzy all that well. But she's buddies with the great Chuck Palahniuk, and Chuck told me Suzy's the bomb. So when I met her and found out she offered editing services (in addition to being an amazing writer), I hired the hell out of her. Long blurb short, she's the real reason this novel doesn't suck. And if you think it *does* suck, well … blame Suzy.

Graham Toseland. Graham, my proofreader from A Fading Street Publishing Services is why this book reads as cleanly as it does—assuming it reads as cleanly as I think it does. If, by chance, you've found any typos or grammatical errors (other than the one's I intended as an artist who's above the rules), let's gang up on Graham and beat his British ass until he's unconscious and/or issues me a full refund.

Angie McMann. Angie is a fellow writer, a selfless supporter of other writers, and one of the few people who responds promptly to my emails. She kindly offered to proof this book when Graham was finished with it—to make sure he didn't ruin my American English with any *English* English corrections.

The Writing Wrong workshop gang. I was fortunate enough to be selected to participate in a writing workshop led by Chuck Palahniuk this past spring. During the workshop, I got the opportunity to read parts of this novel and get beaten Fight Club-style by Chuck and a group of my talented peers until I made many necessary improvements to the book. (Yeah, I realize I already name-dropped Chuck Palahniuk earlier, but when you get to hang out with Chuck Palahniuk for ten weeks, you'd be an idiot not to name-drop Chuck Palahniuk every chance you get. Chuck Palahniuk might disagree, but that is sooo Chuck Palahniuk.)

Maria Novillo Saravia. I always judge a book by its cover designer, and Maria of BeauteBook is one of the best around. She's highly creative … and very patient. Not once did she threaten to murder me for all the changes and tweaks I requested throughout the design process. (Also, special thanks to Andrea Masse-Tognetti of Merimask, who gave permission to use the image of her stunning wolf mask featured on the cover.)

The Internet. I know, I know, the Internet isn't a person. I also know many folks no longer capitalize "internet." But when something does for you what the Internet did for me while writing this novel, hell *yeah* you thank it, and *double* hell yeah you give it a large first letter out of respect. Perhaps even ALL CAPS. Thank you, INTERNET, for providing me with instant access to everything I didn't know but needed to for this novel to seem real. (I'd also like to thank the FBI for not detaining me despite all the creepy Internet searches on child sex trafficking I had to do.)

Mom and Dad. I'd be a real a-hole if I didn't thank my parents for the love and support they've provided while I've thrown my life away on fiction writing. I'm so grateful to them for all the bedtime stories they read to me as a child. They'd read to me every night, no matter how good the cocktail party going on downstairs was. Such devotion instilled in me the passion for words and alcohol one needs to become an author.

You. Yes, *you*. For knowing how to read. Were it not for people like you, I never would have been inspired to ignore my family and friends for over a year to write this book that mostly only they will buy.

And finally … (Warning: Serious shift in tone ahead) …

The victims of child sex trafficking. Nothing even remotely funny to say here. I'd list all the victims by name, but that would be a book in itself—the longest, most heartbreaking one ever written. Also, sadly, it's impossible to know all the names. So I'll just say this: I wish there weren't a reason to write the novel I wrote. But it's good to know that, thanks to all the amazing women and men dedicated to fighting human trafficking, the novel I wrote may one day be TOTAL fiction.

ABOUT THE AUTHOR

Greg Levin is an award-winning author of contemporary fiction. He's gone from being read merely by immediate family and friends to being read also by extended family and Facebook acquaintances.

Greg's novel *The Exit Man* was optioned by Showtime for development into a TV series and won a 2015 Independent Publisher Award (a.k.a., an "IPPY"). He earned a second IPPY with his next novel, *Sick to Death*, which Craig Clevenger (*The Contortionist's Handbook*) called "a tour de force dark comedy." Greg's latest book, *In Wolves' Clothing*, is his most dangerous. He wrote much of it during a ten-week-long workshop led by the great Chuck Palahniuk (author of *Fight Club* and lots of other books Greg sleeps with at night).

Greg resides with his wife, daughter and two cats in Austin, Texas. He is currently wanted by local authorities for refusing to say "y'all" or do the two-step.

Learn more about Greg and his books (and blog) at greglevin.com.